THEATRE OF LOVE

As Staff Nurse Jessica French watched the surfer swooping and swerving between shore and fishing boats, she found herself inexplicably drawn to this powerful, handsome man before her. But her mind was in a further turmoil when she discovered that this was no ordinary man but the eminent surgeon from the military hospital, well-known for his difficult and autocratic personality . . .

THEATRE OF LOVE

BY

LYDIA BALMAIN

MILLS & BOON LIMITED
ETON HOUSE 18–24 PARADISE ROAD
RICHMOND SURREY TW9 1SR

First published in Great Britain 1987
by Mills & Boon Limited

ISBN 0 263 75808 7

Set in 9 on 10 pt Linotron Times
03–0987–67,800

Photoset by Rowland Phototypesetting Limited
Bury St Edmunds, Suffolk
Made and printed in Great Britain by
William Collins Sons & Co. Limited, Glasgow

CHAPTER ONE

'THERE you are; is that better, Mr King?'

Jessica French adjusted the traction from which Mr King's fractured leg was suspended and smiled down at her patient. She did not work on the men's ward much, it was Nurse Hoby's territory, but it was nice to have a change occasionally. Mr King was a cheerful little man in his mid-sixties and a keen gardener who spent a lot of his spare time gazing out of the window at the exquisite gardens below, though it was his hobby that had caused him to end up in hospital. He had told Jessica ruefully that one moment he had been staking artichokes in his steeply sloping terraced garden and the next he had stepped back to admire them. Naturally he had stepped back on air, and had found himself bouncing painfully down towards the sea until a convenient olive tree had stopped his progress, though it had done so by snapping his tibia like a twig.

From there it had been only a small step to the Nelson, for the English hospital dealt with all the ailments in the thriving foreign community, mostly English, German and French, and with the holidaymakers, too.

'That's much better thanks, Nurse. How about a cuppa, then? You make a good cup of tea, you do.'

'I'll just finish my round and then I'll put the kettle on,' Jessica promised. 'I haven't lost the knack of making tea despite having worked in Spain for two years, but I usually have mine with lemon, not milk.'

'Well, with lemons growing in your garden, it's a temptation to use 'em, specially since the milk's hardly ever fresh,' Mr King agreed. 'There's a tree over there in the public gardens that I can't name, but Mrs King's going to find out for me. It worries me, not knowing.'

'Yes, maddening.' Jessica pushed her trolley over to the window, which was open for though it was only April it was still very warm, with a light breeze caressing the leaves into motion. 'Look at those little yachts; you've got to be awfully good to get a speed like that out of them on such a calm afternoon. Oh, to be idle and rich!'

The yachts were racing round a predetermined course, scarlet, white and blue sails puffed out, then flattening as they tacked, then bulging again. The harbour was more than a mile across and one of the deepest natural harbours in the world, so an ideal place for most water sports. Though Jessica had only been working at the Nelson for a week she had seen most aquatic activities taking place as she looked either from the ward windows or from the windows of her flat in the nurses' home further up the coast. Water skiing, sailing, wind surfing, scuba diving, the harbour provided ideal conditions for them all and Jessica hoped to have a go at most of them herself whilst she was working here.

Pushing her trolley up the ward and swishing back curtains round the beds where an occupant indicated he had finished with his bedpan or bottle, Jessica wondered how Pat Hoby was getting on in the female side of the ward. Because of its nautical connections the wards were all called after battles or ships connected with Nelson, so she and Pat nursed on Agamemnon Ward, Aggy 1 was female, Aggy 2 male, and today, because Pat had had to visit the dentist for a filling, they had changed over rooms, though Jessica was the SRN on Room 1 as a rule.

Above them, on the third floor, other nurses shared the work of Victory whilst on the ground floor Sister Albert reigned supreme over Trafalgar. Pat Hoby had returned from the dentist, her tooth no longer aching, but had continued to work on Aggy 1 since she felt it only fair that she should carry the heavier work load caused by her absence.

'Nurse, you can take this now!'

John Simpson had come back from theatre the previous day minus a large bunion and would be going home quite soon. He flourished his bottle at her through the curtains and Jessica hurried over to collect it. Then she plumped up his pillows and settled him down again, assuring him that his cup of tea would not now be long delayed.

'Is that the last?' When no one else seemed to want anything except their tea, Jessica pushed her trolley out through the swing doors at the end of the room and turned left and left again, into the sluice. Rosa, one of the nursing auxiliaries, was already there, snatching boiling hot bedpans out of the autoclave. She turned and sighed at the sight of Jessica's laden trolley.

'I'll do them next, you go and start the tea. Thank goodness for disposable bottles, at least they don't get autoclaved. I'm sorry I've not started the tea but we're behind today, what with Nurse Hoby being away and the students being in school and one thing and another. Still, if you'll get the kettle on it'll help.'

'Why don't the canteen supply after-lunch tea?' Jessica asked, making her way to the door. 'It would save us a job.'

'Meals come across from the military hospital and they cater for Spanish patients, not Brits.,' Rosa explained. 'I've never worked over there but I imagine they don't drink much tea. Did they drink tea in Madrid?'

'I don't think so, though I couldn't be sure. I was a theatre nurse, remember, not on the wards.' Jessica paused, one hand on the door knob. 'If I hadn't suddenly longed for a change I'd have been theatre sister by now. I was due to be made up when the existing Sister left. Still, I love ward work, so I'm not grumbling.'

'Do you miss theatre?' Rosa asked curiously. She was a sweet-tempered, placid Englishwoman in her late fifties, nursing for love of it more than for the money. In fact ever since she had been widowed, she admitted she would have been lost without her work.

Jessica considered. Did she miss it? The excitement, the tension, the thrill when an operation went off smoothly? But it was hard to think of theatre without seeing all over again the face of the man who had made it seem wonderful and worthwhile, until he had gone off with a blonde Scandinavian student nurse, leaving Jessica to gloss over it, pretend she had never been serious, never wanted a permanent relationship.

'Yes, I do miss it,' she said at last. 'But I like ward nursing just as much, perhaps even more, because I never really met my patients before. Theatre work's demanding, but so is ward work. On the wards the hours are longer and the responsibilities are greater. In theatre you've surgeons and doctors all around, but on the wards you're often alone and in charge. I love this place, too. Everyone's so friendly and they all have time for you, not like Madrid.'

'That's big city hustle against small town languor,' Rosa said, nodding. 'Well, you start the tea, Nurse; *mañana* is only allowed if you're a native of the country!'

Jessica left the sluice, turned up the corridor and went into the kitchen. It was a pleasant room, bright and airy, though the windows were set so high that one only had a glimpse of the sky. Pat was already setting cups out on a trolley, her untidy, ash-blonde hair falling in wisps about her face despite a mass of pins which endeavoured to keep it tidy. Her cap was pinned on crooked and one pink cheek was still swollen from the dentist's ministrations but she was a pretty sight in her pale blue staff nurse uniform dress, only partially hidden by the voluminous white apron.

'I don't envy you your patients,' she greeted Jessica, putting her fist in the small of her back with a grimace. 'I've just lifted Mrs Pontin back into bed and strained every muscle I possess. She should have a travelling crane, a human being can't do it unaided.'

'They're trying to slim her down for surgery,' Jessica said, taking dried milk off the shelf and spooning it into a jug. 'Edna said one of the surgeons was quite rude to her because she won't try to lose weight.'

'That's right, I remember your predecessor telling me. It was Perrello. You've not met him yet, have you?' At Jessica's shake of the head she grimaced, lifting the big kettle off the stove. 'A treat in store for you. Perrello doesn't suffer fools gladly whether they're patients or nurses, and he doesn't like the English very much. He's a general surgeon and very good with the knife I'm told, but he doesn't have any sort of bedside manner and often reduces nurses and students to tears. Mind you, I agree with every sarcastic word he said to Mrs Pontin. She really should try to lose weight, it's no joke having your gall stones removed when the surgeon's got a yard of blubber to cut through.'

'True. I've seen patients in theatre for six hours and others for two, for the very same operation. The only difference has been the weight of the patient. Look, can you stay here and finish the tea, or are you still behind? I've got to do the observations and I'd like to get through them before Sister gets back from lunch.'

'We're catching up. The tonsillectomy's feeling better, so Edna's doing observations now. Are you in this evening, or are you going out?'

The two girls shared a flat in the nurses' home. They had been fortunate since, though they had not met for two years, they had done their training together in Manchester and Pat's cheerful and familiar face had been the nicest thing Jessica could have seen when she first entered the Nelson. Pat had been pleased too, especially over her friend's mastery of the Spanish language.

'No one would ever know you weren't Spanish yourself,' she exclaimed after a couple of days. 'I've been over here as long as you have, but I'm nowhere near as fluent.'

'My mother really is Spanish, you know, so I've been speaking the language ever since I can remember, at home,' Jessica explained. She did not add that she had been going out with a Spanish doctor for two years, almost living in his pocket. This had certainly completed her mastery of medical terms and expressions, for Jordi Ramblas had discussed all his cases with her and had been proud of his relationship with the slender theatre nurse with her flame-coloured hair and blue-green eyes, so different from those of his fellow-countrywomen.

Yet his pride in her had not been enough, not when the Scandinavian student had been happy to sleep with him and Jessica had continued to hold back. The sting of his rejection still hurt, though Jessica had got over the worst of it. She told herself that had it been real love she would have been happy to live with him. However, she had held out for respectability and a wedding ring, therefore she could not possibly have loved him.

'Jessica, are you going out this evening?'

Pat's voice was loud enough to make Jessica jump and return abruptly to the present.

'I'm sorry, I was miles away. No, I'm not going out, I'll be at the flat tonight. Why? Are you in?'

'Yes. I may have to do a bit of overtime, so will you get us something to eat or shall we go down to the quayside and pick up a snack?'

'I'll make a couple of omelettes,' Jessica said, leaving the room and returning to the ward. Announcing that the kettle was on and that tea would soon follow, she began to check blood pressures, take temperatures and fill in charts. Ward work was engrossing because the patients were interested in you and you were interested in them she concluded, wrapping the sphygmomanometer around Ted Wilmot's sinewy arm and shaking her head over the collection of rude get-well cards he was chuckling over. She had just filled in his chart and was halfway to the next bed when Mr Ramsey, who had been gazing out of the window through binoculars, uttered a sharp exclamation.

'There he is again! Look, Nurse, see him? The one with the red sail. I reckon he's a marvel on that board-thing.'

Jessica followed Mr Ramsey's pointing finger and saw the wind-surfer. Far out on the blue bay the man and his craft were speeding along faster than a horse could gallop and tacking to catch the slight breeze as though the water beneath the board was only a few feet deep instead of many fathoms. Jessica held her breath; wind-surfing was not like boating, the board had no rudder and the sail could not be reefed, it was controlled solely by the wind, by currents and by the man on board. If he tacked too sharply and fell off out there, in such deep water and far from either shore, he would have a long and tiring swim to safety and he would probably lose his craft.

Taking the next patient's temperature and filling in the chart, Jessica nevertheless managed to keep an eye on the board's progress and presently, knew she was watching a top-class surfer. The man knew how to get the most out of both board and sail. He tore onwards, his wake rocking a cluster of small boards as he entered the harbour, then his sail was sucked flat as he tacked, he lost the wind . . . then was round . . . and the sail was curving outwards once more as he raced back up the harbour as fast as he had just raced towards it.

'Amazing!' Mr Ramsey said, taking his glasses away from his eyes for a moment. 'Watched that feller several times, I have. Amazing! Does things none of the others do; that tacking, it's brilliant. Most of 'em fall off and then climb back on again, but not him. He can stay aboard whatever the weather throws at him I reckon.'

'He certainly knows what he's doing,' Jessica said, moving along to Mr Ramsey and pushing the thermometer into his mouth. 'I've never seen . . . now he's gone too far this time!'

The surfer was rushing straight at a cluster of shipping moored by a jetty but at the last moment he swerved again, a perfect arc, and was swooping between the shore and some fishing boats, poetry in motion. To be able to surf like that, Jessica thought enviously. She voiced the thought aloud and Mr Ramsey nodded, removing the thermometer and handing it to her.

'He's got it taped, all right. You wait till he makes for the shore, you'd think he had brakes and a motor. Watch.'

He handed her the glasses and Jessica put them to her eyes. Immediately the surfer was in front of her, a man and not just a tiny dark silhouette against the brilliance of the sea. He was gripping the sail, his legs braced on the board, his face, in profile, dark and tight-mouthed as the wind whipped his hair back from his brow and the sea sprayed up in a glittering arc.

'He's awfully good, but he's not young,' Jessica said as the man brought his board round yet again. He was coming towards her now, head on, and she saw the harsh lines and planes of his face, the thick hair touched with grey at the temples, the dark eyes, narrowed into slits against the flung spume. Ugly? Certainly not handsome. A powerful, forceful face and figure, the shoulders and chest broad and muscled, the hips narrow, hands and arms strong. Even watching through the glasses you could sense the power and personality of the lone surfer, his determination and skill.

'He's not old, either,' Mr Ramsey pointed out, taking his glasses from Jessica's reluctant hands. 'By heck, he's going to ram . . . no, he's brought her round again. Ah, he's gone out of sight, come in to land, I dare say.' He lowered his glasses and held out his arm for the sphyg. ‘Sorry, Nurse, you can get on with your job now.’

‘I wonder where the surfer comes from,’ Jessica mused as she moved down the ward. ‘He was heading this way only perhaps a bit more to the right. Probably he’s a soldier from the barracks.’

‘Probably.’ No one else was at all interested in the man, apart from his skill as a surfer, Jessica realised. But she found him fascinating even through the glasses. What a time it must have taken to perfect his skill on the board. Idle rich, perhaps? Yet there was nothing of either in his appearance.

‘Tea’s served, gentlemen.’

Pat’s figure, pushing her trolley through the swing doors, got a good reception. She was popular with her patients and the Spaniards fell over themselves to get on good terms with such a very blonde, plumply curving English girl. Now she gave the trolley a push and turned back towards the corridor.

‘Can you manage, Jess? I have to go back, to check the abdominal paracentesis and make sure her drainage bag’s not too full.’

‘I’m fine,’ Jessica said, taking over the trolley and dispensing tea. Now that she had a moment to consider, the man on the sufboard could easily have been heading for the military hospital, next door. It was the military surgeons and consultants who saw all the patients at the Nelson and did all the necessary operations and so on, since the Nelson itself was too small to have a surgical team or theatre facilities. So far, Jessica had only met Dr Imrid, who was the Nelson’s own in-house physician and a Dr Caball, who seemed pleasant, but Pat assured her that, in the fullness of time, she would meet most of the staff at the big hospital next door.

‘Some are nice and some aren’t,’ she had said. ‘We’ve an arrangement with them though, which you should have noticed when you signed your contract. They operate on our patients where necessary and keep a surgical eye on them and we, when occasion demands, help out over there, on the wards or whatever. I’ve been over twice and it’s great fun to nurse the soldiers, though at first the language made things difficult. But I can cope very well now.’

The island of Minestos had a huge military presence since young soldiers came here for their initial training and when possible sick soldiers were sent to the hospital, one of the biggest and best in the area. Even in a week Jessica had grown used to the fact that there was more of the light greeny-khaki colour in the streets than any other, and to the constant presence of handsome, dark young men with conventional haircuts and upright bearing. You crossed the square in Villa Castello, where the nurses' flats were situated, and on each corner was a uniformed man with a rifle held negligently in the crook of his arm. They would smile at you and wolf-whistle, but if you tried to go near any of the buildings they were guarding the rifle was suddenly firmly held, pointed straight at you, and the eyes on yours were very cold and steady.

The afternoon wore on. Teas were drunk and cleared away, the patients were settled down for a siesta. Pat and Jessica reported to Sister Harris and were told to go and sort bedding in the linen room. They were in the middle of folding sheets when the door burst open and Rosa appeared. She looked hot and flustered.

'Leave it, Sister says,' she said quickly, indicating the pile of sheets. 'You'll never guess . . . there's a ward round, during siesta! Perrello's just telephoned and when I came past I could hear footsteps on the stairs! She sent me to tell you . . .'

'A ward round! Damn and damn again!' Pat dropped her sheet into Jessica's unwilling arms and headed for the corridor. 'Come on, Nurse French, this isn't just any old ward round, it's Perrello! Make for Room 2 and . . . oh!'

Sister was approaching them down the corridor, a tall man by her side. She was looking up at him and they appeared to be chatting pleasantly enough but Jessica, impressed by the unflappable Pat's obvious flap, set out after them at a trot. She just hoped they would turn into Room 1 first, giving her time to shoot into Room 2 to check that all was as it should be.

She was doomed to disappointment. Without so much as a glance at Room 1, Sister and her companion entered Room 2, going through the swing doors, fortunately, without a glance behind them to where Jessica and Pat were hurrying in their wake.

'Too late!' Pat hissed, making for Room 1. 'Doesn't matter, not really. Nurses aren't supposed to be prepared for rounds during siesta.'

Jessica took a deep breath, straightened her shoulders and marched into the room. At the very same moment, unfortunately, Sister and the surgeon decided to leave it which meant that the doors, shooting inwards beneath Jessica's impatient push, crashed heavily against their persons.

Sister squawked but Dr Perrello, regrettably, swore, though since he did so in Spanish Jessica guessed that it was only herself who understood. She began to stammer apologies but was cut short by Sister.

'It's all right, Staff, as it happens we were looking for you. Is there someone in charge in there?'

'Nurse Brown's keeping an eye on things,' Jessica said. 'She'll be all right I'm sure, Sister.'

The three of them then made for Sister's office, but when they reached it, Sister waved them in and turned back to the door again.

'I'll leave you now, Nurse . . . I'm so sorry, I didn't introduce you! Dr Perrello, this is Staff Nurse Jessica French. Jessica, Dr Perrello, our senior surgeon.'

For the first time, Jessica actually looked at the man taking the chair on the other side of the desk and, looking, gasped.

There was no mistake, no possibility of error; it was the lone surfer!

It was an odd experience, to meet someone you felt you knew quite well whilst knowing that he could not know you at all, had never set eyes on you, in fact. Jessica knew she must forget all about the solitary surfer and remember that this man wanted to see her about her job, something done badly or not done at all, perhaps. She wished she had had a chance to tidy her hair, rub the shine off her nose, slip into a clean apron . . . but she must forget all that. She had only been here a week, he surely had not discovered anything wrong so soon?

'Nurse French, I begin to believe I've been misinformed, but I was told that you were, until recently, a theatre nurse.'

His voice was deep, his English excellent, almost unaccented.

'That's true, sir.'

'It is? But I was told you worked in the Santa Monica Hospital, in Madrid.'

'That's right, sir. I worked in theatre there.'

He frowned. He had very black, very thick brows and they grew rather close together so that the frown turned them in a dark bar across his forehead. He looked formidable and Jessica swallowed, wondering what was wrong, anyway, with having been a theatre nurse.

'Are you sure, Nurse, that you're the same Jessica French . . . it seems absurd but you are so obviously English that to work in theatre . . . I'd assumed . . .'

'It is me, really it is,' Jessica said rather madly, in Spanish. 'I know I look English . . . well, I am English . . . but my mother was Spanish and it was our first language at home.' Anxiety getting the better of her she added baldly, 'What have I done, sir?'

'Done?' Dazedly she watched the black bar of his brows detach themselves from across his nose and climb into twin peaks. 'What should you have done?'

'I don't know,' Jessica said, 'but I suppose I must have done something or you wouldn't have sent for me. I'm very sorry, but I can't think of anything!'

She was getting rather defiant and heated, she could not help it. He smiled slightly and it was surprising what a difference it made to the dark, rather austere face. He shook his head chidingly and made calming down motions with one tanned hand though, when she attempted to speak again.

'Nurse French, you have done nothing, I only wanted to talk to you. In about fifteen minutes I am to operate on a man with a hernia. It is not a large or a dangerous operation but he was not on the list, so my theatre sister has gone off duty and I am loath to bring her back into Malon for such a small task. I mentioned it in the Mess and one of the men there said he'd noticed that a theatre nurse had just taken a job at the Nelson. He had been interested to find such a one on the Nelson staff so had made a note of your name. But rightly or wrongly he assumed you to be a mature woman who'd been living and working in Spain for many years. When I saw you . . .' his dark eyes raked her from top to toe, their meaning clear, '. . . I thought there must have been some mistake.'

'No, no mistake.' Jessica relaxed. 'Well, I'm relieved it was nothing I'd done, at any rate.'

'I gathered as much. And you've nothing else to say?'

'No, I don't think so,' Jessica said, after a puzzled pause. 'What else is there to say? I'm Jessica French and I was a theatre nurse in Madrid and . . . oh!'

He was watching her, a slight, sardonic smile hovering on his mouth, bringing into prominence the long, deep-cut lines which ran from his nostrils to the outer corners of his lips.

'Well, Nurse? Would you help out in theatre? If you're considering a blunt refusal, remember your contract.'

Jessica stood up and the surgeon followed suit.

'I'll be happy to assist, if you think I'm capable,' she said formally. 'However, you did say your theatre sister was off duty and I never rose to such heights, I was only a staff nurse.'

He shook his head reprovingly at this; he was still smiling.

'Tut, Nurse, as if I'd suggest it unless I thought you capable. My informant also assured me you'd been acting theatre sister for six months and were about to be made up to sister when you gave in your notice.'

'Yes, that's true. Do you want me to come over now, then?'

He passed her and opened the door, holding it ajar for her and nodding as he did so, but once in the corridor she hesitated.

'What about Sister? Shouldn't I . . . ?'

'I've had a word with her. Come along, Nurse, we haven't got all night.'

He strode ahead of her so that Jessica had to trot to keep up. Through the Nelson they went, across the grounds, through a side gate and into the military hospital. He did not glance back to make sure she was following, he was probably well aware that she must stick close to him since she had no idea where the theatres were.

Presently, Dr Perrello flung a door open and gestured

Jessica inside. It was a scrub-up room and the doctor wasted no time. He pulled his shirt over his head in one swift, practised movement and went over to the sinks. He began to scrub and Jessica quickly shed her cap, apron and wristwatch and made for the sink. As she began to scrub she saw him, out of the corner of her eye, flick the taps off with his elbow and turn to the skinny little auxiliary.

'Gown.'

His brusqueness made Jessica blink. Apparently he did not waste even politeness, let alone charm, on someone as low as an auxiliary nurse! But the other girl merely reached for the sterile pack and slit it open. The surgeon took the garment, shook it out, thrust his arms into the short sleeves and glanced impatiently at the girl.

'Fasten the ties.'

He turned his back and Jessica had to smile at the girl's dilemma, for she was a good foot or more shorter than the surgeon and was plainly scared out of her wits at the thought of touching him accidentally as she strained up to the ties dangling loose on the broad, muscular back.

'Excuse me, Dr Perrello, can I fasten your gown for you?' Jessica said, while the girl cast her a grateful glance. 'Nurse is rather short and if she touches anything other than the ties you'll only have to change.'

'Very well, but you should be getting into your own gown,' the surgeon said ungraciously. 'I trust you won't take as long to scrub-up as you do to make-up each morning.'

Jessica's face burned but she finished her task, merely saying woodenly, 'I shall be right behind you when you go into theatre, Nurse can manage my ties without any trouble.'

Finishing his ties she slid into her own gown, the small auxiliary fastened it, and then she and the surgeon put on the sterile shoes, gloves and theatre caps. Then, at a brusque gesture from Perrello, Jessica followed him through another doorway and into theatre.

It was a typical theatre and could have been in any hospital from Madrid to Manchester. The rest of the team, and the patient, were already waiting. The anaesthetist was monitoring his machinery, Dr Caball, who was going to assist, stood by the patient's shoulder and the trolley with all the necessary instruments waited for Jessica.

It was strange, Jessica thought presently, how her mind took one big leap and she was back in the role of theatre nurse, a role which had once suited her so well. She cast a professional glance at the trolley, at the patient and then at the surgeon, picked up a swab and dipped it into the site-cleaning solution. Some surgeons liked to clean their own operation sites, others preferred the staff to do it. This surgeon, Jessica felt sure, would have started to clean at once had he not intended her to do the job. So she wiped off the last trace of the pen which had marked the site, straightened the towels which surrounded it and stepped back, one hand hovering over the trolley.

She was working in a strange theatre for a man she did not know, surrounded by a team whose ways were strange to her, but she felt no flicker of uncertainty, only a confidence in her own ability to do this job. Dr Perrello might be difficult and even unpleasant on the ward but she had no doubt he would make allowances for her here. No one could be expected, for instance, to know what size blade a surgeon preferred until one had worked for him over several months. He would just have to be explicit for a while.

Dr Perrello rapped a command, Jessica gave him the instrument and watched as the surgeon made his first incision. Bleeding started and Jessica reached for swabs and clamps. The operation had begun.

It was neither a long nor a difficult operation but, as Dr Perrello began to close the wound and Jessica and the auxiliary did their last swab count, she knew she was working with a first-rate surgeon. Quick, decisive and unhesitating, his operating technique reminded her that this was the same man who wind-surfed with such skill and daring.

When they had finished and scrubbed they changed back into their own clothes and Dr Perrello led her through to the rest-room which was part of the theatre suite.

'Coffee, Nurse? Black or white?' he poured a cup for her and another for himself and then led her over to the french windows, away from the rest of the team, most of whom were lounging in the big, soft chairs which were scattered across the light green tiled floor. There was a low hum of conversation but Perrello drew her deliberately apart; plainly he did not wish to be overheard.

'You enjoyed that.' It was a statement, not a question, but Jessica answered as though it had been the latter.

'Yes, I did. I don't regret leaving theatre, I like working on the ward, but I did enjoy it.'

'I may need you again. You appear to be good at your work, though it's difficult to tell on such short acquaintance.'

'Thank you,' Jessica said shortly, 'I hope I *am* good at my work, but my work is on the wards, now. I don't think Sister would be best pleased if I suddenly decided I'd rather work in theatre.'

'The decision, Nurse, is not yours.' He gave her a long, considering look. 'Work on the ward may be easier, less traumatic, but that's beside the point. Why did you leave your job in Madrid? Why didn't you stay and take your place as Sister, after doing the work for so long?'

'I wanted a change,' Jessica said evasively. 'I'd done theatre for two years, perhaps I wanted to nurse a patient who could give me a smile, some sort of response.'

'I suppose it was some man,' Dr Perrello said, the sneer in his voice plain for Jessica's ears to catch. 'It's always the way with you English girls, all you think about is having a good time with some fellow. Did he ditch you? Throw you over?'

Jessica stiffened with fury; how dare he! But when the red mist cleared from her vision he had not been struck dead by her silent rage. Instead, he was still standing beside her, looking down at her with that nasty, superior look on his face.

Diplomacy dictated a soft answer to turn away wrath but alas, Jessica was no diplomat. She stared straight up into his face, knowing there were spots of bright colour burning in her cheeks and that her eyes were bright with temper.

'Mind—your—own—business,' she said clearly.

It was a great pity that, as she spoke, one of those inexplicable silences had fallen on the small company so that everyone present heard. A pity, but one of those things. Dr Perrello remained frozen still for a moment, looking down at her, the smile—and the sneer—gradually leaving his face. Then he shrugged and took her arm, turning her to face the window.

'I stand corrected!' he said lightly and aloud, but beneath his breath he added, 'You little vixen!' He did not sound angry any more, but quite amused.

As his fingers closed warmly round her bare arm and his sneer turned to amusement, Jessica felt all her righteous rage oozing away. A little electric shock of feeling ran along her arm and down her spine. She looked up at him and saw, for a moment, the solitary surfer and not the sneering medical man. Something must have made him say that, apart from a desire to bait me, she told herself. Some woman has hurt him badly. Was she English, and a nurse? She would find out easily enough, there's always someone on every ward who knows everything. It would be a help if she knew a few facts about this strange and disturbing man.

Behind them, the team were getting ready to leave; Jessica glanced at her watch, safely on her wrist once more, and saw that it was nearly time she, too, left for her flat. She moved towards the door and immediately his hand fell away from her arm. He turned to face the rest of the room as she did and together, they went over to the door.

'Goodbye, Dr Perrello,' Jessica said as they reached the doorway and turned into the corridor. 'Working with you has been . . . an experience.'

He gave her a mocking smile and inclined his head.

'And with you, Nurse French. An experience that you'll find yourself repeating quite a lot in the months to come. Good night.'

He turned and left her which, as Jessica realised, gave him not only the last word but the last laugh, since without him she was completely and totally lost. She wandered the corridors for a good ten minutes before emerging, more by luck than judgment, in the little foyer with the side door leading to the Nelson.

Hurrying up to Aggy again, to try to catch Pat so that they could go home together, Jessica pondered on his last remark. An experience she would find herself repeating in the months to come? He should be so lucky! She had no intention of finding herself doing two jobs, one at the Nelson and one in theatre. Clever Dr Perrello would have to think again.

CHAPTER TWO

'So I WENT and saw Sister and told her that I'd put in for a ward job so that I could have a change from theatre, and she said she'd do what she could.' Jessica, sorting towels which had just returned from the laundry, sighed deeply. 'Then this morning she called me in to say she'd put it to the Board and Dr Perrello had over-ruled all her objections. In fact, when he said an experienced theatre nurse was wasted on the ward the members agreed with him . . . sharp words were exchanged about our rates of pay, it seems.'

'Yes. We get better paid than the nurses in the military hospital because we're a long way from home,' Pat told her. 'How many Ward 1 towels do you have there?'

'A dozen. Is that right?'

Pat consulted her list and chewed a fingernail.

'Mmm . . . ten, eleven, twelve. That's right. So you're going to do part-time theatre work when the sister's off. How do you feel? You must have enjoyed theatre work once.'

'I did . . . do. It seems hard on Sister, though, to have me being seconded to theatre every time Perrello needs an extra pair of hands. And to be honest I didn't much like Perrello's attitude . . . however, there's no way out, I've got to abide by my contract.'

'You don't like Perrello? Join the club. He's got no time for nurses, particularly English ones. What's he like as a surgeon, though?'

'Awfully good, though I wouldn't say he was renowned for patience and understanding, even in theatre,' Jessica said, after a pause for thought. 'He can be very sarcastic and if things aren't done almost before he's asked he can be annihilatingly rude. But he's first-rate with the knife.'

'Oh, well. Perhaps he won't need you very often,' Pat said hopefully, leaving the towels and beginning on a huge pile of sheets. 'Give me a hand with these, would you? I'll hand you Ward 2 and I'll keep Ward 1—you should have fifteen according to the list and I'll have seventeen.'

'Right. Ah, this one's torn; what happens to it?'

'Put it aside, it'll have to go back for repair. I've got seventeen here, so I'll put them straight back into the linen cupboard.'

'And mine are all here, too. Pat, why doesn't Perrello like the English?'

'Because he was married to an English girl—a nurse, too —about twelve or fifteen years ago, only she left him for some sort of Spanish grandee. It made him very bitter. It put him off women in fact, it's only within the last couple of years that he's actually begun to thaw, as with his theatre sister.'

Jessica smoothed her pile of sheets and turned back to Pat, brows rising.

'He's keen on his theatre nurse, eh? Well, I just hope some of his feeling for her rubs off on her substitute. It would be nice to have a slightly more social atmosphere in the rest-room for instance. The others are so friendly, they chat and laugh and drop bits of information about patients and even their own lives, but Perrello stalks over to the window with his coffee, and scarcely exchanges a word with any but senior medical staff.'

'It's strange when I think of it that you've never met Sister Cruz,' Pat remarked. 'Gosh, more laundry? Oh, draw-sheets. They're like the others, marked in the top right-hand corner and it'll be seventeen for Ward 2 and fifteen for 1.'

'Sister Cruz—what a name! It sounds more like an atomic missile than a woman. What's she like?'

Pat giggled. 'She's dazzlingly beautiful in fact, but she knows it. She can be sharp-tongued, so perhaps she keeps him in his place.'

'Him? Unlikely. He's the domineering sort.'

'Oh, he's just a typical macho Spaniard which means in his heart he thinks women should be chained to the sink by day and the bed by night. They're all old-fashioned and Victorian about women, that's what makes them marvellous lovers and dreadful husbands. My draw-sheets are one short, which means yet another trip to the laundry, more's the pity.'

'It's all right, I've got sixteen, you'd better take one of mine. Is that the lot?'

'Yes, I . . .'

The door shot open and Rosa said plaintively, 'Could someone come? Sister wants one of you to show me how to change a drip.'

'We'll be with you right away, Nurse,' Pat said crisply, picking up the sheets to be mended. 'I'll get someone to take these back to the laundry and then we can come home back to the ward.'

'Give it a bit more height would you, Staff?'

Sister Harris and Jessica were adjusting the spigot and putting up the drip bottle whilst reassuring the patient, a pleasant girl in her mid-twenties recovering from a breast biopsy. Jessica had just got the bottle at the correct angle when she was hailed by a voice from the end of the ward.

'Jessica, where's Sister? Theatre have just telephoned.'

Sister sighed and straightened up.

'I imagine I can guess what they want, but you'd better tell me anyway, Nurse.'

'It's Nurse French, Sister. Could you send her over at once, please? They've got an emergency coming into theatre.'

'Off you go, Staff,' Sister said, taking the spigot. 'I'm sorry, I know you'll be off duty soon, but we can't let them down and it is an emergency. Don't come back when you finish over there, go straight to your flat and let me know tomorrow how much overtime you've worked. And don't walk, Staff, run. Perrello's an impatient man and an emergency in theatre is always important.'

'Right, Sister,' Jessica said, hurrying down the ward, but as she reached the doorway she smiled ruefully at Pat, still hovering.

'What happened to Sister Cruz?' she asked plaintively. 'I'm off duty in fifteen minutes and I was going out for a meal with Dr Gambas; now I'll never make it, even if it's quite a short op. Do you suppose you could let him know, Pat? I wouldn't want him to think he was being stood up.'

'I'll phone right away,' Pat promised, trotting beside Jessica.

'Here, you go down, I'll throw your coat over the banisters.'

'Don't bother, I'll have to come back to the ward anyway, to leave my apron and cap,' Jessica reminded her, beginning to skim down the flight. She raised her voice as she reached the lower hallway. 'Don't forget to ring Gambas, will you?'

Outside the hospital a balmy breeze blew and the sun was gentle and warm. Jessica ran through the hospital garden, down the path and into the Military hospital premises, then began to trot down the long, dim corridors. She had been over here at least half a dozen times and knew the way to the theatres by heart so it was only a few moments after the phone call that she arrived, panting and breathless, at the scrub-up room. It was deserted save for Ana, who often worked with Jessica when she stood in for Sister Cruz. She smiled behind her mask and began to open the packing round a sterile gown.

'Better hurry, Nurse,' she muttered as Jessica began to scrub. 'It's a real emergency, a ruptured appendix, the prep. sister laid up the trolley ten minutes ago, they're only waiting for you and I before they start.'

'I came as soon as I could,' Jessica said, pulling on her gloves with her usual care. Nothing could be more annoying than splitting a glove when you were in a hurry. 'If Sister laid up the trolley ten minutes ago why didn't they ring me sooner?'

'Sister Cruz shouldn't have left, so Dr Perrello was trying to get hold of her,' Ana said. 'He telephoned all round and then sent a runner off to the nurses' room and then came back looking like thunder and told someone else to ring the Nelson.'

'Oh, I see.' Jessica pushed open the theatre door and entered the room with Ana hard on her heels. As the younger girl had said everyone was there, gowned and ready, the anaesthetist fiddling with his dials and the doctors chatting, their eyes on the doors through which the patient would presently be wheeled.

'Nurse French; good,' Perrello said briskly, catching sight of Jessica as the movement of the door caught his eye. 'We're all ready, now. Do a swab check, would you, whilst we bring the chap through.'

'Right,' Jessica said through her mask. She turned to Ana and together they began to count the swabs, from very large to very tiny, hanging on the rack ready for use. Behind her the patient was wheeled in, transferred from trolley to table and the team leaped smoothly into action. Everyone worked hard, attaching the patient to the diathermy machine, adjusting the anaesthetic, getting the patient at the right angle and in the right position for surgery. Used to the routine the surgeon preferred by now, Jessica moved forward with her cleaning swab as soon as the operation site was ready, mopped briskly and dropped the used swab into the empty bucket. Dr Cassim was assisting and he and the surgeon had a brief discussion, then Dr Perrello held out his hand for the first scalpel and they were off.

Watching closely as the surgeon's gloved hands moved, the scalpel neatly opening up the peritoneal cavity, Jessica kept all her attention on the job in hand. She swabbed blood, handed swabs, snatched for instruments seconds before Dr Perrello asked for them. Simultaneously, she kept a private check on the trolley so that she would be able to get the clamps the minute he wanted them.

'Specimen pot, please.'

Jessica watched as the inflamed organ was brought slowly out of the cavity whilst she held the pot ready to receive it.

'There was a faecolith blocking the lumen,' Perrello remarked as he lowered the evil-looking tissue into the jar. 'We were lucky he realised something was very wrong and luckier still that a theatre was clear so that we could operate at once. That little lot could have caused an awful lot of trouble even if we'd only delayed for a few hours.'

'He'll feel a good deal better without it,' Dr Cassim agreed. 'A drainage tube, if you please.'

'We'll do a swab count now, Ana,' Jessica murmured as the surgical team began the methodical work of cleaning the wound and inserting the drainage tube before closing the site. The auxiliary nurse got the sponge holders and began to fish for the swabs, putting them onto the swab rack as they came out so that each could be counted separately. She and Jessica both had a bad moment at the end of the count until they realised a swab had just missed the bucket and was clinging damply to the outside edge of the container. Ana fished it up, giving a nervous giggle which Jessica nearly echoed, for out of the corner of her eye she could see Perrello reaching for the suturing thread. She felt she would rather shoot herself than admit to having lost a swab, though if one remained in the peritoneal cavity it would scarcely be her fault.

'Count all right, Nurse?'

He had not turned away from the patient but the deep voice reached her easily.

'All correct, sir.'

'Good. Send a runner to the path. lab with this specimen pot, would you?'

'Right away, sir. Blanca, take this to the lab immediately, please.'

She handed the specimen pot with its gruesome-looking contents to the runner, being careful not to touch her though at this stage in the proceedings being rendered unsterile was not quite the disaster it would have been earlier. Indeed, Dr Perrello was tying his last stitch and she had a sterile dressing ready with the tape to secure it in place.

'There we are.' Dr Perrello straightened, shrugged his shoulders right up to his ears and dropped them to their normal position, then moved his arms against his sides and straightened, bent and then straightened his knees two or three times. He was stiff and aching from remaining tensely in the same position for so long, Jessica knew, and was trying to ease his discomfort now that the operation was over. He heaved a sigh and turned to the nursing staff, hovering behind him.

'Wheel him into recovery, please.' He turned back to Jessica. 'Well done; come to the rest-room and have a cup of coffee and some sandwiches before you go back on the ward.'

'I'm off duty, actually,' Jessica said, glancing at the clock and coming abruptly back to earth with the knowledge that she was tired and aching and also very thirsty. She might as well go and have coffee, Dr Gambas would have given her up an hour ago and anyway she was now far too tired to enjoy an evening out, all she felt like was a meal, a drink and her bed.

'Off duty? I didn't . . .' he broke off as Jessica smiled and interrupted.

'It doesn't matter, it was good to know you'd caught it in

time and anyway I'll come down to the rest-room, I'm very thirsty, I could do with a coffee.'

He nodded and moved away from her as the team began to cast down their gloves and theatre caps. 'All right, Nurse, see you in a moment. Carlos, before you go I just want a word . . .' the team were all making their way to the scrub room and Jessica followed them.

Later, making her weary way to the rest-room, she glanced at her watch and saw that she had just missed a bus which meant an hour's wait, so a coffee was definitely a good idea. She entered the room to find it unusually quiet for most of the theatre staff must have changed and gone home. However, the glass coffee jug simmered away on its hot-plate and the cups and the dried milk stood ready. A nice addition was a plateful of sandwiches, obviously ordered from the canteen.

Jessica was pouring herself a cup of coffee and contemplating the sandwiches when the door opened and Dr Perrello's head appeared round it. He saw her, hesitated, then came fully into the room.

'Ah, Nurse French. Pour me a *cafe cortado*, would you? It's not good for one to drink it black on an empty stomach but I don't fancy *cafe blanca*, so I'll settle for the in-between.'

Jessica dutifully poured a black coffee, added a dash of milk, and then carried it to the surgeon, who had strolled over to the long windows leading on to the balcony and flung them open.

'Here you are, sir, one *cafe cortado*. Do you want a sandwich? They look awfully nice.'

He took his coffee with a murmur of thanks and turned back into the room, to pick up not one sandwich but the entire plateful; he then carried his booty out onto the balcony, where he set the plate down on a small metal table and hooked a chair forward with one foot. He was dressed casually now, Jessica realised, in a light blue sports shirt and dark blue linen slacks, with navy rope-soled shoes completing his attire. He jerked his head at the chair.

'Take the weight off your feet, Nurse French. Well, this is pleasant—a tête-à-tête, just the two of us. Have a sandwich.'

'I can't imagine why everyone else rushed off,' Jessica said, taking the proffered chair and selecting a sandwich. 'I thought they usually stopped for coffee, or at least they've done so when I've been over on previous occasions.'

'So they do, but it's late so they've all rushed off home to their husbands or wives or loved ones. It is only you and I, Nurse, who would be going home to an empty apartment.'

'I had a date,' Jessica said rather sharply, 'but of course I had to get a message to him telling him that I wouldn't be able to keep it and he'll have made other arrangements by now. Otherwise I'd have been down at Cala Binnarafa, having a meal and possibly a swim, later.'

'Oh well, that's the medical profession for you.' He was not going to attempt to apologise; plainly, he expected her to take such things in her stride. Since she was used to theatre work Jessica accepted that an emergency meant working until the crisis was over, but no one enjoys foregoing an outing and she had really looked forward to this one. However, she did not intend to let herself down by admitting to disappointment. She took a bite from her sandwich and made a noncommittal agreeing sound as she did so.

'What will you do this evening, then, Nurse? Give the boyfriend a ring? Tell him to pick you up in half an hour or so?'

'He isn't my boyfriend, he's never taken me out before,' Jessica said rather stiffly and then, feeling she was being churlish, she added, 'It was Gustavo Gambas, actually, so he'll understand.'

'Gambas, eh?'

Jessica nodded and glanced across at him, to see the black brows were forming a bar across his forehead. She could see no possible reason for the deep frown and raised her eyebrows rather defiantly.

'Yes, Dr Gambas. It was kind of him to ask me out, he knows I'm still very much a new girl here.'

'Kind? I think Gambas is being more self-interested than you give him credit for. Although in your own country your looks must be quite commonplace, here you are unusual, eyecatching. No doubt Gambas feels he's done well to attract your attention. But I must warn you, Nurse French, that we don't encourage flirtations within the theatre team, it can make for a difficult atmosphere when the break comes . . . if it comes, of course. So I'd prefer it if you kept your relationships within the hospital on friendly rather than amorous levels, if you please.'

Jessica stared across the table at his dark, sarcastic face. Two snubs, both crushing ones, in a few short sentences; firstly she was told that her looks were commonplace and then she was warned against amorous entanglements. It was too bad, just who did Dr Perrello think he was? It was tempting to be rude back but pointless as well as quite possibly dangerous. A senior surgeon could make a nurse's life very difficult if he chose to do so. She contended herself with simply not replying, but eating her sandwich with great speed and draining her coffee equally rapidly. There was no need, after all, to remain here to be insulted by her companion.

'You really were hungry, Nurse, that sandwich disappeared in no time! More coffee?'

He reached for her cup but Jessica put her hand over it, shaking her head. She was tired, she would go back to the flat, have a shower, a meal and then go to bed. And although she had no intention of telling Perrello so, she would jolly well accept every invitation from any man who asked her, be he medic or hospital porter! No one would dictate to Jessica French when it came to her personal life.

'No more thank you, sir, I must be getting back to the apartment,' she glanced at her watch and suppressed a gasp of dismay. Unless the bus was awfully late and she ran like anything she would either have to walk back to the nurses' flat or wait an hour for the next bus. But she did not intend to tell Perrello that; she stood up, pushing back her chair with a squeak across the tiles, and the doctor followed suit and rose to his feet.

'Did you know you'd just missed the bus?' he said blandly. 'However, I'm returning to Castello in five minutes or so—can I give you a lift?'

By now, though, all Jessica wanted was to get away from Perrello; I and my commonplace looks would rather walk than ride if the penalty to riding is to be constant criticism she told herself firmly.

'It's quite all right, I'd just as soon walk, and I've got to go back to the ward to change,' she told him. 'I don't know how long I'll be, but the fresh air will do me good.'

It was the wrong thing to say, she realised twenty minutes later, making her weary way along the main road towards Villa Castello, when a car swished to a halt beside her. It was an open sports model and Perrello sat behind the wheel, smiling slightly as he opened the passenger door.

'In this car you can have all the fresh air you desire,' he said lightly as Jessica climbed slowly into the vehicle and sank back on to the smooth leather seat. 'I'm sorry, Nurse, if I seemed harsh back in the rest-room, perhaps it was not necessary to warn you off quite so bluntly. But in my defence I've had good surgical teams ruined by affairs of the heart between doctors and nurses.'

'I can appreciate that,' Jessica said. 'But I did tell you, sir, that Gustavo and I are barely acquainted.'

'Yes, I stand corrected. I wonder . . .' he paused, glancing across at her. It was dusk and she could not see the expression on his face in the gloom but only the flash of his eyes as he turned them in her direction. '. . . Would you allow me to buy you a meal to make up for causing you to miss your evening with Gustavo? Just something simple, so that you don't go home and have to start cooking?'

'It's awfully kind of you but I'm not dressed for going out, and anyway I'm sure you've plans of your own for the evening,' Jessica said uncertainly. 'I'll be all right, I'm used to missing dates—as you said earlier, that's the medical profession for you.'

'Did I say that?' His smile was slight, but she caught a flash of his white teeth in the dark. 'Well, it may not have been very tactful in the circumstances but it was all too true; none of us ever knows for sure that a bleeper won't go or a telephone ring. Now don't worry about your dress, which is very pretty and quite suitable for the restaurant I have in mind. Let your thoughts dwell on iced melon, then lobster salad, then sorbet, or gateaux, or . . . well, whatever you'd enjoy. And then say you'll keep me company.'

It was so charmingly said that Jessica would have felt a

refusal to be ungracious, but she still felt she must impose a condition on her acceptance.

'Dr Perrello, I'd love to have dinner with you, my mouth's watering already, but if I come will you promise not to talk shop? Anything else you like, but not hospital talk.'

She was sitting with her hands in her lap looking straight ahead through the windscreen and hoping he would not be offended, when he touched her hands in the lightest of gestures. Startled, she looked across at him. He was watching the road, his eyes steady, but he nodded.

'Fair enough; no shop. Shoes, ships, sealing wax, cabbages and kings but no hospital talk from either of us. Is it a bargain?'

'It's a bargain. I can't shake hands on it since you're driving, but I promise. Where are we going to eat?'

'Do you know Tonio's Cave, down by the harbour at Villa Castello? I often have a meal there when I'm working late, and I leave my car there and go home by boat. I live on the opposite side of the harbour to the town, you see. Then in the morning I get the boat back, pick up the car, and presto, I'm in the hospital in time to start my clinic or my list or whatever the day holds for me.'

'I've seen the cave restaurant but we usually go to a snack bar,' Jessica confessed. 'The local food is good but prices are too high for us as a rule. It will be a treat to be waited on.'

'I'm glad.' He turned the car down the narrow road to the little harbour and presently helped her out of it and walked her across the stretch of paving and into the restaurant, which was hollowed out of the rock and decorated with fishing nets and preserved marine life, with huge, red-shaded lights which cast a soft glow over chequered tablecloths, the dark-clad waiters and the diners.

The proprietor approached them, greeted Dr Perrello and cast a speculative glance at Jessica.

'Good evening, *señor*; your usual table?'

'Please, Tonio. Could we have a bottle of chilled white wine right away? We've had a long day.'

The meal, which arrived just in time to accompany their second glass of wine was excellent, the talk as far-ranging and interesting as Perrello knew how to make it. Jessica found herself chattering far more than she had intended but the doctor was a good listener, his questions intelligent and perspicacious. Without realising quite how it had come about, Jessica found herself telling Perrello a good deal about her family and early life.

'My parents met, in Spain, about twenty-seven years ago,' she told him. 'Dad was a Londoner but he spoke good Spanish so he was sent over by his bank to work in Madrid for a year. Mum was just a girl, a teller, working in the same branch and Spanish, naturally. They fell in love and married, and moved back to England when Dad's year was up, but of course we came back to Spain every summer and I used to move in with my grandparents for two or three months at a time and pretend I was a little Spanish *niña*, like my Cortezo cousins.'

'That accounts for your fluent Spanish; yet you trained in an English hospital, did you not? In Manchester?'

'That's right. After I qualified I came over to Madrid to see my grandmother—my grandfather had died the previous year—and saw the job advertised, applied and got it. I stayed there very happily, living with my grandmother, until I—I felt like a change. That was when I applied for the job at the Nelson, and got it.'

'And your parents? Your home? Do you go back to England often?'

'Not often, because my father died shortly after I came here and a year after that, Mother married again. He's probably very nice, but he's a lot younger than my father was and I don't feel comfortable in his company, so I only see Mum now when she comes over to visit her sister in Valladolid or my grandmother, in Madrid.'

Dr Perrello had been listening intently but now his black brows rose and he shook his head at her.

'There should not be ill-feeling within a family. Surely you understand that your mother needed to marry again? Can you not accept her new husband not as a father-substitute but merely as a companion for your mother?'

Jessica smiled but shook her head in her turn.

'No, I can't. Oh, I understand that she felt lonely and needed someone, but Richard isn't my type—all he thinks about is his herd of pedigree cattle, how to get his hands on yet more land, and whether to try some new sort of fly on his next fishing trip. So boring!'

'An English country gentleman, eh? And you, Miss French? Do you consider yourself English or Spanish?'

'A mixture,' Jessica said promptly. 'I want to live in Spain, though I enjoy England at holidaytimes.'

'You seem Spanish in some ways,' Dr Perrello said thoughtfully. 'You are such a hard worker and so efficient in theatre.'

Jessica could not help smiling. Plainly, Dr Perrello wanted her to be more Spanish than English to explain her virtues. Her vices, when he discovered them, would doubtless be totally English.

'I think the English, particularly nurses, are both hard working and efficient as well,' she told him. 'Don't be taken-in by holidaymakers or by the fact that we love the Spanish sunshine and perhaps drink a little more than we usually do because we're abroad. When we aren't holidaying we come over here and work very hard, then return to our foggy island to work just as hard over there, probably bringing up families into the bargain.'

'Yes, that's true of some nurses, but there are others . . .' he stopped, glowered into his wine for a moment, then said abruptly, 'I was about to break our bargain. Let us change the subject completely. Do you sail, Miss French?'

'Yes, I do, and I've seen you surf-boarding so I take it you sail as well? Oh, incidentally, couldn't you call me Jessica, now that we're off duty? I've noticed in theatre that you use first-names for most of the team, though you always call me Nurse French. Unless you feel that such informality isn't allowable as I'm actually Nelson staff.'

He laughed and leaned across the table, to put his hand over one of hers. Jessica felt the blood surge in her veins as her heartbeat quickened. His fingers on hers were warm and firm, yet she knew it was the solitary surfer who set her tingling and not the surgeon.

'You are quite right, I shall call you Jessica whilst we're off duty. My given name is Diaz which you must use when we're outside the hospital. Now that I know you like to sail, perhaps we could go out in my yacht, one afternoon when we aren't on duty; there are some very beautiful bays which can only be reached by water. If you would like to visit them we must arrange a day and a time.'

Jessica, nodding, felt that things were really looking up. To make a friend of a man generally believed to be both difficult and surly could make her life very much easier and anyway, he was proving himself a delightful companion as well as an efficient and gifted colleague.

It was nearly midnight before they moved from their table. Dr Perrello paid the bill, then took her arm—electric impulses raced up her arm and charged giddily down her spine—and led her to the edge of the harbour, pointing downwards as he did so.

'See that motor boat? She's mine, I'll take you home in her, I can moor her at the quayside by the nurses' home.'

He climbed down and held up both hands. Jessica took his fingers, tried to jump down lightly and found herself for one breathtaking moment actually in the surgeon's arms before he stood her down on the bottom-boards.

'You're a lot more substantial than you appear, Jessica.' He slid along the seat until he was behind the wheel, then patted the leather cushion beside him. 'Come and sit here. One day you can try your hand at driving her, but it's best to steer for the first time in daylight.'

Perrello started the engine, switched on the headlight and they were off, moving smoothly across the dark water, heading for Villa Castello. It was cooler now and Jessica was glad of her cardigan, but the journey was not a long one. All too soon they were drawing near to the shore again and the surgeon was cutting the engine, letting her drift and then jumping lithely ashore, to tie up to a worn concrete bollard.

'Here we are. Can you manage?'

Jessica could. She climbed out and smiled at him, holding out her hand as he turned away from the boat.

'Thank you, Diaz, for a delightful evening, but don't feel you have to come any further with me. The nurses' apartments are just across the grass and through that belt of trees, I'll be quite all right, you go off home now.'

Diaz however, shook his head and took her arm.

'Independence is all very well, but this is a garrison town and there are bad men in every army as well as good ones. Suppose someone was lurking in those trees? It's not unheard-of for a girl to be attacked. I shall see you to your door.'

Ignoring her half-hearted protest he strolled with her up the path which led to the square and then across the grass and through the trees. In their deep shade Jessica found herself very glad of his presence. It was spooky with dappling shadows and shafts of moonlight and there were thick bushes at intervals which might, as he had said, have contained anyone or anything. But they reached the nurses' flats without incident and stood for a moment in the small, brilliantly lit foyer.

'Thank you very much. Good night, Diaz, there's really no need . . .'

'Hush.' He put a finger to her lips, sending a shiver of pleasure through her. 'Which floor is your apartment on?'

'The second, but do you think you really should come up with me? Surgeons don't usually take nurses all the way home, I'm sure.'

'Second floor. Right, we'll go up.' He still held her elbow but now he looked down at her, smiling quizzically. 'And who is going to care or see, for that matter, if this particular surgeon takes this particular nurse all the way up to her room? Most people are in bed and asleep—it's long past midnight.'

They climbed the stairs and, outside her door, Jessica began to stammer good night all over again and then stopped short, looking up into the dark face above her own. He was not smiling, but she could sense that he was amused by her confusion and even whilst she was wondering whether to simply hurry through the doorway and close it behind her, he drew her, gently but inexorably, into his arms.

He bent his dark head and his mouth hovered for a moment before unerringly finding hers. It began as a light, conventional good night kiss, scarcely more emotionally involving than a handshake, and ended differently, simply because, Jessica thought guiltily, of the way she caught fire at his touch. Furious with herself, knowing that she should pull back, she clung, letting her lips soften and part, letting her body mould itself to his until he gently broke the embrace and held her away from him.

'That was . . .' he looked dazed, less than certain. A hand went to her chin, lifted it, then dropped back to his side. 'Thank you, Jessica, for a very enjoyable evening. You are a pleasant companion. Good night.'

The last words were coolly formal and he turned away as he spoke and made for the stairs. He disappeared without once glancing back whilst Jessica leaned against her door, the flush cooling in her cheeks and her heartbeats gradually returning to normal. When at last she turned to unlock the door and go inside she was still considerably shaken by Perrello's unexpected behaviour. What on earth had got into him? A man of his standing and reputation in the hospital did not simply take a liking to an insignificant little staff nurse and take her home, kissing her outside her door with a depth and passion which would have led her to believe, in any other man, that he felt something a good deal warmer towards her than mere friendship.

Getting ready for bed, she thought over what she had been told about Perrello and compared it with his behaviour this evening. A bitter man, Pat had said, especially bitter against English nurses because of his failed marriage. A man generally found difficult to get on with, a man who did not like women or at any rate, who had been put off even taking women out after the way his wife had behaved. Yes, until this evening she would have accepted all these things as part of the picture of the harsh and dictatorial surgeon for whom she worked in theatre. And yet this evening he had been so different—a good companion, charming and thoughtful and, with his good night kiss, a sensitive and caring person who liked her more than a little.

Shrugging, Jessica climbed into bed, turned out her light and pulled the thin sheet up round her shoulders. So he had unbent a little towards her under the mellowing influence of tiredness, alcohol and good food. He had kissed her, allowing himself to forget that she was an English nurse. It would clearly never happen again but she would do her best to see that they remained friends.

But it was not friendship which warmed her as her thoughts drifted into sleep.

CHAPTER THREE

'HAVE you filled in your menus, ladies? Thanks very much, then I'll collect them and take them down to the office.'

Jessica, about to take a new patient down in the lift for X-Rays, darted quickly round the ward collecting the completed menus. She was on Ward 1 today and rushed off her feet because it was Sr Profiero's theatre day and also because they had had several new admissions. Pat was having her day off but was due on the ward in half an hour since the two of them were going out together that evening.

'All done, Mrs Pontin?' Jessica smiled at the patient's round, rosy face. 'Thanks very much, I'll just run these down to the office then since you're the last.'

'Don't forget me, Staff,' the new patient said rather querulously. 'I don't see why I can't walk; I walked in here this morning, didn't I?'

'I know, it's just a rule. Apparently someone passed out on the way down to X-Ray and ever since they've insisted that we take in-patients down in a wheelchair. Shan't be more than a minute.'

Jessica hurried through the swing doors at the end of the ward, glancing at the menus in her hand as she did so. She was still looking at them when someone called her name. Looking up, she saw Pat hurrying along the corridor towards her.

'Oh, Pat, I shan't be a moment, just got to deliver these menus to Sister's office and then I must take a new patient down to X-Ray. You're early, aren't you? It can't be six o'clock yet!'

'I'm a bit early, but only ten minutes or so. Look, shall I take the menus for you? I can't wheel a patient down to X-Ray in my present gear, though.' Pat was clad in skin-tight pink jeans and a low-cut white angora top. She did not look at all like an off-duty nurse and the effect was enhanced by her hair, which was loose and tumbled down past her shoulders in soft waves and curls.

'Ten to six? Oh, lord, then I'm late.' Jessica thrust the menus into her friend's hands and turned to go, remarking over her shoulder as she did so, 'Is Mrs Pontin allowed to eat *pestinos con miel*? I see she's ticked it on her lunch menu for tomorrow.'

Pat stopped dead in her tracks, heaved an exasperated sigh, and then headed for Sister's office once more.

'That woman would probably commit murder for a piece of honey and almond cake! Never mind, I'll cross it out and write yoghurt instead. I wish she'd remember what Perrello will do to her if her weight isn't down by the time he does his next ward round!'

She disappeared into the office and Jessica hurried back to the ward, seized the wheelchair and began to wheel it and its occupant down between the beds. She was just manoeuvring the chair through the swing doors and into the corridor when Nurse Millar, about to start her shift, came up the stairs. She smiled at Jessica and then greeted the patient with easy familiarity.

'Hello, Mrs Schaefel, so you're back with us? Same trouble is it?'

Mrs Schaefel began to list her ailments and Jessica slowed the wheelchair but was very grateful when Nurse Millar seized the handles from her.

'Mrs Schaefel and I are old friends, Nurse, and you're almost due to go off duty, so if you'd like to let me take over, I'll go down to X-Ray with her.'

'Are you sure you don't mind? I would be grateful,' Jessica said, gladly relinquishing her place to the other girl. 'I'll make my way straight to the cloakroom, then.'

Once there, however, she was immediately pounced upon by Pat.

'Don't be long, will you? The film starts at seven and I've booked a table at Pedro's for ten.'

'I shan't be long,' Jessica said reassuringly. 'It's lucky that I wasn't called over to theatre, though. That really would have mucked up the evening.'

As the two girls walked down to the bus stop, Pat reminded her friend that the following night they were going to go out in a foursome with her friend Eduardo and his friend, Jaime. Both young men were army officers working at the military base, and since they were extremely career-minded, Pat did not think they wanted anything beside friendship and someone to take out occasionally.

'I saw Eduardo earlier, and he suggested we go to see the flamenco dancers at La Galia, and then have a meal on the waterfront, in one of those fish restaurants which line the harbour,' Pat said as they climbed aboard the odd little bus which plied regularly between Puerto Malon and Villa Castello. 'They're a bit basic, but great fun.'

'The officers?' Jessica asked, smiling. 'Or the restaurants?'

Pat laughed. 'What a question! The restaurants, of course. It's all charcoal grilled fish, coarse brown bread, that sort of thing. But delicious and not too expensive. I don't think officers rate much more than nurses when they're young.'

'I'm used to eating inexpensively,' Jessica said. 'Pedro's isn't exactly *haute cuisine*, is it?'

'No, but it's awfully good. It was just that I remembered Perrello took you out a few nights ago. I bet that wasn't fish and chips!'

'No. But it wasn't a particularly smart place,' Jessica said. She sighed to herself and turned the conversation, but she could not help remembering that night out with Perrello wistfully. At the time, she had really believed it might be the start of a pleasant friendship, but it was soon clear that whatever the evening might have meant to her, to Perrello it had been something best forgotten.

He had simply behaved as though their better understanding had never happened. In theatre, in the rest-room afterwards, when he met her on the ward, he spoke coolly or ignored her altogether. He always moved away from her in the rest-room and confined his conversation, as he always had, to other doctors. In short, the entire episode might have happened in another life, to two different people.

'Why the sigh?' The bus lumbered to a halt at their stop though, and any questions which Pat might have asked were diverted by having to get past a tight bunch of chattering, gesticulating teenagers who filled the doorway and were far too busy with their own affairs to think of moving without a hard push and a shrill '*Perdonne, perdonne.*'

The film, when they took their seats in the cinema, was an English one with Spanish sub-titles, but Jessica was tired after a long day on the ward and she let her mind wander well before the interval. Why had Perrello asked her out, treated her like a friend, kissed her warmly, and then apparently forgotten the entire incident?

After the film finished and she and Pat had emerged into the warm dark, Jessica managed to dismiss Perrello and the hospital from her mind as they ate paella and drank chilled white wine. She had enjoyed her evening and it was nice not to have to think about making a meal for once, but she agreed to catching a taxi home to the flat as soon as her food was finished and knew she would be asleep as soon as her head touched the pillow.

'It's fine for you, having had a lazy day, but I'm really tired,' she said as the taxi dropped them outside the flats and they made their way up the stairs. 'I must have been mad to say I'd go out two nights running. I'll be a wreck by the time Jaime and Eduardo have left us.'

'No, you won't. You're on early tomorrow, but that means you'll be off by four,' Pat said bracingly. 'You can come straight home here and get some sleep. The fellows aren't calling for us until after eight.'

'I might do that.' Pat unlocked the flat and the two girls went inside and straight across the little hall to the kitchen. Pat ran water into the kettle and Jessica got out cups and some plain biscuits.

When the drinks were ready Jessica picked up her cup and made for her room.

'I'll set the alarm for seven o'clock,' she said. 'Want me to wake you, or does your alarm work?'

'Yes, it does, but I usually go back to sleep again,' Pat confessed. 'Give me a shout when you're out of the bathroom.'

'Right. Good night.'

Jessica got ready for bed at top speed, and climbed quickly between the sheets. She was tired, she had enjoyed her evening, and now she must concentrate on getting to sleep so that she was fresh for the morning.

'Staff, I'm just off for my lunch but there's a new admission in the waiting room, could you deal with her? You'll find her file on my desk, better read it through before you take down her details. She's a Mrs Begonia Chase.'

'Of course, Sister.' Jessica had only just returned from her own lunch, which she had eaten, today, in the canteen of the military hospital. It had been a very good meal but it was not much fun eating alone and she had not been sorry when her food was finished. If one of the other nurses had managed to come over with her it would have been different, but she had spent nearly two hours in theatre this morning and had gone straight up to the canteen from there.

Usually, she and the other ward nurses used a sandwich bar quite close to the Nelson, or made use of the hospital's own tea and coffee facilities, but today she had decided to treat herself to a proper meal.

And as she walked into the canteen, Perrello had walked out. With a woman. She had taken no notice of his companion because she had been staring straight at him, waiting for him to smile or say hello. Instead, he had not even appeared to see her, so intent was he on the conversation taking place between him and the girl. Head tilted and bent towards her, for she was not very tall—that much Jessica had seen—he had passed by without so much as a glance.

There was no reason why this should have spoiled her lunch, but it had. She had felt downright grumpy and had deliberately shaken her head at the cheerful indication, by Dr Caball, that she might share his table.

So now, making her way to Sister's office, Jessica was not her usual sunny self. She sat down behind the desk, picked up the file, and began to read and knew at once that a day which had begun badly was not about to turn suddenly easy.

Mrs Chase was suffering from thyrotoxicosis, and Jessica could remember from her training days on the ward in Manehester how difficult nursing such patients could be. One needed all one's tact and skill as well as an ability to calm fears and right now, she did not feel at all capable. She felt hot and ruffled and prickly. Telling a patient to get back into bed at once and behave would have come far more naturally than her usual practical, friendly approach.

However, reading through the file she grew a little calmer and it helped that every moment Mrs Chase spent alone in the waiting room would increase her feeling of victimisation. Presently, Jessica reminded herself severely that she was not a lovesick teenager, ignored by the man of her dreams, but a nurse who Perrello had treated no differently from all the other nurses. She reflected that this was absolutely true—he was not on friendly terms with any of the nursing staff and very soon she had got her temporary bout of annoyance and misery under control and was able to make her way to the waiting room.

As soon as she entered the room, however, she realised that her worst fears were about to be realised. Mrs Chase was a pretty woman in her mid-forties with the wide-eyed, frightened look and the sweat-streaked skin typical of the disease. She had just risen to her feet, her suitcase in one hand, her sling-bag on her shoulder, obviously about to leave. The sight of Jessica in her uniform seemed, if anything, to increase her panic.

'Oh . . . oh, Nurse, I'm awfully sorry, but I really don't think I can stay here. My friend, the one who brought me in, won't have gone far, I can telephone her from the nearest café. If you'll just tell the doctor I'm sorry . . .'

'There's no need to apologise, Mrs Chase. If you want to leave you're at liberty to do so, though it seems a shame now that we've a bed vacant. However, I do have your file here, and there are some questions I'd like you to answer if you don't mind, even if we have to put them away for the next time you're admitted. Would you mind awfully just letting me get my paperwork straight?' Jessica took the case, very gently, and put it down on the ground, smiling reassuringly at her patient. 'You wouldn't want to get me into trouble, I'm sure.'

'Oh no, of course not, but when no one came and no one came . . .'

'Yes, it's too bad of me to keep you waiting, but I'm afraid

I've only just got back from lunch. We've had one of those days, do you know the sort? Everything that could happen has done so. I work partly on the ward and partly in theatre, and since I was in theatre for a couple of hours the ward has been short-handed, but now I'm back . . .' Jessica gave the woman's fluttering, nervous hands a squeeze and indicated the easy chair. '. . . If you could sit down there I'll sit here, and we'll get my forms filled in, between us.'

Mrs Chase sat down but she was perched on the extreme edge of the chair and looked as though taking off and running for the door would be her next move. Jessica, to set a good example, sat down herself and leaned back, the file spread out on her lap. She said nothing but merely looked expectantly at the patient and presently, with a little laugh, Mrs Chase, too, leaned back in her chair.

'I'm sorry. What happens next?'

'After I've taken down your details, do you mean? Well, I'll show you to your bed and ring through for some lunch and then you can relax. As you must have been told you won't have your operation for several days, because you'll need rest and medication at first. However, when the medication has begun to work the surgeon will come and see you and you can decide together whether you feel you're ready for surgery.'

'Yes, I understand that, but you see there's so much . . . everything is on me now, since Martin's death . . . I don't think I can spare the time to lie in bed doing nothing. Besides, I get so hot in bed, I . . .'

'The wards are all air-conditioned and we've made up your bed with thin cotton blankets,' Jessica said soothingly. 'Besides, the treatment will ease most of your symptoms. Just think, Mrs Chase, how nice it will be not to have to worry about anything for a few days. And you'll sleep well at nights, too, we'll see to that.'

'Not to worry? To sleep? Oh, Nurse, you've no idea what it's been like since Martin died. I can't sleep, I long for England and a foot of snow, people who understand me . . . but all I've got is Minestos and this terrible heat.'

'I promise you that very soon you'll begin to feel more like your old self,' Jessica said earnestly. 'Now, we'll start with your full name and address, if you don't mind, though I do have it on the file. You are Mrs Begonia Ellis Chase of the Rookery, San Miguel?'

Just filling in the forms seemed to calm Mrs Chase and, as Jessica had hoped, by the time she stood up to show her new patient to the ward the older woman was a good deal calmer. She admired the long, cool ward with its windows facing the wooded slopes of the hill and said that her bed, in a corner and a little way from the others, looked comfortable.

'I'm afraid everyone's in the day-room at the moment,' Jessica said, swishing the curtains round the bed. 'I'll help you to undress and get into your nightie and then you can join them, if you want. There's a very sweet person in the next bed to you, a Mrs Pontin, she'll tell you all about meals, and . . .'

'Irene Pontin, Nurse? Well, that *is* a surprise. Irene and I used to play a lot of bridge together once, when Martin was alive. Her Sammy was a good friend to us, but of course Martin's illness meant that I had to lose a lot of my social activities . . . I haven't played bridge for two years. Well, well, Irene in here at the same time as me—that is a coincidence. I wonder if there's anyone else I know?'

'Bound to be; it's not a terribly large island,' Jessica said, lifting Mrs Chase's nightgown tenderly from the case. 'My goodness, what a pretty nightie!'

'Yes, it's nice, isn't it? I bought it just before Martin fell ill and I've never actually worn it, but it seemed suitable. Lawn is cool and yet not transparent or anything. It buttons down the front too, which is useful because I find buttons so difficult —my fingers slip, you know, because I'm hot all the time.'

'Well, do you want me to help you, or would you rather I went and came back when you've changed? I can easily find something to do on the ward.'

'No, I'd rather you stayed,' Mrs Chase said quickly. 'If you could undo this dress . . . it has a zip right down the back.'

Jessica helped the older woman to undress and get into her nightie, then she went with her to the day room and introduced her to the other members of her ward. After that she hurried along to Sister's office and phoned down to the canteen, who promised to send over a tray-lunch for one in ten minutes.

They were as good as their word. Presently there was a knock at the door and a kitchen worker in green cotton with her head tied up in a kerchief handed Jessica a neatly laid out tray with a main course under a metal cover, fruit juice and a cold trifle.

Jessica took the tray along to the day-room, but Mrs Chase had already left so she went to the ward. Her patient was sitting on her bed looking tired and frail. She was skeletally thin, the result of the disease Jessica knew, but even so she could not help feeling very sorry for the older woman. She gave her a bright smile, however, and handed her the tray.

'Your lunch. I hope it's something you like but tomorrow, of course, you'll be able to choose. The menus are quite good and very varied I think you'll find.'

Mrs Chase took the tray and lifted the metal cover. Underneath, the roast meat, roast potatoes and fresh green beans looked quite inviting.

'It looks rather good,' Mrs Chase remarked, picking up her knife and fork. 'It's odd, you know. I eat and eat but I never put on an ounce, in fact I've lost. Ever since . . . well, for a year or more I've been terribly skinny. But there, my neighbour is envious, she wishes she could eat and stay slim.'

'Slimness is nice, but I do agree you could do with a bit more flesh on your bones,' Jessica said. 'However, it's a symptom of thyrotoxicosis that you can't gain weight, and one which will disappear under proper medication. So before you know it, you'll get your nice figure back.'

'This is tasty,' Mrs Chase announced. 'I had to come out of the day-room though, Nurse. It was terribly noisy and I get agitated by too much noise. I wonder if I might have a sleep after lunch? I am quite tired.'

'Of course you can. Mind you, the first day is always a busy one, so I doubt you'll sleep for long. People from other departments will be round, they may want you to go down to X-Ray . . . certainly they'll want to take blood samples, though I don't suppose they'll do an ECG today. Still, rest whilst you can.'

Jessica left Mrs Chase presently and went along to Sister's office, where she found Pat, back on duty and being very efficient with someone on the telephone. Pat raised her brows, mouthed something, then said goodbye to her caller and replaced the receiver.

'You had a late lunch, didn't you? And Sister was even later. Looking forward to our date?'

'Our . . . oh, you mean watching flamenco dancing with those fellows. Yes, of course I am. Pat, there's a thyrotoxicosis patient on Aggy 1, she's been widowed fairly recently I think. You'd do well to keep an eye on her.'

'Mrs Chase? Why? Is she a very nervy one?'

'She is. Have you ever nursed thyrotoxicosis before?'

'No, I don't think so. I should have read it up last night, I knew she'd be coming on the ward today, but it was late when we got home and I haven't had time today. I know the theory, of course, or used to, but I'm a bit fuzzy about symptoms. How could you describe her?'

'In a state of almost permanent high tension, very hot, very edgy,' Jessica said succinctly. 'I wouldn't leave her alone for too long, if I were you. Not until the medication gets under way.'

'Oh. Right. Is that a hint?'

'Of course not, you can't be everywhere at once. But I've got to change dressings in Aggy 2 as soon as Rosa is free to give me a hand and I wouldn't want to be responsible if the Chase bird has flown by the time you get down there.'

Pat sighed, heaved herself out of her chair and set off for the door.

'No peace for the wicked! Who'll answer the phone until Sister gets back, though?'

'Whoever happens to be passing. We'll leave the door open, so if you hear it you come in and if I do, I will. But she won't be long now, I shouldn't think.'

Jessica and Rosa were just replacing a dressing on an extremely neat incision which was healing nicely, when the phone rang. Jessica waited but when it continued to ring she left Rosa to tape the dressing into place and made her way quickly along to Sister's office. To her considerable surprise the voice on the other end of the line was that of Perrello—and he recognised her immediately.

'Nurse French? Perrello here. I've an emergency just come into theatre, come over right away, please.'

'I'm afraid I can't,' Jessica said apologetically. 'I'm halfway through a dressings round, Sister's still at lunch and Nurse Hoby has a new admission. If you could just wait until Sister comes back, then I'm sure . . .'

'At once, Nurse.'

He put the receiver down so sharply that Jessica nearly dropped her own instrument. Then she put it back on its rest and turned towards the doorway. Whatever should she do? She could not possibly go off just like that, with a ward full of men, their dressings carefully peeled off, waiting for replacements! Yet Perrello plainly expected instant obedience. She had better ask Pat.

But Pat was in no mood to worry about a surgeon's feelings. She was dealing competently with a patient, just back from theatre, who was vomiting into a bowl and whose drip had become detached. She raised a harassed face to her friend.

'Bless you, Jessica, for turning up when I need you most! Can you get me a clean bowl while I fix the drip?'

'Yes, right . . . Pat, Perrello rang, he said I was to go down at once but Sister's not back and I'm halfway through the dressings and . . .'

'Did you tell him no?'

'How could I? Besides, he didn't wait for a reply, he just repeated, *at once, Nurse*, and slammed the receiver down.'

'Ring theatre and tell them you can't,' Pat said briefly. 'Can you cope with the dressings alone and lend me Rosa?'

'Yes, I . . .' Rosa's head appeared round the door at the end of the ward. Jessica sighed and suppressed a desire to shriek at the other nurse to get back to her work. Rosa would not have abandoned the task in hand had she not had some urgent reason for so doing. She began to work on the drip, then stopped and ran for a clean kidney bowl, raising her eyebrows at Rosa as she did so.

'What is it, Rosa? I won't be . . .'

'Ward round,' Rosa said briefly. 'Only Sr Escutia, but he's got some students with him. He's only got one patient on the ward but you know what he is . . . he looked at me and barked,

"Get me a *real* nurse!" as if I were made of plastic!'

Jessica felt her temper begin to simmer. She slapped the clean bowl into the sufferer's hands, picked up the full one and headed for the sluice. Over her shoulder she said roundly, 'Fix that drip for Nurse Hoby! I'll speak to Escutia!'

And speak to him she did, in rapid Spanish, at the end of which he said, quite meekly for a man with a reputation as the most arrogant surgeon in the hospital to keep up, 'I'm very sorry, Nurse, I had no idea you were so short-staffed. If you could possibly just tell these young gentlemen which patient is suffering from . . .'

He became technical and so did Jessica. For ten minutes she explained to the students what Sr Escutia should have been explaining and then she hurried out of the ward and back to Sister's office. She rang through to the theatre suite only to be told by someone that Dr Perrello was operating and could not be disturbed.

'So much for needing me at once,' Jessica remarked angrily under her breath to Rosa, as they finished off the dressings. 'Thank goodness Sister will be back soon, though.'

But in this at least she was wrong. Sister came back, to be sure, but only to tell her nurses that she was very sorry to do it to them when they were rushed off their feet, but she had to go to a senior staff meeting.

'I'll be as quick as I possibly can,' she said, 'but since the meeting is all about staff needs, I can scarcely miss it. I shall tell them how hard we're finding it now, with Nurse French being called away to theatre four or five times a week, and perhaps they'll be more sympathetic to the idea of additional auxiliaries, even if they won't hear of more staff nurses.'

Despite the fact that she had been on an early shift and so should have been free at teatime, Jessica worked on until Pat, too, was able to leave. The two of them, really exhausted, decided that the crowded bus was not for them on this occasion and went halves for a taxi.

'I shall probably fall deeply asleep and snore all through the flamenco dancing,' Jessica said gloomily, as she and Pat put the finishing touches to their appearance in the flat. 'As for a meal afterwards, I don't think I can face eating that late. Why don't we just get ourselves some chips and come home here?'

'Bring the fellows to the flat? Well, I don't know, I don't usually bring people home . . .' Pat began, but was interrupted.

'Not them, idiot, us! We can have some chips and then go to bed. We'll tell them how tired we are and I'm sure they'll understand.'

'We'll probably wake up; that's what usually happens to me,' Pat said wisely. 'I start out thinking it's all I can do to drag myself down to a dance and suddenly find it's two in the morning and I've been leaping around the dance floor for hours and never a creak or a groan.'

'Well, perhaps. But we went out last night, remember.' Jessica swirled, and the fine Indian muslin skirt of her dress swirled too. She put her hands on her hips and surveyed herself critically in the mirror. 'Who would think I'd been on my feet for more than twelve hours? Come on, where are we meeting them?'

'Outside the courtyard where the flamenco dancers do their stuff. Ready? Then let's get on the bus this time. It won't be so crowded and besides, we can't keep shelling out for taxis.'

It was a good evening despite Jessica's fears. Jaime and Eduardo were a handsome couple and bent on giving the girls a good time. The flamenco dancing was excellent and afterwards the four of them sat on the quayside and watched the comings and goings of boats in the small harbour while eating huge mediterranean prawns, charcoal grilled, with great thick slices of brown bread spread with creamy, unsalted butter. They drank the house wine, which was cheap but good, afterwards ate large pink ice creams in dark brown cones.

After this, they strolled along the waterfront, then made their way up the hill into the town. It was quiet now, because it was so late, and when they reached the nurses' flats, surrounded by trees and bushes, both girls were glad enough of a soldierly arm round the waist until they reached the foyer.

Once there, Pat gave Jessica an appealing look which Jessica interpreted as 'do we ask them up to the flat?' Upon reflection, she thought that it was the least the young officers deserved, so gave Pat a nod.

'Would you like to come up to our flat and have a hot cup of coffee before you go back to your island?' Pat said as they stood in the small, brightly lit hall. 'We've both had a lovely evening, we've really enjoyed ourselves.'

But both young men shook their heads.

'I'm sorry, but we have passes only for another thirty minutes,' Eduardo said with obvious regret. 'The boat will leave in ten minutes . . . otherwise we would have to swim.'

'Well, thanks very much,' Jessica said briskly, holding out a hand. She was not much surprised to find her hand taken, but only in order that Jaime might pull her fully into his arms. He began to kiss her and out of the corner of her eye Jessica saw Pat in a similar position. She smiled to herself, but broke the embrace and turned towards the stairs.

'Coming, Pat? Good night, Eduardo, good night, Jaime.'

'Wait! I am off again next week . . . would you come out with me once more? I would very much enjoy your company.' Jaime gave Jessica an appealing look. 'It is very lonely here, where we know no one,' he added.

Jessica laughed.

'Get on with you, you're here with hundreds of soldiers and I bet all the local girls chase after you,' she remarked. 'Still, I have enjoyed this evening . . . what did you have in mind for next time?'

'Oh, anything you would like—a meal, a boat-trip? You choose.' Jaime smiled again. He had a dimple in one cheek. 'I am very proud to be seen with such a beautiful girl,' he finished.

'In that case, certainly, I'll gladly go out with anyone who pays me such pretty compliments,' Jessica assured him. 'Here, I'll write the telephone number of the flats on one side of the menu and the number of the ward on the other, then you can reach me either at home or at work.'

Having made their arrangements the young officers made their way out of the building, leaving the girls to go up to their flat alone.

'They really are nice,' Jessica said, as she and Pat drank

cocoa in the kitchen and mulled over their evening. 'It was pleasant to be able to spend an evening with a guy without being mauled afterwards.'

'I was mauled, not that I objected . . . so were you, I saw out of the corner of my eye!'

'Oh, Pat, really. I wasn't mauled and nor were you. We were properly and politely kissed good night. You've been in Spain long enough to know that some Spaniards expect very much more from English girls than a good night kiss!'

'Do they? I wouldn't know.' Pat laughed as Jessica aimed a blow at her. 'I'm off to bed now. I hope you realise that next time you meet Jaime it will just be the two of you? Eduardo isn't off duty for another ten days.'

'Can't say I'm worried,' Jessica confessed. 'You were right, they are both polite and career-minded. In fact they treated us just like two nicely reared Spanish girls and that is quite a compliment.'

'Is it? Good, because I really do like Eduardo.' The girls reached their bedroom doors and stood by them for a moment. 'Well, thank heaven we're both on a late tomorrow. Night!'

'Night, Pat.'

Jessica went into her room, closed the door, undressed in a few seconds flat and was soon in bed. She decided sleepily that she really did like Jaime; he was awfully good looking, very kind, and seemed fun as well. Much handsomer than Perrello, she decided, still hovering on the brink of sleep.

The thought, however, jerked her awake. Much handsomer than Perrello? Whatever was she thinking of? It did not matter whether Perrello was as handsome as a filmstar or as ugly as a pan of worms, he was not interested in her and she was not interested in him.

Frowning at her own foolishness, she concentrated grimly on thinking about Jaime until she fell asleep.

CHAPTER FOUR

'NURSE FRENCH . . . could you spare a moment?'

Sister's usually placid face looked harassed and there were wisps of hair coming out from under her cap. Jessica, who had spent the morning doing two people's work on the ward since an auxiliary had been moved from Aggy down to help Sister Albert on Trafalgar and was bed-making alone, looked up hopefully. Was this the moment when Sister would tell her about more staff?

'In the office, Sister?'

'If you wouldn't mind. I won't keep you long.'

Jessica finished off the bed and glanced swiftly round the ward. The men were mostly in the day-room but old Mr Whitworth was snoozing in his bed and John Rogers was sitting in his visitor's chair, reading the newspaper.

'I'll be in the office, Mr Rogers, if anyone wants me,' she called. 'Shan't be long.'

She did not pause to tidy her hair or to make sure that her apron was straight but just hurried straight along to the office. Sister was sitting behind the desk working but she glanced up and smiled as Jessica entered.

'Sit down, Nurse. I won't keep you any longer than I have to, but I thought we should have a word. For a start, I'm afraid I wasn't very successful in my efforts to get more staff on the ward, though the board did agree to second an auxiliary over from the military hospital when you're needed in theatre.'

Jessica pulled a face.

'That really isn't fair, is it, Sister? We're two people short on days, and shall be from the sound of it. I mean the girl on Victory isn't going to be back for a month, and Nurse Hoby said that Nurse Sumner was taking her home-leave and might be away longer!'

'I know. The board seem to think that allowing me the odd auxiliary whenever the military hospital has someone to spare is good enough and it isn't, but for now, we must do our best to see that we cope. It may mean working a bit longer, but we're all used to that. I'm sorry to give you what must be rather bad news.'

'It wouldn't be so bad if I could get out of going over to theatre whenever Dr Perrello rings for me,' Jessica pointed out. 'I'd like to know just what's wrong with Sister Cruz, that she seems to spend half her on-duty time off-duty! Surely she can be told that such behaviour isn't good for the hospital?'

Sister looked rather self-conscious.

'You're right, of course. If it was someone nursing at the Nelson I'm sure Dr Perrello would soon put a stop to such an attitude, but as it is, we have to leave the discipline of his staff to him.'

'And put our patients in jeopardy? Surely not,' Jessica said, really upset at what seemed to her an unfair attitude. 'Sister, if you spoke to him surely he would see that Sister Cruz is being unfair?'

'I have spoken to him. Apparently Sister Cruz has an elderly mother who has been in poor health. Señora Cruz lives with an older daughter some way away, and Sister goes over whenever she can to help.'

'Oh, I see. Then shouldn't the big hospital get a replacement theatre sister? After all, they can afford to transfer someone more easily than we can, with our smaller staff.'

Sister looked even more harassed.

'Dr Perrello says they will replace Sister Cruz, if and when she decides to leave altogether. Until then, he says you know the work, you fit in well with the team, and obviously can be more easily replaced temporarily than a theatre sister.'

The obvious truth of this kept Jessica silent for no more than ten seconds. Then she had another idea.

'Yes, I do see. But surely Dr Perrello could train up another staff member to stand in for Sister Cruz? After all, if she really is going to leave, he'll need someone then!'

'Well, no, Nurse French.' Sister was really looking worried now, and slightly apologetic too. 'The fact is, Dr Perrello wants you to apply for the post of theatre sister when it falls vacant. He says . . . and there is some truth in it . . . that he can get ward sisters without too much trouble but that theatre sisters who speak the language like natives and who are living on the premises and far more available, so to speak, are not easily found.'

'Spanish girls speak the language like natives,' Jessica said crossly. 'Why can't he replace Sister Cruz with a Spaniard?'

'Because, Nurse, as you very well know, Spanish nurses usually live out, and for another thing, Spanish nurses rarely speak excellent, idiomatic English. Do I take it that you don't want the job, then?'

'Oh, dear! I don't want to be difficult, Sister, but I really do love ward work and to be honest, working with Dr Perrello isn't always easy. He doesn't like women much, does he?'

Sister smiled.

'No, Nurse, not very much. But it's clear that he likes you! When he came storming up here yesterday evening after you'd left, telling me some tale about ringing you up and demanding your presence, I thought he was about to demand your dismissal. I explained about the pressure of work here at the moment, and assured him that, had I been present, you would not even have been told that he had rung, and that made him think. He was scowling down at the desk, tapping his fingers on the edge, and then he looked up, smiled at me, and said, "I see! She was too busy to come down and had no one she could leave in her place. Yes, that is, of course, understandable." And then I explained about my request for more staff being turned down by the board and he got very brisk and businesslike and said that he would be sure to send an auxiliary over each time he "borrowed" you for theatre, and would I please tell you that he would expect your immediate application for theatre sister as soon as the job fell vacant.'

'Well, I don't understand it,' Jessica said plaintively. 'He isn't even polite to me, Sister. I'm not saying he's rude, he simply ignores me, walks away from me as soon as I enter the rest-room, avoids me when he comes up to do a ward round . . . I thought he disliked me, not the other way round.'

'He obviously admires your work. As for you personally, I don't think he can get over the feeling that if you show any sort of friendship for a woman, she'll let you down. His wife let him down, you see, and took herself off with another man no more than six months after they were married. And . . . I don't know whether I should be telling you this, Staff, so please keep it to yourself . . . and six months after she left him she gave birth to a son. He believed it to be his child, but his ex-wife and her lover swore it was not. He became very embittered.'

'That's awfully sad,' Jessica agreed. 'But it was years and years ago. I think his attitude to women should have changed by now. He's an intelligent man, after all.'

'True. They did say at one time that there was something between Perrello and his theatre sister. Certainly I have seen him apparently on quite friendly terms with her. But there, it's only gossip. Now you'd better go back to your work or we shall both be here until midnight.'

Sister smiled dismissively and Jessica, a prey to a good many doubts, made her way back to her ward once more. But even there, working with the patients, her doubts still lingered. She really did not want to work in theatre again for a bit, not on a permanent basis! And particularly not with a surgeon who seemed to positively enjoy making her feel like an outsider.

By lunchtime, Jessica's thoughts had more or less resolved themselves. She would stay on the ward for a full six months, no matter what. Then, if Sister Cruz did decide to leave, and—the big if—if Dr Perrello's attitude towards her was less antagonistic, she would put in for the job of theatre sister. After all, the work which she had been trained to do was important to her and she knew to an extent Perrello was right—it was far easier to get a good staff nurse for ward work than a trained theatre sister.

Having made up her mind she decided to celebrate an end to dithering and go up to the canteen for a meal. And this time she would concentrate on the lovely food and not worry about sitting alone. Indeed, if Dr Caball or one of the other surgeons were eating, she would join them.

However, it was a busy time in the canteen and as she went in she saw that most of the tables were full. A group of doctors ate their way through paella at a big window table, nurses and porters and young doctors she did not know thronged the rest of the big, airy room.

There was a queue, which Jessica joined, for hot food. Peering ahead, she could see that there was no one from the Nelson in the queue but just in front of her were a group of nurses including Ana, who often worked with the theatre team. Jessica tried to catch her eye as Ana glanced about but the queue moved quickly and in a very short time she was choosing her own meal and the nurses in front of her were sitting down at the only unoccupied table for eight left in the room.

With her tray, Jessica cast a rather hunted look about her. A group of porters and ambulance drivers were shouting and eating between her and the military nurses, but there was a little round table for one with a stool beside it still vacant, just behind their larger table. She made a beeline for it, sat down, got out a paperback and prepared to enjoy a good read with her lunch.

However, she had scarcely read a word when the lively chatter from the nurses' table caught her attention. One girl in particular, speaking in a clear, carrying voice, was obviously indifferent to who might hear her remarks. They're just like English girls, Jessica thought, not for the first time, they enjoy male attention and are quite prepared to have their conversations overheard if it turns heads in their direction. At the moment they were talking about someone called Gio; they approved of Gio, who had a soft spot for nurses, but presently the conversation veered round to hospital matters once more and Jessica heard a name which immediately riveted her attention.

'Perrello? He'll be off in a few days, on a course, in Barcelona. He wanted me to go too—there's a seminar for theatre nurses—but it was out of the question because I've missed so much time lately. So here I am, poor old me, stuck with my nose to the grindstone whilst he gads about all over Barcelona with any pretty señorita who has time on her hands.'

Infuriatingly, it was impossible for Jessica to see who was speaking without actually turning in her seat and staring, but being a resourceful girl she reached for her handbag and took out her small vanity mirror. She held it up as though she had something in her eye and tilted it until she could get a confused view of the table behind her, but even so she could only see the backs of heads and a confusion of features too far away to be able to focus. She slipped the mirror back in her bag but continued to listen.

'Oh, come on, Isabel, you know very well you'll have an excellent time on your own, with all that time off. As for the sick mother story . . .'

'Shhh! My mother has been sick and anyway, she enjoys my visits. If I sometimes use those visits for a purpose of my own that doesn't mean the visits are not necessary! But if Perrello starts getting suspicious and tries to stop me going off, then I shall leave and move in with my sister, to be near the shop.'

'What shop? Does your mother keep a shop? Does Perrello know you plan to desert us, Belle?'

There was a trill of laughter and despite her feelings of antagonism against the woman whose absences put her in such a difficult position, Jessica thought that Sister Cruz, if it was her speaking, sounded rather nice.

'Oh really, Maria! My sister and I have pooled our savings and put the money into a small boutique, and behind the boutique we have a very small workroom where we make most of the clothing. If Perrello got to know he'd be very angry, he would not try to understand, so I shan't tell him until I want to leave.'

'It isn't a very kind thing to do,' someone else remarked rather pensively. 'You don't always think before you act, *querida*.'

'No, it isn't kind, but when's Perrello been kind?' the first voice said, sounding a little defensive at last. 'At one time, as you all know, I was wildly in love with him, and what did I get? I got calmly put in my place, told that he did not believe in affairs of the heart between members of the same surgical team! Ach, so cold, so harsh! So now I revere the surgeon but I don't expect understanding from him for human fallibility such as mine. I need money to support my mother, my sister and myself, you all know that. Nursing doesn't pay well enough, so

I must look round for something else, something we can all do. The answer is the boutique. Carmela can sew *anything*, she makes the most beautiful clothes, but she cannot stand behind a counter let alone persuade people to buy. This I can do. So, if the boutique succeeds, I shall leave nursing. And if you think Perrello will be upset, you're quite wrong. He won't mind in the least provided he can find someone equally efficient to fill my place.'

'He's found someone—haven't you heard? What's more, they say he likes her—the little English nurse from the Nelson. He took her out one night last week or the week before, and bought her a meal! Isabel, he did, don't shake your head. They went to Tonio's and then he took her across the harbour in his boat. My cousin is a waiter at Tonio's and he told me; there could be no mistaking Perrello, after all. So you see, he *is* human, and fallible too, because she's pretty, that one, and he held her in his arms when she jumped into the boat—my cousin *saw*!'

Jessica hunched down in her seat and prayed that no one would look round and recognise her. Then Isabel Cruz spoke again, sounding cool and faintly amused.

'Ah, Bianca, what a silly little thing you are. Of course he took the English girl out for a meal—did you not hear why? He demanded her attendance in theatre and she was off-duty, and of course she bungled something or was criticised . . . I don't know precisely what happened but I do know she was annoyed with him, seriously offended. Well, he can be sharp-tongued, we've all suffered. But anyway, you know his feelings about a good team being in accord? He's very fond of saying that no quarrels or arguments should ever be allowed to prejudice the team relationship. So he asked her out, gave her a good meal, buttered her up a little, possibly even kissed her good night. And now she'll work for him to the best of her ability and probably dream of hot Latin lips on hers when she goes to bed at night. That, Bianca, is good psychology, not human fallibility!'

'I don't remember you calling it good psychology when he took *you* out for a meal, Belle,' someone remarked thoughtfully. 'It was all sweet music and violins and being a surgeon's wife as I recall. What is valid for one must be valid for another, surely?'

There was more laughter, echoed again by Isabel's trill.

'Wicked Conchita, you know very well that the *hombre* adores me and is only waiting for me to say yes! Well, that was what I thought at the time, but now I know better. I cannot have an affair with someone so cold, not for a thousand marriages! And as for his being serious about the English girl, there you are very wrong, for he would never dream of taking an Englishwoman seriously, not after that Amanda.'

At this point Jessica's curiosity got the better of her and she bent as if to fish her handbag out from under the table where she had dropped it and glanced backwards.

Ana was there! Sitting with her back to Jessica, fortunately, but still there, perfectly capable of turning round and seeing that the subject of their conversation was sitting no more than a foot away, no doubt listening to every word!

At the next table, however, were a large and noisy group of men and at this point one of them glanced at the clock, exclaimed over the time and the whole group rose to their feet. Jessica followed suit. She walked swiftly towards the counter, keeping the men between herself and the nurses, as if to order another cup of coffee and then, at the right moment, when the nurses had had a chance to glance up and see it was just the porters and return to their conversation, she changed direction and, still with the men between herself and the other girls, she hurried out of the canteen.

Safe once more in Aggy ward, putting her apron back on and combing her hair to neatness beneath her cap, she thought about the conversation. So he had only taken her out to ensure a good relationship with the team had he? But why should he do such a thing, when she was only occasionally a part of the team and when, in any event, all that was necessary was a degree of politeness to her? And the kiss . . . hearing Isabel Cruz talking about it had made her got hot all over . . . had it really been nothing more than a means to an end? The end, in this case, being her own efficient work and co-operation in his theatre team?

She emerged from the staff room still feeling annoyed, both

with Isabel Cruz and herself, for she had been eavesdropping and should have ignored every word of the overheard conversation. But, being only human, she had been annoyed to think that perhaps there was more than a grain of truth in it. Perhaps Perrello really did think that an outing and a kiss would make her into a nice little doormat for him to trample on. Well, if so, he had another think coming! Jessica French was far too independent to change her attitude just because she had been kissed—kisses, she told herself crossly, were her due, not something particularly precious!

Pat, coming out of Sister's office, stopped short at the sight of her scowl.

'What's up? You do look cross! Didn't you manage to get a hot lunch?'

'Yes, thanks. Sorry, was I frowning? The truth is I've just been in the canteen, and I saw Isabel Cruz.'

'Really? She really is beautiful, isn't she, if you like that very upper-class Spaniard look. What did you think of her? Did you chat?'

'Not really . . . I shouldn't have said *I'd* seen her, because I still haven't, not really. She was sitting behind me. I heard her, though.'

Pat fell into step beside her and the two of them walked down the corridor together. Pat was smiling.

'Oh ho! And what did Sister Cruz say to bring that black look to your face?'

'It's silly, it was just idle chat, I ought not to mind. I shouldn't have been listening, anyway. Apparently, it's common knowledge that Perrello took me out for a meal that evening and she was telling the girls at the table with her that it was good psychology. He had upset me—that bit's true—and wanted to calm me down so that there was no dissension to mar the good team spirit, so he took me out for a meal, buttered me up a bit, and hey presto, good relations!'

'Was it like that?' Pat asked as they went through the swing doors. 'I wouldn't have thought he cared much about people's feelings.'

'I didn't think it was like that, but to tell the truth ever since he's been awfully abrupt with me. Now I wonder whether he did it for the reasons the Cruz missile gave and then felt obscurely guilty and has been naggy with me as a result. What do you think?'

'Do you want the honest, unvarnished truth?'

'Oh dear, I suppose I do.'

'I think you're reading too much into the whole affair. Perrello was tired and hungry and felt a twinge of remorse because you missed your date. He took you out for a meal. Full stop. No strings, no intentions, no psychology, good or otherwise. But you both felt easier with each other afterwards, no doubt, which was a bonus.'

'That's the bad part. I thought things would be easier, but so far as Perrello's concerned, the evening never happened. He avoids me. Really. In scrub-up he's very cool and detached, in theatre he only speaks about medical matters, in the rest-room he walks over to the window and either talks to the doctors or not at all.'

'Oh,' Pat said rather blankly. 'Yet he's asked for you to continue working in theatre. What an odd chap!'

'I know. Oh, by the way, how's Mrs Chase?'

'A bit more relaxed. She speaks quite good Spanish which is a bonus, so right now she and Sancha are quietly chatting while Mrs Chase does some embroidery. Mrs Pontin came onto the ward and loudly envied Mrs Chase her slim figure, which was nice, Mrs C. preened a bit. But I do think you were right, we'll have to keep her quiet yet occupied and see she's not much alone.'

'I'm glad you agree with my far from expert diagnosis. Life will be a lot easier for all of us, her as well, once she's on regular medication. Is she already taking potassium perchlorate, or are we going to put her onto Lugol's iodine when the surgeon thinks she's fit enough?'

'I don't know, I haven't seen the medication they've written up for her,' Pat admitted, looking hunted. 'Hasn't it been an awful day? Just one thing after the other.'

'Pretty bad,' Jessica admitted. 'Well, I'd better go and take over from Ettie now; she'll be only too ready to go back to Trafalgar, after a hectic couple of hours on Aggy 2.'

* * *

Jessica had never been a clock-watcher, but by six o'clock her feet were throbbing, her hands were almost as slippery with perspiration as Mrs Chase's, and she was really longing for the flat and a long, iced drink. She had done all the odds and ends of preparation for the night staff to take over and was actually on her way to the end of the ward when the swing doors swung open and Sister appeared.

'Nurse French; telephone for you.'

Wondering audibly who on earth would ring her here, Jessica made her way down the ward, along the corridor, and into Sister's office. She picked up the receiver and spoke with unwonted crispness.

'Staff speaking. Yes?'

'Ees zat . . .'

Jessica immediately began to speak in Spanish.

'Jaime, is that you? I'm just about to go off duty, you were lucky to catch me.'

'Ah, good,' Jaime replied, 'then it is not too late to ask if you would like to come out with me this evening. I have a late pass.'

'I'm afraid it *is* too late,' Jessica said. 'Thanks very much but I do have a previous engagement.' She knew if she said the previous engagement was with a meal and an early night she would find herself repelling strong persuasion.

'Ah. I see.' There was a pause during which, she imagined, Jaime went through the duty rota giving him his off-duty period for the next week. 'How about next Thursday?'

'I think I'm free then,' Jessica said cautiously. 'What were you thinking of doing?'

'Oh, a meal, a stroll along the waterfront . . . Jessica, do you fish?'

'With a rod and line, do you mean? In a boat?'

He laughed. 'Well, with a rod and line at any rate! Have you ever tried it?'

'No. It always looks pretty dull. Why?'

'I thought we might have a go late in the evening. I know a spot where you nearly always find big fish . . . Are you game to try? I think you'll enjoy it. At least, afterwards, you will know just why people do fish.'

'All right then, for a little while. I'm off duty on Thursday at eight. Would that be about the time you had in mind?'

'I, too, am off duty then. Can I come to your flat at about half past the hour?'

'Fine. Cheerio, Jaime, until Thursday.'

Jessica put down the phone and went slowly out of the room and through to the staff room. She changed out of her blue and white into a lime-coloured cotton shift, then walked down the corridor to the top of the stairs. Should she bus, or take a taxi? But taxis cost money and she had a bus-pass. It had better be the bus though at this time of evening they were always crammed with home-going office workers. Pat had gone two hours previously so she would be by herself which meant, of course, that she would have to bear the whole cost of a taxi.

It was very hot outside, the sun still streaming down from a brassy sky. Jessica walked slowly to the bus stop and waited, trying to will herself to stillness and hoping that coolness would follow. After ten minutes the bus pulled up, but although two people did get off, about ten got on before she could get near the entrance. The bus pulled away and Jessica began, resignedly, to walk.

She had only reached the main road, however, when she heard a car coming up behind her. It came fast, and there was a familiarity to its engine note that made her turn her head.

Dr Perrello! Deliverance! He would give her a lift, she would be home in no time, and . . .

But he was passing, eyes fixed to the front, mouth grave. He was alone.

Jessica, who had stopped walking and actually stepped towards the kerb, moved forward once more, her cheeks more flushed than the heat merited. He had seen her, she was sure of it! How could he have pretended not to, how could he swish past her in a cloud of dust, leaving her struggling home, hot, weary and now depressed?

She had gone what felt like five miles but what was probably more like half a mile when another car passed, but this one drew up just ahead of her. It was the anaesthetist, Dr Fagandini. He leaned over, opened the passenger door, and called her.

'Miss the bus, Nurse French? Come along, room for a little one!'

The car was bulging with staff from the military hospital. Jessica, thanking him profusely, climbed in and squeezed up on the back seat, exchanging moans about the weather and the fullness of the buses with the girls already there. It was only a short run to the flats but he insisted on dropping her off right outside and then drove away to continue to deliver other members of the staff.

He's a real gentleman, quite different from Perrello, Jessica told herself crossly as she climbed the stairs. How selfish can you get though—Perrello had rushed out of the hospital with never a thought for other people also going in his direction. He had probably never given a lift in his life unless of course he had an ulterior motive in so doing. Well, that settled it. He was just a rude, arrogant boor and she would treat him as such in future. She could be every bit as cold. She couldn't wait to see how he liked it!

Diaz Perrello had been sitting in the car-park when Jessica had walked by. She had looked trim and cool in her lime-coloured dress but he was not fooled for a moment. She was too pale and her face had that sheen which denotes exhaustion. Even her lovely, glowing red-gold hair seemed limp and lifeless after a day such as she had lived through.

He nearly got out and called to her, but refrained. What a fool he would look if she simply told him to get lost . . . she was capable of it, he knew that she did not lack spirit. He sat back in his seat again and watched her join the bus queue. She would never get on it, she was far too late.

Then he brightened. Presently the bus would arrive, she would not be able to board it, and she would walk. Or, possibly, remain at the stop hoping to catch the next one, which would not arrive for twenty minutes. He would drift up beside her when she had gone a little way and offer her a lift—one would do the same for anyone in this heat, it would not mean a softening of his attitude towards her.

She began to walk and he revved the engine, let her get out onto the main road, then he drove after her. He was almost upon her when his courage failed him. You must be mad, he told himself, his foot steadily increasing its pressure on the accelerator, you nearly got involved with this one before! She's a woman, what's worse she's English, if you start letting yourself get to know her you'll only get hurt. Look at Amanda . . . and you were fifteen years younger then!

He saw her falter, turn towards the road, but kept his eyes sternly to the front and his hands on the steering wheel. He also kept his foot on the accelerator. Keep all working relationships just that, he adjured himself. If you want a woman then there are plenty of well-brought up Spanish girls. Or there are mature women, who understand a man's needs and don't want to embroil him in the business of loving, giving, being understood and understanding in your turn. Keep away from the young, the romantic, the very creatures who tug so sweetly at your heartstrings, just as Amanda had once tugged.

He looked in the rearview mirror. She was walking along, arms swinging, head held high, her absurd little ponytail of glorious hair no doubt bobbing defiantly up and down on her back as she walked. She was not for him! Too young, too full of life, too . . . too tempting. He rounded a corner on two wheels and frowned, slowing the car. No point in letting his mind stray back along that dusty road to that valiant walker. He had taken her out once, recognised the dangers, and made up his mind to steer clear. Now all he had to do was stick to his resolve and all would be well.

Five minutes later, he realised that he was simply driving at random and had long passed the turning he intended to take. Cursing under his breath he did a fast, three-point turn and headed back down the road again. There were a thousand pretty girls and he did not intend to lose his head over any of them, particularly one who happened to be a useful theatre nurse!

CHAPTER FIVE

AFTER having been passed on the road by Dr Perrello, Jessica found herself called to theatre several times but remained firm in her resolve to treat him as coolly as he treated her. It was not easy, because she was used to working with a team who were all friendly and natural with each other, but she soon learned. She could joke with Dr Gambas, tease Ana and Bianca, tell Sara and Felipe all about her home in England, but with Dr Perrello she remained extremely polite, detached and remote.

Sometimes she fancied that he was looking at her with warmth and interest but such moments were few. For the most part he treated her as she treated him—with restraint bordering on antipathy.

Not that anyone noticed. Dr Perrello had always more or less ignored the female team members, she gathered, unless they did something to incur his wrath. Then it was a different matter! If you made a mistake Perrello was always the first to notice it and he never failed to draw attention to it, usually with some sarcastic comment about your lack of efficiency.

And excellent surgeon though he was, there was no doubt about the relaxed atmosphere which prevailed in theatre after he had left for his course in Barcelona. Dr Gambas took his place for a couple of days but then a newcomer arrived on the scene, Dr John Mariano, and the first time she was called over to work with him, Jessica was astonished to find that he, like she, was half English.

'More than half, actually,' he told her as they relaxed for twenty minutes in the rest-room whilst theatre was cleaned down after a big operation. 'My mother is English and my father half English, half Spanish. But I was born and bred over here and only sent to Britain when I was twelve and old enough, they felt, for public school.'

'I thought one started public school at thirteen,' Jessica said from behind a large cup of coffee. 'It's usual, isn't it?'

'I was a genius, naturally.' Mariano grinned at her. He was a tall, slim young man with toffee-coloured hair and matching eyes. His skin was tanned to a light, clear brown and his eyes looked even bluer against the darker skin. 'I studied medicine in London and practised there for a year and then came winging back to Spain.'

'And now you're here. For how long?' Jessica asked. He was pleasant company, and the fact that he obviously found her attractive and flirted lightly and amusingly with her as they worked was balm for her wounded pride.

'A year. I'm really here to stand in for Dr Perrello when he's away and to learn all I can from him. I understand he's a first-rate surgeon.'

'Yes. First-rate. When does he come back, incidentally?'

'In about three days, I believe. Or so Isabel told me.'

'Isabel? Do you mean Sister Cruz?'

'Yes, I mean Sister Cruz, Jessica.' He reached out and took her hand, wagging it lightly back and forth. 'I asked permission to call you by your first name within an hour of working with you. How could I do less with the fascinating Señorita Cruz?'

'You're welcome to call her Izzy, if it gives you pleasure,' Jessica said, returning his smile. 'Personally, I call her the Cruz missile, but then I'm not a susceptible male.'

'How true . . . and I am! When are you going to come out with me? Do you like to dance? To swim? To drink in the little tavernas? Then I'm game, if you are.'

'Dr Perrello wouldn't approve,' Jessica told him. 'He likes work and play kept absolutely separate.'

'I should hope so! I shan't suddenly lean across the operating table and seize you in my arms though, I shall save that for our dates. So what's wrong with that?'

Jessica shrugged. 'Ask Dr Perrello,' she advised lightly.

'He sounds an ogre. What's he like really?'

'Like an ogre.' Jessica laughed and jumped to her feet as the red light that indicated scrub up and theatre were ready for them glowed above the door. 'Come on, mustn't keep our patients waiting.'

Watching him as he worked though, Jessica knew that John Mariano would be very good one day, possibly as good as Dr

Perrello. But not yet. He was quick, he watched Gambas and Imrid and imitated them, he had self-confidence and flair, but he was not, as yet, a match for the ogre himself.

Working by him though, Jessica did realise how very much she enjoyed theatre work—if it was not spoiled by the presence of someone who disapproved of her and only glanced across at her to find fault. With Mariano operating she found she was quicker, neater and more self-confident. If only Perrello could pretend he liked her—but she must not ask the impossible. It was clear that the man was a woman-hater, she must come to terms with that. If a memory of that kiss strayed across her mind now and again to disprove Perrello's misogynist leanings, she dismissed it as a fluke.

She and Jaime had been out twice since that initial date to watch flamenco dancing. She liked him and got on well with him but they had still not gone fishing because he always wanted to fish around midnight, when he swore the biggest fish came in from the deep, and Jessica was always too tired. However, she managed to get two days off and when Jaime rang the flat on the afternoon of the second day and asked rather plaintively if she would consider fishing that night, she agreed that it might be fun. He was being moved on in the unreliable way the army had, and though he thought that it was only manoeuvres and that he would be back in a month or so, it would still be their last opportunity to go night-fishing for a while.

At eight o'clock that evening Jaime knocked at the door and was let in by Pat.

'Hello there! I'm off to a concert in Peurto Malon, so don't go drowning my flat-mate, will you?' she greeted him, ushering him into the kitchen where Jessica was giving her hair a last comb. 'Have a nice time, though I think you're mad, fishing! See you later, Jess!'

Jessica turned to Jaime.

'Jeans and a floppy shirt; is that suitable for fishing?'

It was a blue and pink checked shirt and the jeans were worn and figure-hugging. It did not need Jaime's nod for Jessica to see that he approved of her outfit, his eyes said it all. She smiled at him, then the two of them set off.

'First a meal, then a few drinks, then fishing,' Jaime said, heading determinedly for the harbour. 'If we climb right along the ridge of rocks I have in mind we reach deep water far more quickly than you would imagine. I have my rod and line and bait and we'll have good sport, you see.'

They had their meal first though, and Jessica walked out of the restaurant into the warm, windy night thinking that the best part of the evening was probably behind her.

She was wrong. As soon as they reached the place where the harbour was bounded by great reefs of rocks she realised that the setting alone would make their fishing expedition memorable. Huge stars blazed out of a cobalt sky and the moon, a sliver of silver, floated serenely above the dark and glinting sea. The rocks stretched out, a solid barrier besieged by the tiny waves which sucked and lapped and sighed against them. And when you looked down into the deep sea, you could see the fish. Huge, dark, silent, they drifted by, unworried by moonlight or sun, simply gliding along in the depths of the ocean.

'See? Down there! Now find a comfortable ledge of rock, shaped like a seat, and I will cast for you.'

Jaime cast. He looked like a Greek god against the night sky, his arm curved in the immortal gesture of hurling a line, and the line itself, silvered by starlight, added its own mystery to the night.

'There! Now hold the rod and if you have a bite you'll feel it right through the line.'

Jessica took the slender rod. 'Isn't this gear a bit slight though, if we hook a big one?'

Jaime laughed. 'It is slight, but extremely strong. You'll find that you need only strength and not weight, when you hook a big fish.'

After that they chose a comfortable ledge of rock and sat down to wait while Jaime, in a low murmur, told Jessica of his various fishing trips and the huge catches which had resulted.

When the tug came on the line it was so light, so tentative, that Jessica thought it merely the result of a larger wave, but Jaime had heard the tinkle as the rod tip dipped and immediately sat up straighter and put a hand on her arm.

'You've got some . . .'

It was the last calmly spoken phrase either of them was to utter for some time. Jessica had indeed hooked a fish, and a big one, too. It must have known, Jessica thought as she was careered from one end of the reef to the other, that it had an amateur on the other end of the line. It behaved, first of all, as though it was determined to tow not only herself but the entire reef if necessary, out into the open sea beyond the harbour. Then it went deep . . . the line, changing direction abruptly, nearly severed her foot . . . then it jerked and Jessica fell to her knees and was only able to scramble up again when her enemy—for by now the fish was her enemy—decided to make for the open sea once more.

Jaime tried to help, but a lot of his advice was double-Dutch to Jessica and quite often, even when she understood, she was unable to act on it before her fish had changed tack. She was rushed up and down the reef, tripping, cursing, bruised and soaked in sea-water. She had her hands blistered by the rod and cut where she had been foolish enough to grab the line as it unreeled.

They were actually both desperately holding onto the rod, which was bent into an arc with the titanic struggle, when the line either broke or the fish snagged it on a rock. At any rate, the two bruised and battered fishers found themselves abruptly pulling on a rod which did not resist. Naturally they both fell backwards, with humiliated cries, to land in a deep sea-water pool, Jessica underneath.

It says a lot for their friendship that no one uttered a word of reproach as they struggled out of the water and made for the beach. They were both laughing, both breathless, and Jessica's pink and blue checked shirt was ripped from collar to hem where it had caught on a tooth of rock, whilst they were both soaked to the skin and considerably bruised. Jessica was showing Jaime the damage which had been wrought by rod and line to the palms and fingers of her hands when an icy voice broke into their breathless exchange.

'What the hell . . . ? My God, it's Jessica!' Above them, on the quayside, Diaz Perrello stood, looking down on them as though he could not believe his eyes. 'My dear child . . .' he leaned down and took her hand to help her up onto the quay and as he did so, turned and addressed Jaime. 'What do you think you're doing, soldier? If you've hurt a hair of her head . . .'

'We've been fishing, sir,' Jessica said quickly, pointing to the ruined rod dangling from Jaime's hand. 'It's quite all right, only I hooked a huge one and it knocked me into the sea and . . .'

'And where is it? This huge fish?'

Jessica looked up into a remarkably cold pair of dark eyes.

'Well, it . . . it got away,' she stammered, furious with herself for her dishevelled state and lack of conviction. 'Th—that's why I fell in the water, and Jaime was trying . . .'

'I have a very good idea of precisely what Jaime was trying,' Perrello said, his tone sharp with sarcasm. 'And I can see you were all in favour—until, of course, you realised you'd bitten off more than you could chew! I think, Miss French, it's time you went home.'

'I don't think you understand,' Jessica said, scarlet-cheeked. 'Jaime and I were only fishing, we weren't doing . . .'

'Nurse, a fully-grown shark could not have torn your clothing and bruised your person the way . . . What's your name, young man? Rank? Regiment?'

Jaime was as red as Jessica and obviously just as annoyed. He said stiffly, 'My name is Jaime Tenono and I'm a subaltern at present attached to the base here. I must take my young lady back to her home now, sir, but if you wish to discuss the matter further you can find me in half an hour back with my regiment. My late pass expires in twenty minutes or I would explain more fully right away. Not that I think explanations are called for. You heard what the señorita said.'

'I think, Lieutenant Tenono, that your young lady would be a good deal safer with me . . . she is, after all, one of my nurses. I'll take her back and then come to your base for an explanation . . .'

'I am not a child!' Jessica cried. She wrenched one arm free from Perrello's grasp and the other hand out of Jaime's. Then she ran across the pavement and dived into a waiting taxi. 'Can you take me right to the door of the nurses' home, please?' she said breathlessly to the driver. 'Apparently these gentlemen have business to discuss!'

The driver, chuckling, did as he was asked and Jessica leaned back against the worn leather upholstery and tried not to shed tears with the frustration of her stormy encounter. Really! There had been absolutely no need for Perrello to behave in that high-handed fashion. Obviously he believed Jaime had been making a pass at her, possibly that she had been responding. It really did not matter, it was none of his business. He had more or less forbidden her to go with any members of his wretched surgical team but Jaime was a lieutenant in the army, not a doctor. Perrello had, she felt, humiliated them both and made them both look fools, whereas the only fool present on the quay had been Diaz Perrello, jumping in with both feet and trying to make something sinister out of a perfectly innocent event!

She was still fuming ten minutes later when she let herself into the flat. Pat was in the kitchen, hair in rollers, sprawled in a chair filing her nails having obviously just had a bath. She raised her eyebrows as Jessica stalked in and flung herself into the chair opposite.

'Hello-ello-ello! I say, you are in a mess! What's the matter? Oh, Jess, your poor hands!'

'We hooked a huge fish, it got away, I fell in the sea, and Perrello suddenly leapt out from behind a bush and accused Jaime and me of behaving badly. Pat, it was really dreadful, so embarrassing! He simply refused to believe we'd been fishing and he was so high-handed! He tried to insist that he took me home instead of Jaime, and he asked him for his name, rank and number and said he was going to demand an explanation . . . I was really ashamed of the way he behaved.'

Pat got to her feet and busied herself making hot drinks. When the water was boiling she made two cups of cocoa and then returned to her seat opposite her friend.

'Well, frankly I can see why,' she remarked, pushing one of the cups over to Jessica. 'You are awfully bruised and battered . . . your hair looks like a bird's nest and your lovely shirt's almost ripped in two . . . so if he leapt to the wrong conclusions he won't have been the only one.'

'Oh, rubbish! Other people know that fighting a huge fish is tough work. And anyway, Pat, he's my boss, not my keeper—nor my father, which was what he sounded like! What's more, he made me sound like an irresponsible child. I'll never forgive him, never!'

'When you've had a hot bath, a good night's sleep and a substantial breakfast you'll probably look at the entire episode in quite a different light. You'll probably think it was quite touching that he was annoyed with Jaime,' Pat said soothingly. 'Come along, Jess, I'm sure Perrello meant it for the best.'

'Oh, well.' Jessica got to her feet, picked up her cup of cocoa and followed Pat out of the kitchen. 'At least a good night's sleep will restore my sense of proportion. Right now, all I can see is what an idiot I was made to look.'

As it was, she was so tired that she nearly fell asleep in the bath and had to scramble dizzily out of the cooling water and drag on her nightie over limbs still damp and trembling with fatigue. Once in bed, sleep came instantly and she slept straight through until the alarm roused her next morning.

'It's quite all right, Mrs Ferguson, Doctor only wants to check that your wound is healing properly.' Jessica peeled back the large dressing with great care, revealing Mrs Ferguson's wound to be clean and healthy.

Together, she and John Mariano examined the site, then the young doctor straightened and grunted approvingly.

'That's fine. Thanks very much, Mrs Ferguson. You've no pain round the wound any more?'

'No, it's been quite all right since last night, thank you, Doctor.' Mrs Ferguson smiled up at the two faces hovering anxiously above her bed. 'I'm feeling better than I've done for a long time, in fact. I'm really looking forward to going home and getting on with all the things I've been putting off until I felt capable of tackling them.'

'You'll be away from here in a day or so, if the wound continues to heal so well,' the doctor assured her. 'Can you put a clean dressing on, Nurse Roberts? I just want a word with Nurse French.'

They left the auxiliary busy with her wound dressing and

moved away to stand by the window, Jessica with her eyebrows raised.

'Yes, Dr Mariano? Is anything wrong?'

'Not today, no. But yesterday!' he rolled his eyes expressively up towards the ceiling. 'Dr Perrello came in, we had a talk, ran through some of his cases together. I told him who I'd discharged in his absence and he seemed satisfied. And then Sister Cruz came in and had a word with him and when she'd gone out I commented that, good though she was, I found Nurse French even better . . . and it appeared he's annoyed with you.'

'Did he say why?' Jessica gazed out through the window, at the blue of the sea and sky, wishing that she did not know the answer, but she was sure she did.

'Oh, sure, eventually. He wants you in theatre full-time, when Sister Cruz goes, and he doesn't think you'll apply for the position. And . . .' here Dr Mariano cleared his throat and looked as embarrassed as a young, self-confident man is capable of looking. '. . . it appears he thinks you might be in some sort of trouble. He suggested that I might find out if you were in need of moral support. Apparently he came upon you with a young army officer . . . it's all right, don't start raising your hackles, he said though at the time he had been annoyed with you he realised afterwards that the fault must have lain with the chap. Anyway he went round to the barracks next day . . .'

'He did *what*?' In her astonishment and annoyance Jessica raised her voice and was promptly the cynosure of all eyes. She sank it to a whisper. '*What* did he do?'

'He went round to the barracks, just to have a word with the young fellow. And he'd gone. Applied for a posting. So naturally . . .'

By now Jessica could not contain her annoyance. She strove, however, to keep her voice respectably low.

'So naturally he assumed I was in trouble and Jaime had fled! Dr Mariano, can I tell you about it?'

'You mean Dr Perrello got hold of the wrong end of the stick? So, it appears, your Jaime's commanding officer assured him. He got very on his dignity and you can be sure that

Perrello did the same. Confusion all round. Which is why Diaz asked me to have a word with you.'

'Right. I am now in the picture but I think you, John, are floundering in the dark.' Jessica had swung away from the window and was glaring fiercely into John Mariano's clear blue eyes. 'Listen for a minute. I went fishing with Jaime Tenono. I hooked a big one . . . huge, by the way it fought . . . but I lost it. It broke the line. When the line went I did the same, onto my back in a rock pool. I tore my shirt getting out and I was soaked. I was also laughing and quite a bit bruised . . . see that?' She showed him the livid abrasion which ran from elbow to wrist on the underside of her arm. 'We came up from the rocks onto the quay and there was Perrello. He leapt to a totally wrong conclusion and was so offensive that I simply jumped into a taxi and left. That, dear John, is the truth. What you've been told is . . . is the ramblings of a lunatic mind!'

'And Lieutenant Tenono's absence?'

'A posting to be sure, planned weeks ago. That's why we went out that night, because he was leaving next day. So if our boss thinks what I think he thinks, then he thinks wrong. There was nothing going on, nothing had been going on, nothing would have gone on even if we'd been there all night. Can you convey that to Dr Perrello forcefully enough, do you think?'

'Yes, of course. He'll be relieved . . . no, don't start frowning again, for goodness' sake, Jessica, he was concerned for you! No, don't shake your head, he was. I'm sure that a rational explanation would have been immediately understood—why didn't you tell him? Why did you just run off?'

'Because he wouldn't listen . . . I tried to tell him!'

'Oh come, now. He told me that he rang through twice the next day trying to speak to you and you were busy.'

Jessica stared. Had he really tried to get in touch with her? If so, then perhaps she might possibly be able to look him in the eye the next time they met. But why had she not been told?

'I must have been busy,' she said slowly. 'No one told me Perrello had rung. I'll ask Sister.'

'You do that. So I can go back and tell our boss that all is forgiven, and that you'll put in for the job when it comes up?'

Jessica was in mid-nod when Dr Mariano added the last phrase, which turned the nod into an emphatic shake.

'Oh, no! I'm not at all sure I want to work full-time in theatre. Anyway, who knows when Sister Cruz will leave? It might be months and months. Let's just leave that part of it in the lap of the gods, can we?'

'Yes, I think that's fair enough. And now to more personal matters; how about showing me round Puerto Malon this evening? I could do with a decent meal and some company other than my own.'

'I think it would be most unwise,' Jessica said with some asperity. 'Dr Perrello doesn't like team members getting involved with each other socially. And after all the trouble I've been in after a perfectly innocent fishing trip I think I'll stay at home evenings, for a while.'

Dr Mariano laughed but turned away from her.

'Right, we'll give it a few days before putting it to the test,' he said cheerfully. 'Coming to the canteen for lunch?'

'Not today.' Jessica moved slowly up the ward as Dr Mariano, apparently taking his dismissal in good part, disappeared through the doors in a flurry of white coat and stethoscope. She was relieved that the misunderstanding over her fishing expedition was to be cleared up but annoyed that Perrello had actually tried to sort it out himself and had been unable to speak to her. Why had Sister not relayed the message? It seemed very odd. But it did not take her long to discover what had happened.

She was taking Mrs Pontin along to the bathroom to weigh her when Sister's office door opened and her head appeared.

'Nurse French! A word, if you've a moment.'

'I'm just checking Mrs Pontin's weight,' Jessica said. 'I'll be along in five minutes.'

With Mrs Pontin balancing her enormous bulk uneasily on the small scale whilst Jessica slid the weights along until the right one was reached, mutual disappointment was expressed, though Jessica decided that recriminations were useless. Her patient knew very well why she had not lost weight, though of course she would never admit it, and it was hard on her. She knew she was being foolish but her appetite had ruled her head for more than half a century, it did not take kindly to being disciplined now.

'No loss. Well, Dr Perrello has put you down for surgery at the end of the week, Mrs Pontin, so if you can possibly try even harder, I think you'll benefit from it. Dr Perrello's bound to come round before you go down to theatre and he's not going to be very pleased that you've lost nothing.'

'I will try, Nurse. But I've been trying—I've scarcely eaten all week, you know that. I'm one of those people who simply can't lose weight . . . I only have to look at food . . .'

Jessica let her run on, saying nothing about the chocolate bars bought from the hospital shop or the number of times other patients had offered her a few biscuits and had discovered, afterwards, that the packet had mysteriously shrunk to empty.

Sister, however, was not so restrained.

'That silly woman, I really am vexed,' she exclaimed, studying the weight chart with its almost totally steady line. 'She's a prey to so many things with her weight right up there—high blood pressure, diabetes, varicose veins, fallen arches—and as for surgery, well the mind boggles. All that subcutaneous fat! Has Dr Perrello spoken to her about it lately?'

'Not for a fortnight or so. I keep warning her that when he does he isn't going to be pleased, but she gives me a reproachful look and her eyes fill with tears and she tells me no one could try harder than her and that she's felt quite ill from hunger. Yet we both know she's for ever getting her friends to bring her in chocolates and great wedges of fudge, to say nothing of trotting along to the kitchen and helping herself to anything left around. And buying from the sandwich bar when we think she's in the bath or watching television.'

'I think the most difficult part is that she's managed to convince herself that she *is* dieting. It's strange the way an overweight woman will actually believe her own propaganda and see herself as a misunderstood victim of a cruel world,' Sister remarked, slipping the unsatisfactory weight chart back into Mrs Pontin's file. 'I've met women who never actually look at themselves in a full-length mirror, though they may appear to do so. But they're so conditioned that they never let their eyes stray below neck-level, so they manage to retain a totally false picture of themselves and the effect of their grossness on their health.'

'Well, we've warned her,' Jessica said, gathering up the file. 'I really don't know what else we can do.'

'I'll go down in a moment and tell her that Perrello won't operate unless she loses at least another stone,' Sister said, getting resignedly to her feet and putting down the pen with which she had been form-filling. 'You'd think that the pain from her condition would stop her wanting to eat but even that she puts down to being too hungry to be comfortable.'

'I'm getting quite hungry myself,' Jessica said, in the doorway. 'Will it be all right if I bring coffee and sandwiches up to the staff room and eat them in there? Usually I go out, but I thought I'd spent some time with Mrs Chase today.'

'Yes, that will be all right, only don't make a habit of it,' Sister advised. 'Nurses need their rest more than most.'

She hurried away towards a confrontation with Mrs Pontin and Jessica, smiling, made her way down to the coffee bar for her lunch.

'What's that bruise on your arm, Nurse?' Mrs Chase looked coy. 'If I didn't know better I'd think it was fingerprints!'

'It is. The other evening I went fishing and very nearly got pulled in by what felt like a whale,' Jessica said, smiling. 'Have you ever fished these waters, Mrs Chase?'

'No, I can't say I have, my dear. But I used to go walking along the beach with young men, and many's the time I came back with less lipstick than I'd started out with!'

'I know what you mean, but I really was fishing,' Jessica said as lightly as she could. It was so annoying to be generally disbelieved, and she was fairly sure she knew who to blame, as well. And that reminded her, she had never tackled Sister about the telephone messages. She looked hopefully at Mrs Chase's dinner plate. 'Have you finished with that? Shall I take it down to the trolley for you?'

'No, it's all right, I'll take it down myself. I usually have a cup of tea with the others, in the day-room,' Mrs Chase remarked, standing up and putting her cutlery neatly in the middle of her plate. She had eaten well, as she always did. 'Now where's my magazine?'

Jessica left her, fussing happily over what she should take through to the day-room with her, and went over to Mrs Briggs, to measure the amount of fluid in her catheter balloon. Having done so, she checked in the Kardex and found, as she suspected, that it was due to be removed later in the day. After that she made sure that the cannula and the intravenous drip were still functioning as they should have been, then made her way to Sister's office.

Sister, rested and fed, smiled at her and waved hospitably to a chair.

'Well, Staff? Mrs Chase passed me as I was coming back from the canteen and it struck me immediately how happy she looked, and how very much calmer.'

'I can't take all the credit; the medication's helping enormously,' Jessica admitted, taking the chair. 'Sister, I wonder if you've had any messages for me lately? Someone said they'd phoned the ward a couple of times and asked for me.'

'Not when I was on duty,' Sister said positively. 'But now that you mention it there was something . . . yesterday, would it have been, when I was in that staff meeting. Yes, that's right. Young Illon was minding the telephone and she left a message. A man rang but wouldn't leave a message and said he'd ring back later.'

'Well, that's a relief. It isn't important, I've sorted it out now, but it worried me when he said he'd been trying to get me. Why didn't Illon call me?'

'Because she thought you were over in theatre; she doesn't know the staff very well yet and she'd somehow muddled you and Felicity Carew. She knew she hadn't seen Nurse Carew, so obviously said you weren't available.'

'Hmm. I hope she doesn't think that just because Nurse Carew and I both have red hair we're interchangeable!'

Sister laughed. 'I doubt it, Staff—your hair is an unusual shade, not really red at all, and poor Carew is bright ginger! I'm glad you got your messages sorted out, anyway.' She paused. 'That's a nasty bruise on your arm!'

'Yes. I got it trying to catch a big fish, and then the line broke so I lost him,' Jessica said rather stiffly. She had thought better of Sister than to believe she would listen to gossip.

'Oh, is that how the rumours started,' Sister said genially. 'Well, I might have known! I don't believe it, I told Sister Brewster. Staff isn't the kind of girl to go getting herself mixed up with a Spanish soldier, no matter how handsome.'

'I was with a Spanish soldier, a very handsome one,' Jessica said, grinning. 'But we were just fishing. I'm beginning to wish I'd never agreed to go though, Sister. If anyone says anything else to you, I'd be obliged if you'd tell them frankly that it's all spiteful gossip.'

'Don't worry; it's a nine-days' wonder and pretty soon they'll be talking about someone else. Now Staff, about Mrs Briggs . . . it's about time we checked her catheter and . . .'

'I've just done it; shall I put screens round her bed and then we can remove it? It's ready now.'

'Yes, please. And Jessica . . .'

Jessica paused, already half out of the doorway.

'Yes, Sister?'

'Don't let gossip worry you, Staff. Hospitals, even the best of them, are hot-beds of gossip and intrigue but in the main it's harmless. Unless you take it seriously, of course. Laugh it off and they'll forget it in an hour; take umbrage and they'll begin to believe it.'

'I won't forget, Sister.'

CHAPTER SIX

'SWAB the site please, Nurse.'

Jessica picked up the disinfected swab and began to clean the marked area, taking care to avoid Ana, who was protecting the radial nerve in the patient's arm by supporting it on the arm-board which had been pulled into position prior to the patient's entry into theatre. The patient was a handsome woman in her mid-forties having a breast biopsy; the surgeon believed she had a large cyst, but even so the precaution of surgery had to be taken.

It was several days since she had explained her fishing experience to John Mariano, but this was the first time that she had been called to theatre to work with the team and the first time, also, that she had seen Dr Perrello since the fateful night when she had jumped into the taxi and left him standing on the quayside. To her secret relief he had been unfailingly polite to her as they scrubbed up and had been cheerful, almost talkative, to the other team members. Apparently he was not going to bear a grudge for her behaviour—though Jessica still thought that his own was far worthier of grudges. However, she did not intend to show anything but efficiency and friendliness towards him, since he seemed equally determined to be pleasant to her.

'That's ideal. Thank you. I'll have a Number 3 blade please, Nurse.'

'Certainly, Dr Perrello.' Jessica dropped her used swab into the bucket and handed him the desired blade, first fitting it neatly into the handle. She watched as the scalpel moved quickly and cleanly, unhesitatingly making an arc-shaped cut around and above the patient's nipple. It was, Jessica could see, the ideal cut. Because the wound followed the nipple's edge so exactly the patient would be unable to find the wound after healing had taken place.

'Hmm, deeper than I thought, but clearly a cyst . . . a big

one . . . and another, and another . . .'

The cysts were in a typical string formation and were gently drawn forth and dropped into the specimen pot which Jessica quickly held out.

'Good. Just check that there are no more within reach.' Dr Perrello probed gently, grunted, found one more cyst and then laid his scalpel down on the trolley once more. 'Close the wound would you, Galdos? Nurse,' he turned to her, indicating the specimen pot. 'Get a runner to take this over to the lab, would you? I'll want a frozen section done immediately—before the patient comes round if possible.'

Jessica held the pot out and Milagros, the fastest of the auxiliaries who worked in theatre, came eagerly forward.

'Take this to the lab please, Mila, and come straight back with the result.'

Milagros took the pot, careful not to touch Jessica as she did so.

'Certainly, Staff; I'll be back before you know it,' she promised, fairly shooting out of the room.

She was as good as her word. The patient was still on the table, the wound neatly sutured, when she reappeared with the result which the team had expected: benign cysts.

'Thank you, Nurse. Staff, would you supervise the patient into Recovery, then come back to scrub up for the next.'

Jessica did as she was asked and later, waiting her turn to use the sinks whilst Ana reached for the packs of new gowns, gloves and masks, she behaved as she always did, though she kept a wary eye on Perrello. She joked with Dr Galdos, teased John Mariano about buying flowers for his new flat before he had even got a teapot, asked the prelim. sister whether she was still seeing one of the porters, Cesar, and if they intended to get married, and all the time her mind was half uneasily, half wistfully, on Diaz Perrello as he moved around the room. It was clear both from what John had told her and from her own experience this morning that Dr Perrello had decided to believe her innocent of having an affair with Jaime, and equally clear that he was doing his best to treat her just as he treated other nurses. But that, she realised dismally, was not what she really wanted. She wanted his friendship, even if she could never have anything more.

Anything more? The thought, coming unbidden, made her blink. Why on earth should she want more from a colleague and a senior colleague at that? Surely she was not fool enough to expect a closer relationship with someone as stern and remote as Perrello? And after what had happened between her and Jordi Ramblas you would have thought common sense alone would have bade her steer clear of doctors for a bit.

For a day or so after the fishing episode she had really thought she would like to drop theatre work altogether rather than face people who believed she had been first seduced and then abandoned by a young soldier. Then, however, common sense had reasserted itself; she was probably happier in theatre even than she was on the ward because she was doing a job she did very well indeed to the best of her ability and actually helping to save lives.

She had also accepted the truth of Sister's statement that she and Jaime were a nine-days' wonder, soon forgotten. Indeed, only by her own behaviour could she make people see that she was not an empty-headed, promiscuous young woman.

So it had come as something of a shock when Dr Perrello had not rung for her to join the team in theatre for over a week. She had wondered, uneasily, whether he had decided not to try to pressure her into doing something she kept saying repeatedly that she did not much wish to do. Then, this morning, as soon as she went onto the ward, Sister had bustled out and told her that Sister Cruz was off all day due to her mother's state of health, and Dr Perrello required her assistance.

The sinks both became free and she and the surgeon scrubbed up side by side. Since they had started at the same time they finished more or less together, Perrello's elbow tipping the tap off just as hers did. As they both turned away from the sinks, Jessica, naturally, met his eye and as naturally, smiled. For a frozen second she thought he was going to ignore her but then he, too, smiled slightly, though he turned away at once, to speak to John Mariano.

'What's next? He's a private soldier, pains in the lower right abdomen. They've done a urine test, I suppose to check for albumen? Not that it seemed like kidney trouble, I saw him on the ward when you did. What did you think, John?'

'Straightforward appendicectomy,' John said, as the auxiliary helped him into his gown. 'I checked the usual tests but they all point to it.'

'Like to do it? There's a cardiospasm next which I really ought to do myself . . . we tried the negus hydrostatic bag but the condition was too advanced, so surgery's the only answer. How about it? I know you've covered for me whilst I was in Barcelona, how about showing me your technique, instead of watching mine all the time?'

'With Nurse French assisting I'm game to try anything,' John said gallantly, giving Jessica a quick, reassuring smile. 'Her efficiency is admirable; she knows which instrument I'm about to ask for whilst the words are still unsaid.'

'How nice you are to me,' Jessica said, as they made their way back to theatre, John and she in the rear. 'That was a really kind thing to say.'

'It wasn't kind, it was true,' John told her as they entered the familiar theatre. 'Some nurses never manage to be anything other than capable, you know. They do as they're told quite quickly but never take the initiative. It's a pleasure to work with someone who thinks ahead and can act virtually before a surgeon has opened his mouth. Wouldn't you agree, Diaz?'

'What? Sorry, John, my mind was miles away. Ah, here comes your patient.'

Jessica, going quietly about her work, seethed inside at his ungraciousness. He could have agreed with John, instead of pretending not to have heard! But it was typical of the man; he might put on a surface politeness to keep the team happy and everyone working at their best, but his deeper feelings of dislike and distrust for her sex in general and herself in particular could not be totally hidden.

'Done all your checking, ladies?' How different was John Mariano's approach, Jessica thought thankfully, as John's eyes narrowed into a smile above the mask. 'Right, then if you'll clean the site, Staff, we'll get cracking.'

Despite a certain slowing down in view of being watched by the senior consultant, Dr Mariano's operating technique stood the test of close scrutiny and when it was over and they were taking a coffee break before the next big operation, John came over to where Jessica stood, by the long windows which led onto the balcony, gazing out over the blue of the harbour.

'Well? What did you think? I thought we made quite a neat job of if, you and I.'

'Well, you did,' Jessica acknowledged. 'And you're very easy to work with, which helps.'

'That's me, fun to be around . . . no, don't shake your head, you may not have said that, but you meant it.' Jessica was still shaking her head and laughing at him when she saw, out of the corner of her eye, Perrello turn and walk towards them. Whether John Mariano saw or not she could not have guessed, but he burst into low, hurried speech.

'Jess, don't mess me about now; will you come out with me? For a meal and a chat? Any evening you're free.'

'Well, you know what I said about . . .' but Dr Perrello was too close; he would hear his name and know they had been talking about him—or *think* they had been talking about him. 'Oh, John . . . yes, I'd like to have an evening out.'

'Great! When?'

'Oh . . . How about Saturday?'

'Fine. What time will you be free?'

Dr Perrello was now too close for a hope to linger that he might not overhear. Jessica threw discretion to the winds. After all, it was not a hospital rule or anything, it was just Perrello's personal feeling that love-affairs within the team could be difficult.

'Call for me at eight,' she said, her chin well up, the sparkle in her green-blue eyes defiant. 'I'll be ready for you by then!'

'How do you feel now, Mrs Webb?' Jessica smoothed the sheets flat and then eyed her patient hopefully. Mrs Webb had a fractured femur and due to her age and general medical condition an immediate operation had not been thought wise. Instead she was on a dextrose drip and had her leg supported on pillows until Dr Perrello judged she was fit enough to have a Smith-Petersen pin fitted. Additionally, the nursing staff had to make sure that the old lady took as much fluid as she could stomach, and whenever possible they moved her around in the bed and persuaded her to sit up as straight as she could. A physio came over from the military hospital once a day to give her breathing exercises and to encourage her to void any phlegm which had gathered in her lungs and poor Mrs Webb, through no fault of her own, was rapidly becoming the bane of Aggy.

The difficulty was, of course, that an intake of fluids means a need to relieve oneself, and Mrs Webb's frail voice was frequently raised in a shout of 'Nurse!' At first any nurse within earshot had come in to see what the old lady required but now at the sound of her voice a nurse complete with bedpan would hurry up the ward. Indeed, as matters became more urgent Jessica had taken to leaving a couple of bedpans under the visitor's stool so that Mrs Webb would not have to wait.

For waiting was just what the old lady could not do, and since she was fastidious and rather autocratic everyone tried their very best to see that bedpans arrived as regularly as did the cool drinks, the cups of tea, the glasses of milk, which had been prescribed.

Jessica, having just removed Mrs Webb's bedpan, re-arranged the pillows round her leg, straightened the bottom sheet which, the sufferer announced crossly, was so wrinkled as to be bound to cause bed-sores, stood back and tried to look calm and relaxed whereas in reality she was in a great hurry to get over to Mrs De Sousa, who was on bed-rest for a threatened miscarriage and who had been asking if someone would pass her knitting for at least ten minutes. If I don't get there soon she'll reach across for it herself, and she isn't supposed to reach, Jessica thought frantically, but she allowed none of these feelings to show on her face. Mrs Webb liked one's full attention!'

'Thank you, Staff, I feel a good deal better.' Mrs Webb smiled graciously and picked up her book. It was not a novel but an autobiography—and of royalty, no less. Mrs Webb might have lived in Minestos for forty years but that had not lessened her fervent admiration for all things British and most of all, for the royal family. She opened the book and showed the page she was reading to Jessica. 'The things I've learned about the Duke . . . I was quite shocked!'

'I can imagine.' Jessica moved slowly away from the bed, not turning her back but simply gliding further from Mrs Webb's vicinity. When she felt it was safe to do so, she hurried across to Mrs De Sousa. She smiled, whisked up the knitting, and put it down across Mrs De Sousa's bulge.

'There you are, one matinée jacket! I'm sorry I couldn't come across earlier, Mrs De Sousa, but Mrs Webb does need a good deal of attention.'

'That's all right, Staff.' Mrs De Sousa picked up her knitting and began, desultorily, to continue with her row. 'Why can't I go home? If all they're going to do is to watch me lie here . . .'

'If you went home you'd fuss around that handsome husband of yours and run errands and do housework and probably, in this heat, you'd go swimming in the afternoon,' Jessica reminded her. 'That's what you were doing when you were brought in. Doctor says that if you can just bring yourself to stay quietly here for another fortnight, then either baby will decide to put in an appearance or they'll start you off. Isn't it worth being bored for a couple of weeks to have a nice healthy baby?'

'Yes, of course it is, really, but I get so weepy when I'm stuck in bed all day,' Mrs De Sousa confided. She was only twenty-one or two, with a thick and curly mop of blonde hair and a pair of round, slightly astonished blue eyes. She reminded Jessica of a doll she had once owned and added to this illusion when she was upset by her rather high voice, but she was a pleasant girl and amusing company when she was not depressed by the prospect of a fortnight in a hospital bed.

'Well, there are mealtimes, and the other patients . . . poor you, not even able to stagger in to watch the television,' Jessica said teasingly. It was a fact which amused all the patients and a good few of the nurses that Mrs De Sousa had managed to catch—and keep—her incredibly handsome husband without the help of more than about three words in Spanish. Furthermore, she made no attempt to learn the language and announced that she did not intend to do so. Whilst her Carl did all the talking for her, why should she bother? So not being able to watch television was a matter of indifference for her since she could not understand a word that was said.

'Oh, I don't mind missing the telly,' Mrs De Sousa said comfortably now, dropping a stitch and using a word that made even broadminded Jessica blink. 'I do miss my social life, though. What do you do in the evenings, Staff? Go out with the local lads?'

'Not a lot. But I'm going out for a meal with Dr Mariano one of these evenings—on Saturday, actually, if I can get away. If you want details of someone's love-life to stop you from feeling bored you should ask Felicity Carew, the nurse with the beautiful auburn hair, or Pat Hoby . . . you know Staff Nurse Hoby, of course. They always seem to have something exciting on. But I'm quite new here, and I find nursing takes up most of my spare energy.'

'Beautiful auburn hair! Ginger, you mean! But I don't see why you aren't up to your knees in swooning Spaniards, Nurse, with that lovely long dark gold hair. Are they all blind or something?' She tossed her own primrose-coloured locks. 'I always had to fight 'em off, mainly because of my hair,' she said smugly.

'Did you, now? Perhaps they like blondes better than reddy-yellows,' Jessica said teasingly. 'I don't, alas, suffer like that. Besides, I'm too busy.'

'Mariano . . . he's really nice looking,' Mrs De Sousa said, apparently suddenly able to bring the young doctor to mind. 'And what about Perrello? I wouldn't call him handsome, but he's got something, wouldn't you say? Amanda says he's cold, but . . .'

'Amanda? Who's she?'

'Didn't you know, Staff? They were married and Carl says people thought they were crazy about each other . . . real love-birds, apparently. But then Señor Alberto Dennuce came back from a business trip and saw Amanda and they fell for each other. Poor old Diaz didn't stand much chance, not when you set his villa and his salary against old Dennuce's millions. So every year about now Perrello goes about looking as if there's a wasp in his shirt because Amanda and Dennuce are up in their big castle in the mountains and he may bump into her any moment! Awful for the poor chap, except you'd have thought he'd have had enough sense by now to have got himself married. Perhaps he's hoping Dennuce will snuff it and he can take over, I don't know, but more likely he just can't be bothered. Men are all lazy; they wait to be caught if you ask me, rather than doing any catching themselves.'

'Mrs De Sousa, you say one thing in one breath and something totally different in the next,' Jessica protested, her head still spinning with the story she had heard. 'I thought you were besieged by eager admirers before you were married?'

'Well, so I was, but I didn't say they wanted to marry me,' Mrs De Sousa said with painful frankness. 'That wasn't what they were after at all, as I'm sure you must know! It was *me* who decided I'd had enough of being single, for all the fun, and picked my Carl out to be the lucky man.'

'Oh? I wonder if he knows?'

'Bless you, no! He's quite convinced it's the other way round. But you show me a man who's eager for marriage and I'll show you a bore!'

'I see,' Jessica said faintly. 'I think I'd better get on with my work, Mrs De Sousa, before you corrupt me totally.'

'Why don't you have a go at Diaz though, Staff? I should think you're his type—very efficient and yet pretty as they come. You ought to set your cap at him and show him not all English girls are shallow, like that Amanda.'

'Aren't you a friend of hers?' Jessica asked as she turned away from the bed. 'That isn't a very nice thing to say about a friend.'

'A friend? Bless you, Staff, Amanda's near enough thirty-five and so sophisticated you wouldn't believe. I'm not just being nasty, either, because I *am* friendly with Roger Michaels and he told me that Amanda's shallow, vain and heartless. So there!'

'What difference does it make that Amanda's thirty-five?' Jessica asked. 'You can be friendly with someone regardless of age, can't you?'

'No. Not when you're twenty-one and married to someone without a huge pot-belly or a huge wallet,' Mrs De Sousa said with conviction. 'She wouldn't look twice at me. Once she dropped her handbag in the *supermercado* and I picked it up . . . do you know she took it without even looking at me? Very regal!'

'Gosh. Did she thank you?'

'No. Not a word. Too grand.'

Jessica shook her head sadly over such rudeness and made her way to the end of the ward, but she had scarcely done more than push the swing doors when a plaintive cry from the end bed made her pause with sinking heart.

'Nurse! Nu-urse! Could I trouble you for the bedpan?'

Jessica was on duty on Saturday, but only on a short shift, from eight until noon. She was hurrying over her work, determined not to leave too much for Felicity, who was doing afternoons, when the swing doors at the end of the ward swung and Dr Perrello's tall figure came hurrying through. He was alone, and rather to her surprise, not wearing the customary white coat and stethoscope.

'Nurse!'

Jessica hurried over to him, trying not to be impressed by the casual elegance of what looked like a cream silk shirt and coffee-coloured slacks.

'Yes, Doctor?'

'I've been meaning to ask you . . . the overweight woman in Room 2, has she lost?'

'Oh, Mrs Pontin, you mean. Er . . . no, sir, I don't believe she has.'

'She's been warned what an operation on all that fat could mean?'

'Well, yes, but . . .'

'Do your best to see that she loses at least half a dozen pounds in the next week or so, would you? I'm relying on you, Staff.' He took her elbow and led her over to the window, where they could not be overheard, though the ward was almost empty save for Mrs De Sousa and Mrs Webb, all the other patients being in the day-room. 'Do you enjoy opera, Nurse?'

'Opera? Well, I suppose . . . why, sir?'

'There's a private performance of *Figaro* being given this

evening. I've been invited to attend and this morning I received two tickets. I wondered if you'd like to accompany me.'

'A private . . . this evening? I'm awfully sorry, sir, I've a previous engagement.' Jessica could have wept, but she could not possibly let John Mariano down, even for such a tempting invitation as this!

'Oh? But surely you could explain . . . make your arrangements for some other time? An opportunity such as this does not come often, not on an island the size of Minestos, though doubtless when you were in Madrid you could watch opera every night of the week if you so wished.'

'I'm awfully sorry, but . . .'

'There are absolutely no strings, Nurse, if that's what's worrying you. I have no interest in you personally whatsoever, save as a companion for this particular evening.' Jessica looked up at him and saw his eyes dark and sombre, his mouth grim. 'I cannot explain just why I need to take a . . . a friend with me, but . . .'

'Dr Perrello, believe me I'm sure you've no interest whatsoever in me,' Jessica said firmly, though with heightened colour. 'Unfortunately I could not possibly break a previous engagement, even for the sake of your . . . your *kind* invitation.'

She was hurt and offended and it showed, as indeed she had meant it to. Dr Perrello opened his mouth, closed it again, stared down at her, then nodded and turned on his heel. He was out of the ward before she had so much as opened her own mouth, though what she could have said to mend matters was beyond her.

'Well, you *are* a dark horse!' Mrs De Sousa sat up in her bed, tossing her pale hair over her bare shoulder and looking very bright and interested. 'Don't tell me Perrello wasn't propositioning you, I know what makes a girl look like that. You did right, to turn him down . . . but don't turn him down too often or you'll stop being interesting and a challenge and turn into someone who doesn't appreciate him!'

'Dr Perrello was most certainly not propositioning me,' Jessica said, her tone biting. 'If I were you, Mrs De Sousa, I'd be a little less nosy and a little more discreet. As it happens someone's given him two tickets for the opera and he wondered if I would like to make use of one of them, but as I told you, I have a previous engagement.'

'Temper, Staff, temper!' Mrs De Sousa said, not at all offended by Jessica's snub. 'I thought you were his type!'

'Oh, nonsense! He doesn't even like me, he told me quite frankly that he was merely asking me out because he had to have a companion and I was the only person he could think of,' Jessica said tartly. But the irrepressible Mrs De Sousa was not at all dismayed.

'He's been hurt, it isn't likely he'd risk another blow to his pride,' she said. 'He'll go at it sideways, like. You mark my words, he's after you.'

'Well, I'm not after him. He's . . .' truthful words about Perrello's nature rose like bile in Jessica's throat and were, reluctantly, swallowed. 'He's years older than I am, and far too serious.'

'You're quite old, and you'll get older. Besides, mature men have got a lot going for them,' argued Mrs De Sousa, secure in the knowledge that she was four or five years younger than Jessica and already married, and that Mr De Sousa was older than she—probably in his mid-thirties. 'Go on, tell him you'll go with him some other time. He may not show it much but he's shy, I believe.'

'Shy! Anyway, he didn't ask me for some other time, he asked me for tonight and I've already got a date which I'm not breaking. If your baby gets born asking questions I, for one, shouldn't be in the least surprised. And furthermore,' Jessica added, warming to her task, 'as you rightly point out I'm older than you, so it follows that I've had more experience, and my experience tells me that he and I don't get on, won't get on, and probably never will.'

'I remember saying more or less them very words about Carl,' Mrs De Sousa said reminiscently, laying down her knitting. 'And within six months . . . no, I tell a lie, more like three . . . we walked down the aisle together. I'll dance at your wedding, Staff, see if I don't!'

Jessica smiled and whisked out of the ward, determined to say none of the things which were bursting to be said. Perrello had every right to ask her out, but no right whatsoever to expect her to accept. He had been cold and remote and really quite nasty to her for a long while now, his surface politeness could not make up for the way his eyes frosted when he looked at her. As for expecting her to break an existing date . . . well, that really did show what sort of a person he was.

But as she made up the drugs trolley from the cupboard in Sister's office and murmured replies as Sister spoke, she could not help wondering whether Perrello had asked her to the opera because Amanda would be there and he had no desire to turn up alone, as good as admitting that he had never got over his broken marriage. If so, despite how she felt about him, it was a pity that she had not been free. An evening at the opera would have been an enjoyable experience, even with the cold and remote Dr Perrello beside her. And besides, you never knew; she might have been lucky enough to have discovered, as they met, that Dr Perrello was having an evening off and it was the skilful and exciting lone surfer who was taking her out. Despite herself, she could not completely eradicate from her memory the feel of his mouth moving on hers.

'Is that the lot, Staff? Good, good. Well, fetch Nurse Roberts and do the drug round and then I think you might as well get away.' Sister thumped down on the chair behind her desk and pulled a pile of papers towards her. 'I'll get going on these. Have a good weekend!'

'Thanks, John. I really enjoyed that.' Jessica, with her hand tucked in Dr Mariano's arm, had almost succeeded in forgetting that she might have been sitting beside Diaz Perrello and listening to the heady strains of *Figaro*, up in the castle on the mountainside above them, or indeed wherever it was being performed. Instead, she and her escort left the little restaurant and walked out into the darkness of Bastion Square, with the soft golden floodlights illumining the old, grey-stoned tower, the bridge and the blosson on the trees which grew around the plaza.

'I'm glad. You don't get out a lot, do you.' It was a statement, not a question, but Jessica said defensively, 'I do go out. Pat and I go off sometimes, have a meal out and a drink.

But I haven't been here much longer than you, you know.'

'I bet I know more of the island than you do! Have you visited any of the big beaches? Or the old town? Or the ancient monuments? There are the remains of a Paleo-Christian church no more than ten miles away, right up against one of the best beaches you could wish for. I've not done much myself yet, with work and one thing and another, but it would be fun if you'd come out with me.'

'It's very kind of you, and I'd enjoy it, but we'll have to sort out our off-duty times,' Jessica said. 'What would you do, hire a car, or use local buses?'

To her surprise, John slid his arm round her waist and gave her a squeeze before answering.

'Jessica, I'm glad you're here too! I dare say you won't believe it, but a fellow can get lonely just the same as a girl can when he's a long way from his home town.'

'Oh, go on, don't tell me you're lonely! Look at all the nurses who think you're the best-looking doctor ever to work at the Nelson!'

'You can't enjoy someone's company just because they think you're good-looking,' John said. He smiled down into her eyes. 'It's got to be a two-way thing, this attraction business. And I, John Mariano, find you, Jessica French, very very attractive.'

He squeezed again and Jessica gasped, laughed, and decided he really was good company and pushed Diaz Perrello's predicament, alone at the opera, further from the forefront of her mind.

Or tried to do so. Presently, having strolled down to the waterfront, John Mariano pulled her into the shelter of a doorway and put both arms round her. He was smiling, with the hint of a query in his eyes.

'Jessica?'

He kissed her, his mouth warm on hers, and Jessica waited for magic. It did not come, but even so, it was a pleasant experience, and his hands, tightening on her waist, caused her to feel that at least she was appreciated by someone.

The door, opening abruptly and hitting Jessica quite painfully on the bottom, broke their embrace. They moved apart, both equally conscious, as the light streamed out on to them, of dishevelled hair and, in Jessica's case, of smeared lipstick. A woman stood there, paused for that moment of transition from light to dark, then stepped forward, passed them. She did not see them, Jessica was sure, but the man who followed her out certainly did.

'Good evening, John. Good evening, Miss French.'

Perrello's dark face showed no emotion as he moved past them but Jessica felt colour flood her cheeks. How embarrassing! Had he seen them kissing? Even if he had not seen though, he must have guessed. A man and a woman did not usually go into a dark doorway for any purpose other than lovemaking.

'Hello, Diaz!' John said jauntily. He put his arm round Jessica's waist and drew her out of the doorway and on to the pale paving of the waterfront. 'I didn't realise that was a club or a pub, you nearly knocked us into the road, opening the door just as we reached it.'

Perrello turned. His eyebrows climbed but he nodded.

'Yes, it's a club. May I introduce . . . but I believe you know each other, it's just Miss French who hasn't come into contact with Señorita Cruz, I believe.'

Face to face for the first time, and both smiling, they eyed one another. Isabel Cruz was about five foot six inches tall, with thick, glossy hair as black as a sloeberry. Her skin was perfect, smooth and pale. Her eyes, large and lustrous, were fringed with black, upcurling lashes. Her nose was small and straight and her mouth was a pretty shape and when her lips parted her teeth were so white they looked dazzling and very even.

In short, she's one of the most beautiful women I've seen, Jessica told herself as they murmured greetings. And not merely beautiful either, but with a sort of twinkling sweetness in her smile which was most attractive. Beside her, she knew John was instinctively straightening his shoulders; he had probably seen her every day for a fortnight but only as a nurse. Now he saw her as a lovely woman and was, Jessica could tell, quite impressed!

'So we meet at last, Miss French,' Sister Cruz said. Her voice was low and prettily pitched. 'How strange it is that you and I are constantly in the company of these two, so charming gentlemen, yet we have not before met.'

'I've heard a lot about you, it's nice to see you for myself,' Jessica admitted, smiling. 'Did you enjoy the opera, señorita?'

'The opera? Ah, but you were there too, of course! I'm so sorry, but there was such a crowd and Diaz hurried me away as soon as it ended . . .'

'No, we weren't there, but Dr Perrello happened to mention that he was going to see a performance of *Figaro* tonight, when we were checking a patient's chart this morning,' Jessica said hastily, devoutly hoping that the surgeon did not think she had been about to explain that she had been asked first! 'John and I had a meal at the Blue Cat and now we're walking off all that rich food.'

'Ah, I see. Yes, of course, you aren't dressed for it, I suppose.' Her dark eyes scanned Jessica's cool, beech-green shift and open sandals without criticism. She was wearing a long, ivory silk gown which clung to every curve of her figure, Jessica realised. Her dark hair was pulled up into a coronet of pearls on top of her head, and though her arms were bare she wore elbow-length gloves. 'As you can see, it was a dressy affair, which was no doubt the reason Diaz asked me to go with him . . . I do adore a chance to dress up!'

'You look lovely,' Jessica said frankly, though inside she was seething. What a fool she would have looked in her simple little cotton shift and open sandals, in a crowd of people in evening dress. No doubt Dr Perrello had never given it a thought when he asked her to accompany him, or perhaps he had intended to tell her to buy herself a glamorous gown. Well, what a blessing that she had already promised her evening to John!

'It is nice, occasionally, to feel a little special,' Isabel admitted. 'What do you think of Diaz, then? A change from a white coat or theatre blue, is it not?'

For the first time since their abrupt initial meeting, Jessica looked at Perrello. In a black dinner jacket and stiff white shirt with a frilled front he looked incredibly macho, the harshness of his features set off by the stark black and white. He smiled at her as their eyes met and it was, for a moment, as if the two of them were totally alone. Just for that moment Jessica knew that she and Diaz were two of a kind, that no matter how beautiful Isabel Cruz might be, she could never be the perfect match for the surgeon. She also knew that it was the lone surfer looking at her, just for that second. And then the look faded and she could interpret the smile as mocking, the lifted eyebrow as a challenge to her to think for one moment that he would have preferred her company to that of Isabel Cruz.

'You look very nice, sir.' Jessica said it as woodenly as she could, and with as little real meaning. But he nodded gravely, and said at once, 'Thank you. You look pretty yourself.'

'And now, having exchanged compliments . . . I was missed out, but I dare say none of you noticed . . . shall we go for a drink? There's a good place on the waterfront, a bit further down, where you can sit outside and watch the lights in the water and listen to an old chap who's a wizard with a mandolin, strumming away.'

John's suggestion, however, was turned down after Perrello shot up his cuff and looked at his watch.

'Thanks very much, Mariano, but it's late and I've got a list first thing in the morning. I think I'd better get Isabel back home, so that she's fresh and awake by nine o'clock. Can we give you a lift anywhere?'

'No thanks,' Jessica said quickly, before John could speak. 'I'd rather walk, it's such a cool, beautiful night.'

'Right, then we'll be off. Good night, John. Good night, Miss French.'

'I don't see why you can't call her Jessica,' Isabel Cruz said in her carrying voice as the two of them made their way up towards the town. 'You've called me Isabel for years. Is it because . . .'

They turned the corner and her voice was lost. Jessica grinned ruefully up at John.

'Dear me, she's not shy, is she? Fancy asking Perrello why he won't use my first name. I've been longing to ask him precisely that for ages, though I suspect I know the answer.'

'And what might that be?' John put his arm round her waist once more and they began to walk slowly along towards the bar which John had pointed out.

'He dislikes me quite intensely. I'm sorry about it, but it seems to be just one of those things.'

'Diaz doesn't like you? My dear girl, what a thing to say. He doesn't like any women very much, or hasn't since his wife left him I believe, but as nurses go he's most attached to you. Why do you think he wants you to take over as theatre sister when La Cruz leaves?'

'Because I'm a damned good theatre nurse,' Jessica said frankly. 'And not because he likes my style or person or anything else about me; just my efficiency.'

'Oh! Well, it's a start. Don't expect too much, that's my motto. In a week or so we'll have him call you Jessica as naturally as you please, just wait and see.'

CHAPTER SEVEN

'You'll have to speak to her, Staff.'

Mrs Robyns, recovering well after a nasty dose of food poisoning and then a ruptured appendix, addressed Jessica in a low voice as the younger woman walked down the ward. Jessica, who had scarcely noticed who had been flying out of the swing doors as she herself entered raised her brows.

'Who? What about?'

'It's Begonia Chase. Can we have a talk for a moment?'

Wordlessly, Jessica led the other woman out of the ward and into the small private room, vacated that very day by Mrs Browne. She perched on the windowsill and gestured Mrs Robyns towards the comfortable easy chair.

'Here we are, then, privacy of a sort. What's been happening? I do hope Mrs Chase hasn't been getting upset?'

'Upset! Well, the way she flew out at poor Iris . . . that's Mrs Blakie, you know . . . was enough to upset anyone! I had a word with Sister yesterday, when I could see trouble brewing, but she's a busy woman and told me to speak to you. Only you weren't on this morning and for all the good it does talking to Nurse Encantada I might as well save my breath. I know she's supposed to speak English but unless you mention bedpans or cool drinks all you get is that sweet, blank smile.'

'I believe she does speak English,' Jessica said rather guardedly. In the nature of things she did not come into much contact with her relief, apart from a smile and a nod when they passed in the corridor. Mercedes Encantada was neat and quick moving and Sister did admit, albeit grudgingly, that she was a hard worker, but it was obviously not ideal to have someone working on the ward who spoke almost no English. However, she had no wish to let the patients know of her sympathies. 'Why did Mrs Chase fly out at Mrs Blakie, then?'

Mrs Robyns sighed and shook her neatly bobbed grey head. She was a lively, intelligent woman, the type who, at home in

England, would probably run a large home, a large family and a small job quite effortlessly, whilst being on the Church council, in the Women's Institute, and probably holding office for the RWVS as well. She had come to Minestos when her husband's health broke down and though she worked mornings in a boutique it was easy to see that her boundless energy needed as many outlets as it could get.

'Well, it started off when she was rude to Nell. Nell had some photos in her handbag, the children, her dog and so on, and she was saying how she missed them as she handed the photos round. Begonia said that if there was one thing she couldn't stand it was children running riot and she did hope Nell wouldn't encourage them to come on the ward. It was said quite lightly, I do absolve her from spite, but it hurt Nell. It seems Nell's children really are very wild. Anyway, she went very red and put her pictures away and tried to change the subject, and whilst everyone was chattering to try to ease the atmosphere, Begonia suddenly threw her magazine on the floor, jumped to her feet, said we were all shallow, spiteful creatures and rushed out of the day-room. I know she's ill, Staff, but so are we all, more or less, and it's very unsettling for everyone to have these melodramas.'

'So what were you doing on the ward? And what was Mrs Chase doing flying out of here as I came in?'

'Well, I tried to pour oil on troubled waters; I followed her in here—she was crying—and told her that it was all part of her illness and she must try to be calm. She quietened down a bit, and then I saw Dr Mariano going past the door so I said wasn't he a charmer, such a nice young man . . . and she started really crying, I mean floods, Staff, and shot out of the room.'

'Ideally, someone with Mrs Chase's complaint should have a private room and spend most of her time resting in it,' Jessica explained. 'But as you know, we've only this one room and until this morning it was occupied by Mrs Browne. Now I wonder whether we might move Mrs Chase in here? She could come down to the day-room when she felt able to do so but would not be driven out by feeling she was different if she remained on the ward. She's having a lot of pre-operative medical treatment and attention here rather than at home because her nervous state was so bad that her doctor felt she must come in. I thought she was getting calmer as the drugs began to take effect but it looks as though I was wrong.'

'No, you weren't. She's been a lot calmer. To tell you the truth I had a feeling that someone had said something . . . but it's bad for all of us, this constant nervous irritation. So if you would have a word, Staff, we'd all be grateful.' Mrs Robyns rose gracefully to her feet. 'I'll go back to the day-room and calm feelings down there, knowing that I've left Mrs Chase in capable hands.'

'I wonder where she's gone?' Jessica said rather uneasily, following Mrs Robyns out of the small, pleasant room. 'Sister's office, perhaps? But Sister isn't there, she's gone to a meeting.'

'Oh, you'll find her soon enough, she can't have gone far,' Mrs Robyns said, showing a sublime ignorance of thyroid patients. 'You'll probably find her in the bathroom or the loo, Staff.'

But despite her optimism it took Jessica a good ten minutes' search to track Mrs Chase down to the linen room in which she was hiding. One glance at her patient was enough to show that she was indeed in a pitiable state, her face streaked with tears and hectically red.

'Here you are, my dear,' Jessica said gently, going fully into the linen room once she was sure that the figure sitting in a crumpled heap on a pile of clean blankets was indeed the runaway. 'Don't get yourself so upset, nothing's worth it. What's the matter?'

She put both arms round the other's thin shoulders and gave her a hug, then took Mrs Chase's hot and trembling hands in her own cool, firm grasp.

'I can't tell you . . . she's a wicked, wicked woman,' Mrs Chase wailed, snatching her fingers out of Jessica's hold and scrubbing wildly at her hot, drenched face. 'I want to go ho-ome, I don't care if I die, I wish I were dead!'

'Now, of course you don't wish any such thing. Think of your friends, your beautiful home, your pleasant life here, once we've got this wretched condition under control. The medication has helped, hasn't it? Once you've been down to theatre and had the operation you'll be fighting fit in no time and your old self again. Now tell me what upset you and I'll do my best to put it right.'

'She said . . . she said . . . and I don't blame her, she's right,' Mrs Chase said incoherently, through the fingers spread across her face. 'I wish I'd died, instead of . . . of . . . I can't go on, Nurse, feeling the way I do. I'd be better at home, at least it would be quiet and I wouldn't have to listen to . . . oh, Nurse, perhaps it was only the truth but I felt so . . . if only things were as they once were! If only I could turn the clock back!'

'I know, my dear, but unfortunately it isn't possible. Now come along, who upset you?'

'She said . . . she said . . .'

'Now who's "she"?' Jessica demanded. 'If I don't know who it was I can't do much about it, can I?'

'It was Iris—Mrs Blakie. She said . . .' Mrs Chase rubbed fiercely at her eyes, then surprisingly, calmed right down. Her voice, when she spoke again, was even, toneless, as though the pain she had suffered had numbed all feeling out of her. 'Iris said she wondered what had made Martin marry such a freak, let alone live with her until he . . . until he . . .'

'The wicked . . .' Jessica stopped, to whisk a clean towel off the shelves. Gently, she dried Mrs Chase's tearstained cheeks, talking soothingly as she did so. 'Look, Begonia, it was a wicked, spiteful thing to say, the sort of thing a jealous spinster uses to attack a married woman, and you must treat it with the contempt it deserves. I'm going to ask Sister if you can move in to the private room, now it's free, and all the staff will make sure you aren't lonely and have plenty of people when you want them, but it will enable you to pick and choose a bit. You won't feel you have to stay in a room which contains people like Iris Blakie, for a start! Will that make things easier, do you suppose?'

'Oh, but I don't think . . . I was going home, you see. Don't you think that would be better?'

'Just try it,' Jessica advised. 'Tell you what, we'll go along to the bathroom now, you can tidy up, and then I'll bring you your lunch in the private room and you can see what you think.'

'All right.' Mrs Chase followed Jessica meekly along to the

bathroom and submitted to having her face and hands washed and her hair combed. Then she followed Jessica back along the corridor to the private room. She looked inside, then went right in. A slow smile spread across her face.

'It *is* nice—gracious, it's got it's own television set, and a radio!' she turned rather shyly to Jessica. 'I feel ashamed now, Staff, that I repeated what Iris said, I had been cross all morning, probably I deserved it. But why did you call her a jealous spinster? She's married with three children!'

'Is she? Well, when she said that she had the soul of a jealous spinster,' Jessica said firmly, and was thrilled when Mrs Chase gave a muffled gurgle of amusement.

'Well, I'm going to forget all about it, and ask her along to watch my television the next time she's bored by what the others are watching,' she said generously. 'After all, it only hurt me because I knew she was right—Martin never would have married me if I'd been the way I am now. But quite often I think you're right—that it's just the condition and not me at all—one day I'll be myself again.'

'So you will. Now all the others are in the day-room except for Mrs De Sousa, of course, and the new lady, the one who had her operation this morning, so if you like we can go along now and collect your things . . . perhaps, if you'd go through and start putting them together, I'll just check with Sister that it's all right.'

'Sister's at a meeting,' Mrs Chase said, the ready tears springing to her eyes once more. 'I tried to speak to her earlier.'

'She'll be back now,' Jessica said, looking at her fob-watch and crossing her fingers. 'I shan't be long.'

She was in luck. Sister had just returned to the ward and was sorting out her committee papers. She sat herself down when Jessica entered and smiled hopefully at the younger woman.

'Yes, Staff? I do hope it's something that will give me a good reason for not doing paperwork for a few more minutes. How I hate it!'

'It's Mrs Chase, Sister. She's had some trouble with one of the other patients. If she heard aright, and I'm afraid she probably did, someone was very spiteful. However, as you know Mrs Chase can be trying, so I thought as the private room's vacant, we might put her in there. I know you wanted to do so when she first came in, but Mrs Browne was in situ and didn't want to move so you left it. I have asked Mrs Chase if she'd prefer it and the answer is most definitely yes. Will it be all right, do you think, or have you other plans for it?'

'No, I've no other plans and as you say, Mrs Chase really should be nursed away from as many distractions as possible. Put her in there for now, anyway, and I'll mention that it's engaged to the admin. staff, though we've no one seriously ill coming in that I know about. I think you're right; she needs to be kept calm and quiet and the private room's the obvious answer.'

'Right. I'll move her in right away, then. I told her she could have her lunch in there, to avoid the hurly-burly of the day-room.'

Sister gave her approval so Jessica, feeling very pleased with herself, returned to the ward to give Mrs Chase a hand moving her small possessions. Well before lunchtime, in fact, the new arrangement was complete. Mrs Chase was sitting in her own easy chair listening to one of her favourite light music radio programmes and looking forward, she told Jessica, to her lunch.

As she returned to the general ward to change a bed and put on clean linen, for several of the patients were going home after lunch and would be replaced, tomorrow, by others, Jessica at last found time to wonder about her new relationship with John Mariano. It was pleasant to have someone who looked at one admiringly and who planned treats and excursions. She had enjoyed his company on their night out and he had come in for a coffee afterwards and had charmed Pat with his ready laugh and unselfconscious humour. Perhaps, she dreamed, making neat envelope corners and tucking the thin cotton blankets in firmly, perhaps he would turn out to be the man she was waiting for, if she was waiting for a man. Perhaps he would sweep her off her feet, or at the very least whisk her off in a long sports car to cries of envy. Or perhaps he would just make that stupid Diaz Perrello see what a gem of a girl he was ignoring!

'Staff, can I go for lunch with you? Perrello's got some students in theatre and he's sent word that he'll be doing a ward round at two, so Sister said to come and warn you.'

Vicky Parkinson was a second year SRN student and the sight of her bright, happy little face always gave Jessica's heart a lift. So young and hopeful and so attached to all her patients, she was a marvellous advertisement for nursing as a career, for few people could be happier in their work than Vicky. She smiled at the younger girl now, finished the bed and walked across the ward towards her.

'Yes, of course you can have lunch with me! Shall we go over to the military hospital canteen, or do you want to snatch a sandwich and a cup of tea here?'

'Oh, the canteen please, Staff; I'm always starving at lunch-time, even though I usually eat a couple of packets of biscuits with my coffee. Is there anything I can do to help you before we go for lunch?'

'Not really. We'll be back in plenty of time to get the patients into position for the ward round. There are two new patients though, the hiatus hernia and another breast biopsy, I wonder if they've had blood tests and ECGs? Dr Perrello likes to have all the results of tests in his hands by the time he does a ward round.'

'I'll check.'

By the time Vicky had come back to announce that all the tests had been done, Jessica had finished in the ward. Together, they set off for the canteen.

'You're very much better, Mrs Robyns, so I think you'll probably be discharged before next weekend.' Dr Perrello smiled briefly at Mrs Robyns and moved, with his circle of students, to the next bed.

Jessica, attending the group with the files in her hand ready to take the one Perrello had finished with and hand him the next, found herself contemplating John with some complacency. He might not have all the confidence and skill of the older surgeon but he had good looks, a really good bedside manner and a sort of diffident charm which made the young girls eye him covertly and the older women cluck in a motherly way when he left them. He was not in the least in awe of Perrello either, interrupting with questions when he could see the students did not quite understand what was going on, explaining easily, in his turn, when the surgeon asked him a question, and putting everyone at their ease. It was rather annoying, really, to see how friendly Perrello could be towards the younger man, even when John was doing or saying something of which Perrello could not entirely approve. The surgeon did not hesitate to tell the junior doctor when he was wrong or had not elaborated a point sufficiently, but he did so in a pleasant, easy-going way very different from the attitude he took when reprimanding or even merely speaking to Jessica.

The doctors had moved on now to Mrs Nell Stedlaer's bed. Nell was sitting on the edge of it looking complacent. She had had a myomectomy to get rid of fibroid growths and because of her youth and excellent health had made a spectacular recovery by any standards. She had been in very little pain until the largest fibroid had begun to press against her bladder, and then she had been rushed in for investigation. Dr Perrello, however, had pinpointed fibroids almost at once and so she and he were rather pleased with one another.

'Still feeling no ill-effects, Mrs Stedlaer? That's fine. Then you'll be going home tomorrow.'

'I did tell my husband that if he brought my things tonight and could keep the children quiet for twenty-four hours I might leave tomorrow lunchtime,' Mrs Stedlaer said gleefully. She was only twenty-four, with a mass of slippery, untidy brown hair and a pretty face which she sometimes left alone though at times she daubed it vaguely with heavy makeup. Jessica knew she had married a waiter at one of the big hotels when she had discovered she was pregnant, coming indignantly back six months later to confront him with the proof of their holiday friendship. Fortunately Pedro was sufficiently attracted not to dispute paternity, so they had married eight weeks before the first child was born and Nell had patiently given birth to another one, yearly, ever since. She was probably happy enough and had learned to speak excellent colloquial Spanish, but Jessica often found herself wondering whether Nell would have come quite so far had she known that her marriage would result in her being the mother of four young hopefuls after a mere three and a half years of connubial bliss.

'Very good. Staff will make you an appointment to come back to the clinic in a month.'

Dr Perrello moved away from the bed, talking to Dr Mariano as he did so. 'Now this next patient's interesting, John. She's under night sedation and is on medication during the day to keep her calm because she's suffering from thyrotoxicosis and will have her operation as soon as her condition is under control. Naturally, we've . . .' he broke off as he went to enter the curtained off cubicle, only to find himself facing the empty bed which had once contained Mrs Chase. He scowled blackly, turning on Jessica at once. 'Staff, fetch this patient at once! Why isn't she in bed?'

'Mrs Chase has been moved into the private room, sir,' Jessica said promptly. 'As you know, her condition is hard to nurse when the patient is constantly being excited or irritated by those about her. When some trouble blew up this morning Sister decided to move Mrs Chase into the private room. Mrs Browne was called for early this morning.'

'Sister didn't mention it to me,' Dr Perrello said. He had been careful not to catch Jessica's eye for weeks but he was glaring straight at her now. 'Why wasn't I told?'

'We only moved her just before lunch,' Jessica said defensively. 'It was my idea in the first place, but Sister . . .'

'I might have guessed it! I have a patient waiting for that room, Staff. She's due in tomorrow morning, so you'll have to tell Mrs Chase she must vacate it tomorrow by nine o'clock.'

'Oh, but Dr Perrello . . .' Jessica broke off. Useless to expect him to listen to her, better to get Sister to have a word with him. She was fond of Mrs Chase and knew the dangers inherent in upsetting a victim of thyrotoxicosis. If Mrs Chase really believed they did not mean to do their best for her it was not unlikely that she would run away from the hospital, even though she only had a nightie and dressing gown with her.

'Yes, Staff? You were about to say . . . ?'

'Nothing, Doctor.'

The group moved on but Jessica seized the opportunity, as soon as they left Room 2, to hand over to Pat and hurry along to Sister's office. Sister was tackling her paperwork but looked up as Jessica entered.

'Well, Staff? Ward round over?'

'Nearly, Sister. They've gone along to Room 1, but I came to tell you that Perrello says he has a patient for the private room and wants Mrs Chase moved out of there by nine o'clock tomorrow morning.'

Sister swelled; it was clear that no matter how important he might be, Dr Perrello was not going to get away with dictating to Sister Harris!

'Move my patient!' she said ominously. 'I think I'd better go along and have a word with that gentleman. Move Mrs Chase indeed, when we all know that she needs peace and quiet more than most. As for another patient, and one, moreover, who comes under Dr Perrello's jurisdiction rather than mine . . . well, I've not heard one word about it. Don't say anything to Mrs Chase, Staff. I want her just where she is and what's more, I want her happy!'

Hurrying back to the ward with what amounted to a smirk on her face, Jessica met the surgeon and his party just as they turned out of Room 1. She stopped short, hoping that they would simply turn and go down the corridor towards the stairs but instead Perrello caught sight of her and beckoned. An imperious crook of the finger accompanied by another of those scowls did little to lessen the antagonism she felt.

'Staff . . . I said nothing to you on the ward, but what are my requirements regarding Mrs Pontin's weight loss?'

'A stone, sir,' Jessica said coolly.

'And how much has she lost in the three weeks she's been with us?'

'Less than two pounds, sir.'

'Then why have my explicit instructions been so flagrantly disregarded?'

Jessica eyed him squarely. He knew very well how impossible it was for any one nurse to force a deceitful, greedy and determined patient to lose weight!

'You'd better speak to the patient, sir, and to Sister, of

course. As you know I spend a lot of time in theatre so I can't implement your words to the letter, as I would wish to do, but I'm sure all the nurses on the ward follow your instructions faithfully. It is only the patient who flagrantly disregards them.'

It might have been all right, he might even have backed down and apologised had not someone in the group surrounding him given a low chuckle. Immediately Perrello's mouth tightened and his eyes gleamed like steel in the dim corridor lighting.

'Put her on a diet of liquids only for the next three days, Staff. I shall operate next Tuesday no matter what her condition, but I expect her to have lost sufficient weight in the remaining time to make such an operation safe. Tell her, so that she knows the risks. Is that clear?'

'As crystal,' Jessica said coldly, her own mouth as tight as his and her eyes as chilly. 'If you've finished with me now, sir, I'll return to the ward.'

She marched through the swing doors, back stiff, mind seething with resentment. How dare he! For one thing she could put Mrs Pontin on a liquid diet and her patient could beg, borrow and steal food from the other patients and from the snack bar, which would mean no more weight loss than if they had let her eat normally. He must have done it to make her look a fool, because she, Sister and the other nurses had been telling the patient for three weeks about the dangers of operating on someone as fat as herself. Only Dr Perrello's own voice, thundering threats, was likely to be regarded, because all the nurses had seen how, after a lecture from him, Mrs Pontin actually stuck to her diet for as much as three or four days at a time.

Jessica hurried through the rest of her work, went to Sister's office and worked out a liquid diet for Mrs Pontin, then went and saw Mrs Chase for a few minutes before going off for a cup of tea.

Pat was in the kitchen drinking tea and making up the huge tea-urn for the patients so Jessica got out the biscuits and began to arrange cups on the big, rattling old trolley. They were chatting about the chances of keeping Mrs Pontin away from food when the door opened. Dr Mariano's head popped round it.

'Hello, girls. Jess, can I have a word with you?'

'Of course.' Jessica went out of the kitchen and joined him in the corridor. 'What is it?'

'I just wanted you to know that after you left us we went along to the private room and Diaz was very gentle and charming to the patient there. He said nothing about moving her out, in fact he told her she would be very much better for the quiet. He's a strange man, sometimes.'

'What happened when Sister caught up with him, I wonder? She was breathing fire and brimstone over his daring to say that he'd move a patient on her ward. John, I'm not being vindictive or over-sensitive, but I think he only objected so that he could take me down a peg or two, and I think he invented the other patient. And the vindictive part, is that I hope Sister bawled him out!'

'If she did, she did it in private. He disappeared into her office after he'd finished his round.' John cleared his throat and looked slightly embarrassed. 'It wouldn't have happened if you'd somehow managed to let him know there was an empty bed in the next cubicle . . . why were the curtains round it? I think he thought you were trying to make a fool of him!'

'As if I would! I didn't draw the curtains, the auxiliary did. She probably didn't realise that the bed was empty, or at least she obviously realised there was no patient in it, but she'd have thought Mrs Chase was down in the toilets or perhaps lingering for a moment in the day-room.' She paused, then looked hopefully up into the blue eyes above her own. 'John, could you be a dear and pour oil on some very troubled waters? Could you let Perrello know that was what happened? Because having his constant enmity can make life awfully uncomfortable for me.'

'Certainly I'll tell him. I suppose you couldn't tell him yourself?'

'Me? Haven't you noticed? If I walk towards him he walks away; if I try to exchange a word with him he either pretends he hasn't heard or simply snubs me with a monosyllable. It isn't that I mind, exactly, it's just as I said, that it makes life uncomfortable.'

'Actually, I have noticed. You're quite right, except that it isn't only your life—how do you think the rest of us feel when he's so on edge and quick to criticise?'

'Is he, though? To everyone? That's a relief, in a way, because I thought it was just me. He seems downright pleasant to the rest of you when I'm around.'

John sighed and took her hand, playing with her fingers as he spoke. 'He's always more tense, more difficult, when you're around, to tell the truth. And when you leave there's always an hour or so when he snaps every time he opens his mouth. I've wondered . . .'

'What? Do you mean you've wondered what I've done to him?'

'Yes. Yes, that's exactly it. I've wondered several times if he isn't rather fond of you, and hating himself for it.'

'Good lord, you couldn't be more wrong.' Jessica recaptured her hand and opened the kitchen door. 'Thanks for coming over, John, and if you could speak to Perrello for me, I'd be grateful.'

Back in the kitchen, she and Pat continued to make the tea, but presently Pat said curiously, 'What did he want, Jess? I don't want to seem nosy, but I am!'

'He wanted to tell me that despite Perrello saying that Mrs Chase had no right to the private room, he'd been very nice to her.' Jessica sniffed. 'He wasn't nice to *me*, quite the opposite.'

'He's never been easy, but lately he's getting downright impossible, or so everyone says,' Pat agreed. 'What's biting him, do you suppose? Perhaps he's in love!'

'Who with?'

Jessica had not meant to snap out the question quite so sharply but it had happened before she could do anything to stop it. She saw Pat's glance flicker quickly over her and then away, but when Pat answered it was lightly enough.

'Oh, probably with the Cruz missile, heaven knows she's lovely enough for any man to be forgiven if he loses his head over her. But I was only teasing, I suppose it's more likely that he's overspent, or found his ex-wife sitting on his doorstep demanding that he take her back . . . I don't know. But don't let him upset you, Jess. It's just his way.'

'I won't. Thank goodness tomorrow's my day off, though. I'm going to swim over to the oil tanker and see what it's like over there.'

'By yourself?' The harbour was a mile across and the oil tanker, permanently moored and rusting away, the subject of frequent scornful comments from the staff. Everyone said they would swim out to it one day and see just how badly neglected it was, no one, however, had yet done so.

'No, I'm going with Felicity. She's a strong swimmer too, and wants to take a look. We'll have a picnic down by the harbour first and then swim over.'

'I hope you enjoy it, but for my part I'd rather snooze on the beach. You've not yet visited the beach, have you?'

'Not yet. A pleasure postponed! Actually, John Mariano and I are going one afternoon, but he's on duty tomorrow.'

'Oh, well. Have fun and forget Perrello for a bit,' Pat advised, pouring boiling water from the urn into the big brown teapot. 'Let's get this tea-trolley moving!'

CHAPTER EIGHT

THE next day, Jessica arrived at the appointed spot down by the harbour, lay her towel out on the big, uneven paving stones, and slipped out of her wrap-over skirt and the short-sleeved blue blouse she had worn with it. She was already in her costume, a brief bikini in lemon-yellow silk, but now she smoothed sun-oil on to her skin and then lay down on the towel. She might as well improve her tan whilst she waited for Felicity.

She had had a hectic few days though, and was almost asleep when a hand touched her shoulder. She opened her eyes and a small girl of five or six stood beside her, smiling tentatively.

'Hello!' Jessica said, rolling over and then sitting up. 'What's your name?'

'Maria. Señorita Jessica French?'

'Yes, that's right, Maria. Do you want me for something?'

'I have a message, señorita, from Felicity. She has to work today and is very sorry to let you down. She gave the message to my mother, Joaquina, and my mother asked me to come down to the harbour, find you and tell you.'

'Well, thank you very much, Maria.' Jessica fumbled in her beach bag and found some loose pesetas and a rather battered peach. She handed them to the small girl, bade her buy herself a few sweets, and then, as her small acquaintance made her way up the narrow cobbled street which led away from the harbour, she contemplated her day with a good deal less enthusiasm.

What should she do? She could eat a solitary picnic, then go for a swim when her food was digested, then go back to the flat. Or perhaps sunbathe, although in the late afternoon village lads often came down here to bathe and they would show off and shower her with water and generally do their best to get attention.

On the other hand, if she had a quick swim now she could

take her picnic back to the flat, get into a cool dress, eat her food and then go off by bus to a beach somewhere, or perhaps even visit one of the local beauty spots. She wanted to visit some of the ancient monuments, now was as good a time as any.

She checked that all her things were together on the towel and then walked over to the edge of the quay. Looking down, the water swayed and beckoned, green, cool, inviting. About thirty yards from the shore was a heavy old fishing boat, moored to a buoy, which the nurses had adopted for their own. No one seemed to mind when they swam out to her, sunbathed on the dried out bottom-boards, and kept bits and pieces aboard. She would just swim out to the boat, round it a few times and then come back.

She slid into the water. It was warm as new milk. She was within grabbing distance of the hull when she realised that she was unlikely to be able to get aboard without either a helping hand or the dinghy from which they usually boarded. She sighed and started to swim round the old boat, and then it occurred to her that she might as well have a practise run at crossing the harbour. Even if she did not reach the tanker, she could swim towards it.

To think, with Jessica, was to act. She swerved away from the old boat and headed out into the wide blue expanse of the natural harbour. A strong swimmer and one, moreover, who had swum long distances consistently for years, a mere mile seemed no particular challenge, though it would be an interesting swim. I'll go slowly, she planned, already intent on the task, and then I'll be the very first person from the hospital to visit the biggest tanker in the world!

It will be a lot easier and pleasanter than eighty lengths of the school swimming baths, she told herself, forging steadily through the water. It's deeper, which means more buoyancy, and it's salty too, much more invigorating.

However, swimming a long distance can be boring, so Jessica thought about the tanker. Having built the mammoth craft the makers discovered it was too big for useful work and promptly abandoned it in this huge harbour. It had never, to her knowledge, done more than an odd voyage or two yet now it rusted here, with only a few sailors aboard who made sure that the useless hulk did not get vandalised or cause a nuisance.

Presently, having considered the stupidity of human beings who could create such a vast, iron-clad nuisance, Jessica began to sing to herself. She changed her stroke from the crawl to the breast stroke to a back stroke. She sang a few songs, ballads, love-songs, laments. And the tanker, which had been large enough from a mile away, got larger and larger, enormous, gigantic, until she was so close that it was all she could see. The great black and rust mass of it, the ropes which had looked like string from a mile away but were now steel hawsers as thick as a man's thigh, dominated her entire view.

Jessica swam on, into the shadow of the tanker, where the water was cooler and the depth beneath her somehow more ominous. Once, she ducked below the surface and swam underwater for a bit, looking about her at the hull, bigger than the biggest whale, at the myriad fishes which had sought this spot for the thick weed which flourished below the plimsoll line. When she looked down, though, there was nothing visible but oily darkness and somehow, here in the great ship's shadow, the darkness was frightening, hiding something monstrous which might, if she was not careful, get her.

Jessica arrowed up to the sunlight, her head bursting out into the air again with an audible plop, her heart beating a good deal faster than was its wont. Awe-inspiring as had been the sight of those depths beneath her she wished she had not ducked below the surface, knowing she had to swim the same distance back to reach the safety of Villa Castello. She swam on though, and reached one of the steel hawsers. Hanging onto it, turning slightly in the sunshine as the gentle waves moved her, she peered past the great steel plated body and saw the further bank, which was nothing but a straggle of dusty track and what appeared to be desert with scrubby vegetation and dry, sandy soil. No point in going ashore here, obviously, quite apart from the fact that she would have a seven or eight mile walk to get back to the nurses' home.

Having rested for a moment, she released the hawser and swam right up to the hull and banged on it. A hollow boom rewarded her but although some flakes of rust fell into the water and floated lazily downwards, nothing else happened. No sailors' heads appeared over the rusty rail, to see what strange sea-creature was rapping on their tanker, no diver suddenly surfaced from the depths to see who had summoned him.

Jessica swam back to the hawser and hung on it for a moment, but suddenly all the adventure of reaching the tanker no longer mattered; she wanted to get back to the shallower, happier reaches of the harbour where the water lapped against the Villa Castello quayside, back to warmth and voices, the muted domestic sounds from the houses which crowded along the harbour, the lap of the tideless Mediterranean against the weed-sown walls.

Oddly enough, she also discovered that she felt cold. It was partly the shade of the ship, she supposed, and partly because she was tired, but she found that the mile long swim back no longer attracted her. She was tired . . . a rest would be nice . . . yes, she would haul out of the water, as seals do, lie and sunbathe for an hour, and then, rested, would tackle the swim home.

It was not so easy. She could not get ashore near the tanker because it was so very long and even if she managed to swim to the wall it was both high and slippery, plainly impossible to climb. Steps must surely bisect it at intervals but she could not pick them out with the strong sun blasting down on everything and she was beginning to be uneasily aware that she really needed a rest. She had been silly, swimming so vigorously instead of taking her time over it, now she must rest before facing the return trip. If she swam the half-mile along the tanker's side, then the distance to the wall, and discovered that the only steps were a further half-mile off, she had an uneasy feeling that she might never make it. Not without a rest.

She floated on her back, thinking earnestly. So the tanker was out; there was no means of getting aboard her and no sign of anyone aboard who could throw her a ladder or help her aboard in any way. The near bank, also, was not possible. So that left only the long swim back, without a break or a rest, or the islands. Jessica turned and swam to the hawser, then hung on to it whilst she considered. La Lapitos was a long way off, she could not make it as far as that. It would have been an appropriate place to swim to, since it was the island where the authorities housed all medical personnel who needed a holiday or who wanted to attend one of the courses regularly held there. There was another island, a very small one, but that was just as far as La Lapitos. The island which housed the army barracks was nearer though, scarcely any distance, only it was off-limits for civilians. It was quite large and housed an officers' club, living accommodation for the officers themselves and a couple of large detention blocks where military prisoners were kept.

Jessica stared longingly across at the barracks. She could see every detail of it from here, the barrack square with lines at intervals across it, the officers' club with green shutters and brilliantly coloured awnings at all the windows, the grey and whitewash of the detention blocks. There was a running track around the perimeter of the island . . . she could even see a couple of men in running kit jogging around it.

It was out of bounds; every nurse knew that, but it was also on the way back to Villa Castello and Jessica knew that she was going to risk it. It was no use telling herself that she should not, because she knew it. But she also knew that in her present exhausted state she might never reach land if she tried the mile long swim back to the quayside.

She let go of the hawser and started to swim but even that relatively short distance taxed her strength so that when at last she reached it she simply hung for a moment onto the post of a small wooden jetty, content merely to stay still, too weary to drag herself out of the water. After a moment or two though, she glanced cautiously about, saw no one, and decided to act. She grabbed at the wooden planking, heaved with the last of her strength, and landed in a soggy heap. Land at last!

It was good just to lie on the silvery boards, to feel the sun warming her even as the strain seeped out of her limbs. So good, so good, Jessica thought dreamily. She turned her face so that her cheek rested on warm wood, told herself she must get up, begin to move about and ease her limbs for the return swim . . . and fell deeply asleep, lulled by the sun and by the simple bliss of not having to move her arms and legs through the water.

On the island, men came and went about their duties but no one came down to the jetty so no one noticed the slim girl in her lemon-yellow bikini who lay there in the sun.

It was Diaz Perrello's day off and he had been sailing, but it had not been too successful because of the lightness of the breeze. When he reached home he heard the telephone ringing from the jetty and cursed it but hurried up through the garden to answer it himself. He was off duty and had planned a good dinner and a few drinks in the shade of the trees which surrounded his patio, but the shrilling of the telephone usually heralded a change of plan. Still wearing nothing but shorts and espadrilles he hurried across the cool shade of the living room to snatch up the receiver.

'Perrello speaking. What is it? Oh, it's you, Sancho. I'm off duty; isn't there anyone on call?'

The answering voice was apologetic.

'Sorry, Diaz, I know it's against the rules, and Dr Galdos would come, but it's a good way for him and scarcely two minutes for you . . a chap's lacerated his finger in the penal block, all it needs is a few stitches and a shot of something in case of infection. As you're so near we wondered if you'd mind popping across.'

'Curse you, Sancho, I was sailing right past your place two minutes ago! Yes, of course I'll come, I'll get the motor boat out. Nothing else, is there, whilst I'm there?'

'No, nothing. Or nothing we can't deal with, at any rate. Did you have a good sail?'

'Not too good; no wind. I'll be with you in a few minutes, I'll just tell José to wait until I return for dinner.'

The penal block on the island was no distance, Perrello reflected, replacing the receiver. He crossed to the door, leaving wet footmarks on the gleaming marble tiles, and shouted. When no one replied he continued across the hall and into the modern kitchen beyond. An elderly man was chopping parsley on the big, scrubbed wooden table. He looked up, his seamed, brown face creasing into a smile.

'Ah, you're back, señor! We're having a paella fit for a king tonight, to say nothing of iced melon first and a little piece of fish as sweet as a nut . . . and one of my lemon souffles to follow. And the cheese in Puerto Malon this morning had reached just the right stage of ripeness . . .' he kissed his fingers to the excellence of the cheese.

'Good. I came in to tell you that I'm going over to the barracks on the island. Some fool of a soldier had cut his finger, it needs stitches. I shan't be more than half an hour. Will that fit in with dinner?'

'Sure,' José said, 'but you're off duty, you shouldn't . . .'

Perrello did not wait for the words which he knew by heart to follow; he nodded, raised a hand and made his way back through his cool house and out into the hot sunshine once more. On his jetty he untied the motor boat, jumped into it and started the engine. It roared into life, shattering the afternoon quiet and he swung her round, sat behind the wheel and headed for the island. Arriving almost before the engine had warmed through he turned her off, swung himself on land, tied up and then stopped short, staring.

The body of a girl lay slumped across the jetty. He could see little beside the curve of her hip and a mass of wet, golden-auburn hair, curling across the pale skin, drying almost as he watched.

His heart missed a beat; was she dead? She lay so still, her attitude so abandoned, that it was clear she had not merely chosen to sunbathe in this forbidden spot. He went over to her and knew her at once but simultaneously with recognition came the realisation that she was breathing. The neatly clad breasts were rising and falling and now that he could see her face he could also see the faint, rose-pink flush on her cheeks and the slight trembling movement of her soft, full underlip as she breathed in and out.

Relief came first, then a mixture of hot rage and what he told himself was a purely physical desire caused by her near-nakedness. But she looked so young and defenceless lying there, so different from the efficient, imperturbable nurse in her starched uniform or sexless, saggy theatre gown. He bent over her and shook her roughly; how dare she lie there sleeping and arousing a devil in him that he had thought long conquered! He did not want or need women, she was no exception! He shook her again, harder. Now that he thought about it, he was sure she had come here to meet a man, one of the prisoners, perhaps. Was this where her Jaime had disappeared to, after that fracas on the rocks weeks and weeks ago? Had she sneaked over here, found the fellow, let him make love to her, and then fallen asleep afterwards?

Furiously, he pulled her up by her shoulders and saw the long, dusky lashes lift and a pair of bemused greeny-blue eyes widen as they saw his face so near. She shook her head, frowned, then stared at him again.

'Dr Perrello? What on earth are you doing here? Where am I? Oh, I remember, I'd swum out to look at the oil tanker and . . .'

'You swam? Over a mile? Alone?'

He was still crouching beside her, a hand on either shoulder. She looked confused, a small frown etched on her brow for a moment, then her expression cleared.

'Well, I was supposed to be going with Felicity . . . Staff Nurse Carew . . . only she couldn't come so I swam over by myself. Only I got awfully tired, I swam too fast, and I thought I wouldn't get back without a rest, so I came over here and pulled myself onto the jetty. I didn't mean to stay, or only for a few minutes, but I must have fallen asleep.'

He sat back on his heels, lip curling contemptuously. As if any woman would swim a mile or more just to see a rusty old tanker! The girl was a compulsive liar, she had lied before, over that soldier who had taken her down to the harbour and messed her about, but she had almost convinced him that she was only speaking the truth, then. This time, however, there could be no doubt. Rage gripped him, that she could take him for a fool and, oddly, that she had undoubtedly come over to meet some soldier when he had thought her different from the others. He supposed, dully, that a boyfriend shut up on the island must have been frustrating for her, so frustrating that she was prepared to face a long and dangerous swim just to see him for a few minutes. Had they made love? Was that why she had sprawled out on the planking and fallen asleep?

He stared fixedly down at her, but she was paying no attention to him, or not overtly, at any rate. She was trying to pin the long mass of her hair up and back, off her face. As he watched her he grew calmer; she could not possibly have seen a prisoner for more than a few minutes, perhaps as he was exercising round the running track. Even if she had come to see one of the guards, or an officer stationed here, it was unlikely that the meeting could have encompassed more than a few stolen kisses. He stared harder at her, and when she looked up, let his eyes stray deliberately across her body, at the tiny silk bikini, the rise and fall of her breasts as her breathing quickened with his stare and his eyes seemed to draw a blush over the bare flesh. He must know who she had met and for what purpose she had come here! He did not ask himself why he needed so urgently to know; that was a question he was not yet prepared to face.

'Who is he? The man you came to see? What was the arrangement?'

She shook her head. She was flushed now, but the eyes which stared up at him were wide, seemingly guileless.

'A man? I didn't come to see anyone, this place is out of bounds for civilians, they told us at the Nelson. I wouldn't have come ashore, but the water seemed a lot deeper and more dangerous than it had coming over, and I'm afraid I felt I simply must rest. It was just the nearest land, you see.'

He wanted to believe her yet he could not. Why would she swim such a distance? He stood up, then leaned down and lifted her up as well. It startled her; her eyes sparkled with annoyance and she scowled.

'Hey, that hurt! What's the matter *now*, Dr Perrello? I told you I didn't mean to trespass, but . . .'

'I want to learn the truth!' he grated through closed teeth, still holding her bare upper arms. He was so annoyed that he shook her, to emphasise the point. 'Just stop lying to me and tell me who you came to see—I can soon find out, simply by asking the staff here.'

His hands were hard on her shoulders yet her movement, when it came, was so sudden that it took him by surprise. She gave a sharp exclamation, twisted out of his grasp, and next moment he was alone on the jetty. Jessica was in the water, forging away from him with strong, furious strokes, making for Villa Castello.

'Come back at once! Jessica, I order you to turn back at once . . .'

She took no notice and despite his annoyance he felt a perverse satisfaction that she would not let herself be bullied, she was prepared to throw herself in the water and swim away from him rather than listen to any more of his insinuations. Was he wrong, then? Could it be true that she had come here to rest and had no intention of meeting any man?

But he could scarcely let her go off like that, in a rage and unlikely to reach the harbour before the sun sank. He was about to get back into the motor boat and start the engine when he heard the low thrum of engines and, glancing seawards, saw the Tenerife ferry entering the outer harbour. She was a big ship, one of the biggest to come daily into the harbour, and the stupid, pigheaded English girl was swimming right across her bows. She would be run down, drowned, no one aboard would even know she was there, for a swimmer in the water could not possibly be visible to those high up on the ship's bridge.

There was no time for the motor boat. He was in the water almost as the thought entered his head, swimming strongly towards her, overhauling her with ease, for she had no idea she was being followed.

He caught up, swam alongside, then cut across her, forcing her to acknowledge his presence.

'Go back, Jessica,' he said urgently, 'the Tenerife ferry . . .'

She snorted rudely, flipped over and continued to swim towards Villa Castello, oblivious of the throb of the mighty engines as the ship got nearer. Plainly she was still far too angry with him to take the slightest notice of anything he might say. Yet they were both in deadly danger unless they got out of the ship's path at once. He ducked under the water and saw her, oddly, from beneath, the slim legs stretched out straight, the feet moving methodically in the paddling motion of the crawl whilst her arms appeared one by one, outlined in bubbles, as she tried to out-distance him.

He came up quickly, shockingly, taking her as some undersea predator might, holding her under water until she went limp in his arms. Only then did he begin to swim strongly for shore, a hand supporting her neck, carrying her with him.

It was not easy, with her dead weight, to climb out onto the wooden jetty, but he managed it. She stirred and coughed; he flipped her over onto her stomach, supported her up into a crouching position and then watched for the second time that afternoon as she regained consciousness and slowly sat back on her haunches. He put a hand on her arm, intending to ask her if she was all right, but she turned on him like a tigress.

'Get your hands off me! Let me alone! I'm going back to Villa Castello whether you like it or not!'

She would have struggled to her feet and thrown herself back in the water, but Diaz Perrello had no intention of letting her escape a second time. He put both arms round her and held her for one throbbing, dangerous moment hard against his chest.

'Don't blame me . . . look over there!'

He swung her round, still holding her, so that she had no option but to look. He watched her eyes widen as she understood the significance of the Tenerife ferry ploughing placidly through the very stretch of water which had, two minutes earlier, held her furiously swimming body.

'Well, Jessica? If you can't bring yourself to thank me, at least acknowledge that I was right to bring you back here.'

He still held her. She was pliant against his chest. He could feel the rise and fall of her breasts as she breathed, and her flesh against his was silky smooth, her hair smelt summery and young.

'Well, young lady?'

Her chin came up and she glowered at him, eyes smouldering. She was no longer pliant; he knew she was resisting his embrace with every fibre of her being yet it was with great reluctance that he released her.

'If you hadn't called me a liar I wouldn't have jumped,' she said crossly. 'However, I'm glad I wasn't run down, even if you did find it necessary to knock me cold and nearly drown me in the process. Are you going to take me back to Villa Castello in your boat? Because after what you've put me through I very probably would drown if I tried to swim.'

'How gracious!' He smiled at her, fighting a ridiculous desire to take her in his arms again and risk her undoubted wrath just for the pleasure of touching her. 'Very well, I'll take you away from this forbidden place. And I'll also apologise for doubting your word.'

'Thank you. But please refrain from talking to me whilst we go back, because it seems to me you can only be rude!'

He inclined his head, his lips twitching. She was just like an angry kitten with the little tendrils of red-gold hair standing up all round her face and her eyes wide and sparkling.

Five minutes later she turned to him, frowning.

'Where are we going? You're taking me in the wrong direction. Turn the boat round again and head for Castello or I'll . . . I'll . . .'

He put a finger to his lips and gave her the benefit of his most saturnine grin. It was she who had forbidden him to speak to her, after all!

'Oh!' He could see she was struggling not to return his smile and felt absurdly triumphant over this first sign of softening. Perhaps it would be possible for them to be friends; it was for the good of the team, he reminded himself hastily. Life had been uncomfortable in theatre lately, because of their mutual antagonism.

'I'm sorry, I shouldn't have spoken to you like that. Put it down to being half-drowned by my superior officer.' She was smiling properly now, showing her white teeth, and a dimple had appeared beside her mouth. 'May I know where we're going, Dr Perrello?'

'I'm taking you to my place, Miss French,' he said formally. 'There you can borrow a warm wrap, have a stiff drink, and share my dinner. After that I shall prescribe a quiet boat-ride back to the mainland, a couple of aspirin, and a good night's sleep, to take your mind off your experience.'

'It's kind of you, but I'd rather go straight home,' the girl said stiffly. 'I'm in no state to go visiting.'

'I live alone, with a manservant who is both old and discreet,' Perrello assured her. 'Besides, in this heat who can be surprised by two people entering a house, one in a swimsuit and the other in shorts? You're tired, you need a meal and a drink. No more arguments, is that a deal?'

She hesitated, then nodded quickly. Despite her pluck he guessed she must be really very tired and darkness was falling quite quickly now. He put the boat alongside his own jetty, tied her up, climbed out and held out his hands. She put her own in them and came ashore, swaying a little. It was sufficient reason to slide a hand round her waist; he did not want her fainting and falling, after all!

They were actually about to enter the main living room through the french windows when she gasped and put a hand to her mouth.

'Oh, I've just thought . . . Dr Perrello, may I use your phone?'

'Certainly. Am I allowed to ask why?'

'Of course. I had a date . . . I'll have to explain why I shan't be there.'

He led her over to the phone. He felt vindicated. If she had a date then she most certainly would not have swum over to the island to see some soldier or other, she was not that kind of girl. He moved away, so that she could make her call in private, then stopped just outside the door. He would just linger for a moment—he certainly did not intend to eavesdrop, he would go as soon as he knew who she was calling! He listened.

'Hello? Oh, it's you, Sally. Is Dr Mariano on duty still, or has he left? Oh, never mind . . . do you have his home number, then? I've not got a pencil, but I'll dial it at once. Yes, got it. Thanks.' She put the phone down and re-dialled whilst Diaz stood outside the door, a prey to mixed emotions. John Mariano! A member of his team, and he had told her quite unequivocally that he did not want members of his team dating one another. She and John had seemed quite friendly, John had more or less said that he met her socially, yet he had not allowed himself to think of them as actually going out with one another. Now, facing facts, he found himself hot with a feeling that he did not wish to acknowledge or analyse.

'Hello, John? Yes, it's Jessica. I'm awfully sorry but I shan't be able to dine with you tonight, I'm afraid I'm absolutely worn out . . . no, I'm not at home so you can't very well come up, I'm with a . . . a friend. I was looking forward to the evening more than . . . what? Oh. Yes. Yes, that would be lovely. I really am sorry to mess you about like this, if there was any way . . . no, 'fraid not. No. Right. Right. See you in the morning, then. Me too. Bye.'

As she replaced the receiver Perrello re-entered the room. He beckoned and she followed him into the hall. He pointed to the stairs.

'Up there, first on the right, you'll find a bathroom. Clean up, in nice hot water, you'll find a towelling wrap behind the door. If you leave the bathroom by the other door, not the one you came in by, then you'll find yourself in the spare room. There's a big wardrobe with a variety of clothing hanging up in it. I've a sister and a niece who leave bits and pieces here, you should find something that fits at least approximately. When you come down, come back to the room with the phone in it and I'll have a drink poured and ready. Whilst you're upstairs, I'll tell José that a friend is dining with me.'

She nodded and trailed up the stairs, her exhaustion clear. Perrello watched her until she rounded the corner, then went about his self-appointed tasks, the first of which would be to ring Sancho at the barracks. They had better arrange to take the patient to the military hospital, after all.

The tasks completed Perrello found himself thinking smugly that at least this little adventure had put paid to her evening with John Mariano, which was a good thing—she would have to make do with himself!

CHAPTER NINE

'MRS PONTIN, you wouldn't be so silly as to *eat* that?'

Jessica swooped, taking the unopened box of chocolates out of Mrs Pontin's frightened hand with sufficient authority to cause the lady to do little more than moan slightly at the theft. 'Really, you know what Dr Perrello said, you've been so good and you're down for surgery tomorrow!'

'I know, but I've lost the weight, Staff, just like he said, and I can't lose much more between now and tomorrow, so I thought a little treat . . .' Mrs Pontin did her best to look starved and pathetic, not easy for a fifteen-stone woman blessed with a happy nature and rosy cheeks. 'Remember, after the operation I may not feel like eating chocolates for days and days. Oh, Staff, look out of the window!'

But not the most blatant and engaging tactics could attract Jessica's attention away from the subject of her horrified gaze. Ignoring her patient's cry, Jessica bent and fished out from under the bed a gleaming bedpan. Inside it was a large packet of shortbread biscuits (Real Butter! declared the label) and a bunch of bananas. She gazed accusingly at Mrs Pontin who gazed equally accusingly back. Obviously she thought that a good nurse would have had more tact than to look inside a bedpan!

'Mrs Pontin, how could you? I'll have to take these things away and if I hear you've been looking for them I'll report you to Sister first and Dr Perrello second. You know very well we're not doing this to be cruel, we're doing it for your health's sake. We want you to get over the operation as quickly and comfortably as possible.' Her curiosity got the better of her indignation at this point. 'Just when did you intend to eat this lot?'

'Before midnight, naturally,' Mrs Pontin said with the injured air of a completely misunderstood innocent. 'I wouldn't be so silly as to eat and drink after that. I don't want to make things difficult for myself. But . . . but I couldn't see the harm in having a good feed first.' She glanced quickly at Jessica and then down again, into her lap. 'Suppose I die on the operating table, Staff? Suppose I'm one of the unlucky ones and don't make it? Then I'd be sorry I hadn't had something nice before I went, wouldn't I? And you'd be sorry as well, because you'd stopped me having the only sort of enjoyment I can have, cooped up in here.' She cast a piteous glance at Jessica and a covetous one at the loaded bedpan. 'You're a kind girl, Staff, you wouldn't want to think of me going down to theatre tomorrow hungry and unhappy, I'm sure.'

'I don't care how hungry and unhappy you feel tomorrow morning, provided you wake up feeling hungry tomorrow afternoon,' Jessica said. Frankness seemed the only resort. 'Mrs Pontin, if you'd sat here at ten minutes to midnight and eaten all that food, can't you see what it would have done to you? You see, as you say you've been awfully good, but that much food on an empty stomach could cause all sorts of problems, especially for the surgeon who's going to operate.' She patted Mrs Pontin's hand, however. 'You were probably thinking of the condemned man being allowed a hearty breakfast, I suppose, but remember what happens to him after breakfast! Now you'll live to fight another day, and to eat lots more delicious meals, I don't doubt.'

'I wouldn't have eaten all of it,' Mrs Pontin said wistfully as Jessica, arms laden, turned away. 'Still, I dare say you're right—if I had one chocolate now I'd be longing for a second in five minutes.'

'Yes, and before you knew it, the box would be empty and you'd be planning how to get another box before midnight,' Jessica said, smiling over her shoulder but continuing to walk down the ward. 'You'll thank me for this when you come round in the Recovery room, feeling that you're starting a new life with a nice, freshly cleaned out gall bladder.'

She carried her find through to Sister's office and put it, bedpan and all, on the desk without a word. Sister looked up and shook her head wonderingly.

'Don't tell me—it's Mrs Pontin's winter store! Oh well, it looks as though you found it before she'd started eating and tomorrow we can stop all the absurd precautions we've been taking for the past couple of weeks. Now, Staff, you've got a full list for theatre tomorrow, you can go off at four if it would help.'

'It would be lovely, if you're sure,' Jessica said gratefully. She pointed to Mrs Pontin's booty. 'Shall I take that lot down to the canteen kitchens or the snack bar on my way out?'

'Yes please, Staff, if you wouldn't mind. It seems a sort of justice, that the snack bar should have the stuff when you take into consideration all the food she's taken from there since she arrived on the ward. I feel we've done awfully well, though. How much weight has she lost this past fortnight?'

'Thirteen pounds. A really remarkable loss. But of course Perrello came in and put the fear of death into her, which helped. Sister, if you're sure I can go, can I go right now? I can catch the 3.55 bus if I run.'

'Yes, we'll manage very well this afternoon, we're full strength for once.'

Jessica left the ward and ran down to the snack bar, where she handed over the biscuits, bananas and the box of chocolates. The girl demurred at first but when Jessica explained which patient had given them up she laughed and accepted them.

'Did you know that Dr Perrello was here one day, buying a salad sandwich, when Mrs Pontin made one of her surprise raids? He caught her red-handed . . . he said such dreadful things, too! Told her that stealing was stealing, even if she did intend to pay for everything she'd taken over the weeks. Told her that if her daughter knew what she was doing it would make her ill . . . reduced the woman to tears. But she hasn't been down since then, to my knowledge.'

They exchanged a few more pleasantries and then Jessica made her way out of the hospital grounds and out on to the main road. She went over to her bus stop and waited there, and presently she looked out to sea. A yacht with scarlet sails tacked around a buoy and the Tenerife ferry came slowly and majestically into view, its rails crowded with people.

The sight of it took Jessica's mind back to that eventful

evening when she had so nearly been run down, and back to her rescuer and his beautiful villa.

The bathroom, when she reached it, had been pretty awe-inspiring for a girl used to small English flats, small Spanish flats and nurses' quarters. Mirror tiled walls, cork tiled floor, and a bath, shower and handbasin in avocado green. The towels matched, the shower was instantly adjustable, the water soothed away not only the sea-salt and the sand but also the aches and pains and a good few of the worries of the past few hours.

The bedroom, as he had promised, yielded feminine delights—perfumed talc, a large mirror with beautiful, silver-backed hairbrushes and an ivory comb and a big wardrobe with louvred doors. She found a thin, wrap-around beach dress in some soft, silky material, put it on, looked at herself in the mirror—and promptly took it off and hung it back in the wardrobe. It was far too revealing, showing clearly that she had no underwear beneath it! However, a further search brought to light another beach dress but this time in a very fine towelling material and in a pretty shade of dark gold. With the tie belt firmly fastened around her waist and a pair of borrowed flip-flops on her feet she descended the stairs, feeling that she looked at least a good deal better than she had done twenty minutes earlier, as she wearily climbed them.

The rest of the evening passed in a dream; it was the lone surfer who greeted her as she entered the cool, shady drawing room and he remained with her through the course of an excellent meal, coffee, a liqueur and then the boat-ride back across the water to Villa Castello. She did not know who it was who walked beside her through the trees to the nurses' flats but whether it was the surgeon or the surfer, neither one of them kissed her.

In a way, though, it had been a relief. The first time he had taken her out he had kissed her, and afterwards, for ages and ages, he had been cold and cross with her, as though he despised himself for his weakness and her for accepting it. And now that she looked back, it was true that ever since her marathon swim, Dr Perrello had been far easier with her. Not yet as natural and jokey as other members of the team, but easier. So she would not repine over merely being told to sleep well and never to go swimming alone—she would not. She would simply count her blessings and be glad that they were on easier terms than before.

A car, drawing up beside her, startled her out of her dream. She blinked, then smiled.

'Oh hello, John!'

'Hi, Jessica. Going my way?'

'I'm going back to Villa Castello, if that's what you mean.'

'Hop in, then.'

Jessica climbed into the passenger seat and settled the seat belt round her. Then she leaned back and sighed.

'Gosh, lovely to have a lift, thanks very much, John. Did you have a good day?'

'Pretty good. Jessica, I know you had to miss our last date, but why can't we arrange something for this coming weekend? We're both off and I'd like to hire a car and take you round the island. Neither of us know it at all, really.'

'I'd love it,' Jessica said at once. After all, it had been two whole weeks, more or less, since Perrello had given her dinner in his villa and he had not once attempted to ask her out since. She certainly did not intend to spend her time fretting! 'Look, if you're hiring the car then I'll provide the picnic lunch. Is that fair?'

'It's generous,' John told her. 'What time shall I pick you up? I'd like to go to La Playa de Merenda, it's right over the other side of the island but very beautiful. Lots of small coves, the bathing's excellent and there's a big hotel up on a cliff where we can have a drink or some tea when we've swum enough. Or we could drop in on a monastery that one of the fellows told me about. They make their own wine and cheese and things like that, it's right up in the mountains, very remote spot, we could pop in there.'

'I've heard of Merenda, I'd love to go there,' Jessica said, and the rest of the drive was given up to planning their day out. Hopping out of the car outside the nurses' flats and thanking John sincerely for an enjoyable drive, it occurred to Jessica that he was in a car already so surely would not have to hire one for Saturday? She voiced the thought and John laughed.

'This is Gambas's car, on loan for two hours only. I wondered when you'd ask!'

He drove off and Jessica made her way slowly up the stairs, reflecting as she climbed that delightful though the day out which John had sketched might be, it could not compare to a ten-minute chat in the rest-room with Perrello.

Startled at her own thought she stood stock still for a moment, staring at her own front door. Was she mad? It was plainly useless and stupid to become attached to Diaz Perrello, who only wanted her as a friend, if indeed he wanted her as anything other than a theatre nurse. She knew he wanted no entanglements with women, he had been married disastrously and it had given him a distaste for her sex and anyway he was too old, too powerful and too rich to consider a very ordinary little English girl as anything other than a momentary distraction, someone to kiss once, absently, because she was pretty enough, within arm's reach, and all too obviously willing.

Slowly, she fitted her key into the lock, opened the door and went through into the kitchen. But that kiss had not been absent at all, it had been . . . forget it, she shouted soundlessly to herself, just forget it! He'd be strong meat for anyone, let alone someone like Jessica French, who had been too busy making a career for herself in nursing and then falling in love with a complete rotter like Jordi Ramblas, to have much experience with men. Stick to fellows you can handle, she told herself severely. Nice fellows like John Mariano, who want to take you out, give you a good time and exchange a few kisses and a bit of a cuddle. Only an idiot wants to wrestle with a tiger when they could cuddle a domestic tabby cat!

Having thus rudely put John and Diaz into their respective places, Jessica began to make herself some tea. She told herself crossly that it was about time she learned some common sense. She should be able to stop her mind from wandering giddily around after Diaz Perrello when it should have been fixed on someone worthy and commendable like John Mariano. So as she cleaned lettuce and sliced tomatoes, she turned her thoughts to Mrs Pontin's gall bladder and to the trials of getting Mrs Chase fit enough for surgery.

It was annoying that mentally reviewing a gall bladder

operation meant that she kept seeing those dark, firm hands going through his surgical routines, and the way his eyes could smile above the mask though she could not see his mouth at all. But at least it was better, she told herself, setting the table, than thinking about a kiss that was weeks and weeks old and should have been long forgotten!

'Specimen jar, please. John, you'd better get the stones out and put them into the wretched jar or the woman will accuse me of deliberately losing her gall stones.' Dr Perrello put down the cholecystectomy forceps and held out a hand, not wasting words, but Jessica needed no instructions. She already had the T-tube ready for insertion and the necessary materials for ligature. Mrs Pontin had given them over two hours of solid slog and it looked as though it was not over yet. It had been bad enough getting through the layers of subcutaneous fat but there had been heavy bleeding to contend with and the swab rack was well-laden. In an ordinary abdominal operation Jessica and Ana kept up a regular swab count, but with Mrs Pontin's gall bladder, they had been counting and getting out the sponge-holders about twice as often as usual.

'Blood pressure's rising again,' Dr Fagandini, the anaesthetist, said quietly, in the momentary silence whilst Perrello fixed the T-tube in place. 'And the diathermy's registering a change in heartbeat. Will you be long, now?'

'Not long.' Perrello grunted and held out his hand again. 'I'll start closing the wound now; say a further twenty minutes at the outside.' He peered up at the clock and Jessica reached up with her cloth and quickly patted the perspiration which was trickling down from beneath his cap. 'Thanks, Staff. How much time did we allow for this one?'

'A good deal less than it's taken, which means we'll be working late,' John Mariano contributed, from his place at a side bench, where he was tinkling stones into the specimen jar. 'Imagine what it would have been like if she hadn't lost that extra stone! I wonder whether it would encourage patients to watch their weight if we showed a video of the stuff that lards up their guts?'

'It might cause a good few people to faint, I should think,'

Jessica said from behind her mask. She turned to the auxiliary. 'We'll do one more swab count, Ana, and we'd better check the instruments once more as well.' She nodded towards the swab bucket, in which a few swabs still lurked, and the once-immaculate trolley, now laden with used surgical implements.

'Check the number of dilators carefully, would you?' Perrello asked. 'Thank God the military don't run to fat as a rule. What's next?'

'Hernia. The next three are hernias.' Dr Gambas grinned, his eyes narrowing over his mask. 'All fairly slight, as I remember.'

'Good.' Perrello glanced up at the clock again, as though to verify that too much time had not passed. 'We'll take a proper coffee break after this I think, twenty minutes.' He finished closing the wound and stood straight, sticking his fists into the small of his back in a gesture which Jessica knew well. 'How are things your end now, Fagandini?'

'Better. The diathermy reading has settled down, and the BP hasn't risen any more. If you're ready I'll get blood and saline on now and then she can go into Recovery.'

'Right. Everyone else to scrub up, then.'

The team made their way out of theatre, though Jessica stayed for a moment to take a look at Mrs Pontin. Her patient's face looked very pale but she was breathing evenly. Dr Fagandini was instructing the theatre porter to move Mrs Pontin into Recovery and the staff were buzzing round. Through the half open door Jessica could see the blood bottle and the saline drip being manoeuvred into position. It was clear that Mrs Pontin was about to start on the protracted business of having the drip and the blood connected, and herself taken out of theatre and brought back to consciousness, there was no need for her to hover anxiously, everything was in hand.

Making her way to scrub up, Jessica reflected that it was strange that she, who had just seen the T-tube inserted, should also probably be the one who would deal with the drainage and see that the patient was propped up in bed at the correct angle and ate the right sort of food. Strange, but rather nice. The best of both worlds, she thought complacently, taking her turn at the sink as John Mariano left it.

Perrello had not scrubbed up first, obviously, as he usually did, for now he took the sink next to hers. They were both out of their operating gear, he in dark slacks and a tired-looking white shirt, she in her trusty orange shift dress. She glanced sideways at the surgeon and to her pleasure he was looking at her, and did not scowl or look quickly away but smiled too.

'Well? Tired? Despite her fat I think your patient will make a good recovery. She's strong and fit, and without all those gall stones she'll be even fitter.'

'I'm glad. She's a friendly soul and kind to the other patients, despite her own problems.'

Perrello finished at the sink as she did and they turned away together, but then John joined her and the surgeon walked over to Gambas and made for the rest-room in close conversation with the younger man. She wanted Dr Perrello to know that she and John were going out together—not because she wanted to make him jealous, she was well aware that jealousy would probably be the last thing on his mind, but because she did not want him to think her deceitful. He had, after all, warned her against socialising with members of his team, but John seemed to think that provided they did not start a world-stopping romance, or move in together, Perrello would not mind at all.

'It isn't the moving in that would bother him anyway,' John had confided the previous day when they met over soup and a salad in the canteen. 'It's the moving out. He's against emotions which go wrong and effect other people than those actually involved. He won't mind me taking you out, I'm sure of it.'

So now, the two of them walked into the rest-room and took their places around the coffee jug. Perrello was pouring his own as they entered, but he turned round, raised a brow at them, poured two more cups and pushed them towards John.

'Thanks, Diaz,' John said, whilst Jessica murmured her own thanks. 'Shall we go onto the balcony?'

It was a lovely morning, but already very hot. The three of them walked onto the balcony however, heading for the solitary patch of shade, but after only a few moments Jessica went back to the cool of the rest-room once more. Air conditioning, she decided, had its good points!

The two men stayed out for a few more moments, then turned to come indoors, but once through the french windows, Perrello turned towards Gambas and Fagandini whilst John came over and joined Jessica.

'I just mentioned to Diaz that you and I were going to the beach on Saturday.'

'I'm glad. What did he say?'

'Nothing, really. Just muttered something about the heat, but I told him we'd probably move on during the worst of the sun, in mid-afternoon. I meant to tell you, incidentally, not to bother bringing anything to drink. The beach bar's pretty good and you won't want to carry heavy bottles. Besides, they have ice, which you'd find difficult.'

'True, though you can always dangle the bottle in a seawater pool. I wonder, John, if I'll get time to pop up to the ward around lunchtime? Just to check on Mrs Pontin, you know.'

'I shouldn't; sir might not be pleased. Wait until the list's over, which shouldn't be much after three o'clock, and go over then. Unless Diaz decides to do some visiting of his own, of course, in which case we can all blow off for ten minutes or so.'

Presently, the team began to saunter back to scrub up, and Jessica joined them in time to hear John and Perrello in conversation, and a conversation, she gathered, that she was not meant to hear.

'. . . unsuitable,' Perrello was saying as she went across to the sink. 'You don't know what it can be like down there . . . you've never been before, you think it's all very modern no doubt, but . . .'

'Diaz, old fellow, you wrong me,' John was saying jocularly. 'I'm an old-fashioned bloke myself, I wouldn't dream . . .' he broke off as he saw Jessica out of the corner of his eye, and nudged the surgeon with one elbow. 'So you won't join us, you and your latest conquest?'

Jessica felt alertness creep over her body as a physical thing; if she had been a dog ears would have pricked, hackles risen and fur would have stirred all over her body. As it was, she gave all her attention to Perrello's answer, whilst appearing absorbed in the long and thorough hand-washing which theatre work calls for.

'My latest . . . I don't know what you mean; or should I say who?'

'Well, who did you take to the opera, Diaz? Rumour has it that you've a soft spot for your theatre nurse!'

'Oh, La Cruz! No, I wouldn't dream of taking her to Fontells. Does that prove to you how unwise . . .' he broke off, shrugged and turned away.

Jessica finished her wash, nudged the tap off and turned to find her sterile towel. Soon, fully gowned and masked, she was making her way back to theatre for the next operation.

'Well, it's all over, Staff.' Mrs Pontin opened her eyes and a smile stole across her face. 'And aren't I glad I'm still alive? I don't feel too bad now, either, since they let me have a little drink.'

'You look very good, all things considered,' Jessica said, sitting down by the bed. It was late afternoon, the sun was well down the sky and Mrs Pontin was fully conscious, though sleepy still. 'How about a mouth wash? I can do that for you, if it would be nice.'

'Mouth wash?'

'That's right. There's an oral hygiene pack . . . would you like it?'

'I would, very much.' Mrs Pontin managed her small, tired smile again, a very different one from the big, rather self-satisfied beam with which she usually greeted the world. 'Begonia's been very kind. She's been in and out ever since I got back on the ward, had a little chat, held my hand for a bit . . . oh, ever so kind.'

'She's an extremely nice person,' Jessica agreed. 'I'll just pop out and fetch a kidney basin and so on, I shan't be a minute.'

She was not in uniform since she was off duty, but went into the changing room, got her clean apron and slipped it on, then went along to the dressings room for the necessary equipment.

She had almost finished Mrs Pontin's mouth wash and was

tidying up when the door at the end of the ward swung and a tall and familiar figure in a dark green shirt and khaki riding breeches came up the room towards them. It was Perrello, looking extremely military and efficient with shiny boots and a peaked cap held lightly in one hand completing his appearance.

'Hello, Mrs Pontin; how are you feeling?' He raised a hand to acknowledge Jessica's presence but did not address her directly. Mrs Pontin smiled, with a little more life than she had previously shown. It must be the uniform, Jessica decided with an inward chuckle; the sight of a handsome soldier had revitalised her patient.

'Oh, Dr Perrello! I feel very much better, thank you, very much better. Sister says I may have soup for my meal tonight and perhaps a little icecream or milk pudding. I'm looking forward to it.'

'Good, good. But having shown us all not only how you can use your will-power but what a pretty figure you have, I hope you won't backslide.'

Mrs Pontin fluttered her eyelashes and smiled coquettishly. She sat up a little straighter against her pillows and even glanced down at her nightie as if to make sure that its voluminous folds hid her large expanse of bosom.

'You may be sure I shan't be so silly again, Doctor,' she said earnestly. 'Having lost the weight I definitely won't put it back on again.'

'Well done. The wound, you understand, was a large one. You are feeling no discomfort from it?'

'It aches,' Mrs Pontin acknowledged. 'But other than a feeling of muzziness I'm fine.'

'That's what we like to hear, isn't it, Staff?' Perrello actually smiled at Jessica, who had leapt to her feet as he approached the bed. 'Are you off duty? If so, I wonder if I might have a word with you?'

'Of course,' Jessica said with alacrity. They had not exchanged much social talk since her marathon swim, though he had begun to include her in the casual chat in theatre and in the rest-room. Was this a further break-through, she wondered, following him meekly out of the ward.

Once outside in the corridor he advised her to put her equipment away and take off her uniform.

'When you've changed I'll walk down to the car-park with you,' he said. 'I'll run you home if you're going back to Villa Castello.'

'Yes, I am. Are you going in my direction?'

'Well, in a way . . . look, we'll talk in the car.'

Entering the changing-room sedately, Jessica promptly became a whirlwind. She tore off her apron and dress, attacked her hair with a brush, examined her face and decided she needed a good wash, then had to put on a dab of make-up and some mascara. Yet even after completing her toilet by doing her hair in a pony-tail and spraying cologne with a prodigal hand, she was out of the room in under ten minutes.

'You look very clean and fresh,' Dr Perrello said as she emerged and they both turned towards the stairs. 'How did you think Mrs Pontin seemed? It was a long operation, a good two and a half hours. She's a plucky woman, sitting up there and beaming at everyone.'

'She's strong, and she responded well to oxygen,' Jessica said. 'She doesn't fluster easily, either, which is always good. Nurse Floyd said despite her weight they had no trouble with her in Recovery. She came round placid and smiled after a few breaths of oxygen and kept the mask on without any fuss until they wanted it removed. Some people get very tense over the mask.'

'True. Have you ever worked in Recovery?'

'Not really, though I did a stint during my training and when I first started ward work I went in and out of Recovery with my patients.'

By this time they had reached the car-park; Jessica hesitated and Dr Perrello immediately took her elbow, led her over to his car, and settled her in the passenger seat. He went round to the other side, opened the door and slid behind the wheel. Then he looked across at her, with something in his expression which Jessica could not quite define.

'I'm on my way to a . . . a meeting, so it will have to be straight back to your flat and then on, for me. But . . .' he stopped talking whilst he started the car, revved the engine and drove out of the car-park, only recommencing his sentence when they were purring smoothly along the road. '. . . but I wanted to ask you whether you really wanted to go to Fontells with John, at the weekend.'

'Oh? Well, of course I do. Swimming in the harbour is great fun but nothing compares with a real beach and the open sea.'

'I agree. But there are girls who wouldn't go to Fontells with a man.'

'Oh? It's remote, I know, but I certainly don't mind that. Why should I mind?'

He snatched a quick glance at her, brows low over his dark eyes, then shrugged and looked back at the road.

'You know what those beaches are! Besides, there's been a plague of jellyfish. The harbour's fairly clear but they seem to congregate in those narrow coves.' He turned and scowled at her. 'Why not tell Mariano you'd prefer to swim in the harbour? With the jellyfish about he wouldn't disbelieve you . . . I can't think you'll feel comfortable at Fontells.'

'I'm not worried by jellyfish and as I said, I'm longing to swim from a real beach,' Jessica said. 'If you think . . . if it's such a quiet spot . . . if you mean that John might start something, like . . .'

'Like Jaime?' His smile was at its worst and most sardonic. 'But I thought you and he were just fishing!'

Jessica felt the heat fly to her cheeks and knew she must be scarlet. He was too bad, bringing her out in his car simply to find fault with her, and over a silly little thing like a trip to a beach, too! If it was jealousy that would be delightful and gratifying, but it was pretty clear he was merely being a dog-in-the-manger. He did not want her making love to John on some lonely beach though he had no desire to make love to her himself!

'No, *not* like Jaime, because we *were* just fishing and John and I will be just swimming and sunbathing,' she said firmly. 'I was going to say like the way you thought Jaime behaved but then I thought it would be a mean thing to drag that old business up again. You, however, had no such qualms.'

'No, none at all. Jessica, you are a very good theatre nurse, and I don't want to lose you. If you and John have an affair, however much you may both enjoy it, it'll affect your performance—and his—in theatre. When . . . or if . . . you split up there will be an atmosphere. I did ask you, if you recall, not to choose boyfriends from the team. Yet now you and John Mariano are going to a lonely beach where you will both . . .'

'We shall not!' Jessica snapped, not waiting for him to finish a sentence which could well, she felt, end in a way she would find very offensive. 'It sounds like a line from an old TV movie, but we are just good friends and want to stay that way. Now can we change the subject, please?'

He turned the wheel and the car swung into the driveway before the flats. He braked viciously, so viciously that Jessica was flung against the seat belt and gasped with surprise as it bit into the soft flesh across her breasts.

'Are you telling me you trust John to behave . . .'

'Goodbye, Dr Perrello; thank you for the lift,' Jessica said in a tightly controlled voice. She got out of the car and made for the foyer without another glance in his direction. She heard his door slam and then his footsteps but she was across the hall and flying up the stairs before his voice came echoing up to her.

'Jessica! Wait, please. I did not mean . . .'

But she was at her front door, her key fumbling for the lock. Then she was in the flat, shutting the door behind her. She was trembling, partly with annoyance of course but also because she had wanted so badly to turn and run down the stairs and let him tell her again that she was being a fool.

And then I suppose you would have meekly agreed and cancelled your day out, she said crossly to herself. Jessica French, you very nearly made a fool of yourself, because he doesn't want you, but he doesn't want anyone else to have you either.

It was only later, after the kettle had boiled and the first sip of tea was cooling her temper, that she reflected her choice of phrase had been unfortunate. She did not want anyone to 'have' her, not Dr Perrello or John Mariano. All she wanted was a pleasant outing! She had been badly hurt by Jordi, she did not want another passionate relationship with anyone. Not even Diaz Perrello. Though there was something about him which transcended his harsh, dark features and his rather chilling manner, some chemistry which sparked her feelings in a way that a handsomer and more charming man never could.

Sighing, she repeated her advice to herself not to be a fool and began, rather slowly, to put together a meal for when Pat came in later.

CHAPTER TEN

'JOHN, it's beautiful!' Jessica got out of the car and walked to the start of the sloping, narrow little beach. 'The colour of the water . . . and those rocks . . . the sea's so dark, so clear . . . it's perfection!'

'Yes, it's pretty nice. I thought you'd prefer to bathe here and we can go round to the main beach later for a drink.' John jumped down onto the sand and Jessica followed. 'Let's put our things down here, in the shade, and bathe at once, shall we?'

'Lovely.' Jessica unwrapped her skirt and pulled off her top to reveal her trusty yellow bikini. John blinked approvingly.

'I say! Where's the prim Nurse French now? Come on, straight in!'

The water was mildly warm, the marine life abundant. Great spider crabs stalked between patches of underwater rock, colourful little fish fluttered over to the fascinating white arms moving so leisurely through their domain. The little waves rocked and caressed, livelier between the narrow rocks of the cove, cooler than the water in the harbour.

'Had enough?' John said after half an hour. 'You've seen most of what's to see in the cove, how about that picnic?'

It had been good to swim in the sea again, and it was equally good to sit in the shade of a palm tree, leaning against a rock draped with a towel, and eat. Jessica had brought chicken patties, salad and big bunches of ripe purple grapes. They ate everything, their appetites sharpened by their swim, and then, replete, they re-arranged their towels in the sun and lay down side by side for a little sunbathing.

After forty minutes of slowly turning over, like chops on a griddle, Jessica sat up.

'I think more sea is called for,' she said, examining her darkening tan and distrusting the rosy flush that was slowly appearing on her shoulders. 'What about that drink? Is the main beach far?'

'Not so very. Are you up to swimming round there, though? I can put my money in the pocket of my shorts and we can pick up our clothes later, when we've got ourselves something long and cold and refreshing.'

John, too, had sat up, now he stretched, yawned, and then stood, holding out his hands to her. 'Come on, then, if you're feeling energetic.'

They wrapped their things in the towels, put them in the shade and then ran down to the sea. Jessica wanted to know which way she should swim but John simply told her to follow and plunged.

They swam out of their own cove, into the open sea. It was fresh and exhilarating to be swimming out there and Jessica was thoroughly enjoying herself when John, swimming strongly to one side of her, advised her that they should head in for the shore.

'I'm not absolutely sure how many coves we pass before we reach the main beach,' he explained. 'But I wouldn't mind taking a look at one or two. I found ours by chance, but there may be another one just as lovely and equally quiet situated a bit nearer the bar!'

'I wouldn't mind a spell on land,' Jessica agreed, so as they rounded the next spur of rock they turned in to the cove.

As she swam she realised that this was a considerably larger cove, and hearing voices, decided that this was probably the main beach, not so far from their secret cove as they had thought. She put a spurt on, calling to John over her shoulder as she did so, 'Race you!'

They clambered out of the water onto a ledge of rock, and Jessica, still going first, walked along it and dropped onto the sand. It was hot beneath her feet and she winced, turned to speak to John and warn him, and stumbled right into someone walking in the opposite direction.

For a second she was completely stunned; then she whipped round and grabbed John, almost sending him flying.

'Get back! John, get back . . . this isn't the main beach, it's . . .' without finishing her sentence she turned and ran back down the beach, to plunge straight into the sea and retreat from the land at a steady crawl though presently, when she was a safe distance out, she hauled herself out onto a rock and sat there whilst John followed suit. She saw that he was shaking with laughter and laughed herself, though her cheeks were still hot with remembered embarrassment.

'Oh, John, wasn't that awful! I've never been so embarrassed! That man hadn't a stitch on and when I looked past him there was a woman completely bare as well. It must have been a nudist beach, and we walked slap bang on top of them!'

'No wonder Diaz made snide comments when I said I was bringing you down here,' John said ruefully, though still with a grin etched on his face. 'Did you see that lot playing cricket? I don't want to be vulgar but I thought they looked downright obscene. I've seen some sights since I started doing medicine but at least the naked women in hospital aren't bowling overarm . . . and thundering up the sand . . . oh, my God!'

He began to laugh again, rather to Jessica's annoyance.

'Do you mean Perrello thought we were going to a nudist beach? How dare he think such a thing!'

'Oh, come on, I said Fortells, and didn't think to add I meant a cove near Fortells. Look, are you up to swimming along to the main beach, do you think? It must be another quarter of a mile or so.'

'Yes, of course I am, so long as we stay well out and don't have to face up to any more nudist colonies.'

They slid off the rock into the sea and still swimming side by side, began to make their way along the coast once more. They had covered most of the distance and Jessica, turning her head as she swam, could see the umbrellas and tiny figures which dotted the main beach when she saw, bobbing in the translucent green of the sea head, her first jellyfish.

'Look, John! Perrello said something about them, better swim round it, but isn't it lovely?'

It was. Its mushroom shaped body was almost completely transparent save for green and purple patterns traced on the top and tiny, fluorescent dots which followed the scalloped edge, but the long trailers, darker and cloudier, could be seen quite easily as they dangled beneath the pulsating cap.

Jessica, however, did not admire it for long; she gave it a wide berth and never even saw the tentacles whose stings trailed across her thighs, burning twin tracks of agony across her tender flesh. She cried out and John swam towards her, even as another searing pain whipped across the middle of her back, then another and another, catching her hips, her thighs, her calves and ankles, almost paralysing her leg movements as her muscles snatched in spasm after spasm of pain.

She sank, then rose to the surface, spluttering and coughing up sea-water. John was near her but one glance at his face convinced her that he, too, had been attacked. She turned for the shore, shouting to her companion, in a thin voice, to follow suit, and felt—or thought she felt—more tentacles touch her. She moved violently in the water, ducked her head under to see just what was happening, felt a touch on her cheek followed by more burning pain . . . swam . . . collided with a rock . . . feebly splashed her way round it, collided with another, tried to climb . . . and was hauled ashore by a strong hand which picked her out of the water by the back of her bikini rather as a mother cat lifts her kittens.

'You damned little fool!' the words were harsh, but the hands that supported her into a wobbly standing position were gentle. 'Jellyfish?'

Her eyes were blurred with tears and one lid was swollen by a passing sting; she could see nothing of her rescuer save that he was a tall man in navy shorts and espadrilles but she did not need sight to tell her that it was Diaz Perrello. She said, her voice choked with sobs of pain, 'Yes, it was jellyfish. About a million.' She sagged against him; no use pretending to be resolute and independent when pain had reduced you to a child again.

'Well, I did warn you. You all right, Mariano?'

'I'll live.' John was beside them, Jessica realised. He touched her shoulder lightly. 'Poor old girl, you must have been right in the middle of a swarm of the things. You must be in agony.'

Reaction was catching up with Jessica. She nodded, unable to speak, then began to shiver, hot though it was. Great shudders shook her, but when Perrello put his arm firmly round her she screamed . . . the pain of a touch on the stings was unbelievable.

'Go ahead, John, would you? You'll find my car parked at the top of the beach outside the hotel. Here are my keys; get my bag out and go into the hotel and ask them . . . tell them . . . to set aside a room for my use for an hour or so. We'll get analgesic cream on the pair of you and perhaps you'll live to fight another day. I shan't be far behind you, so hurry.' Jessica saw John's blurred figure hurry for the beach, then Perrello addressed her. 'You can't walk, so I'm going to carry you. I'm afraid it'll hurt, but try not to struggle, I don't want to drop you. Ready?' He sounded very impersonal.

Jessica nodded but had a job not to scream and fight him when he caught hold of her and lifted her. With the best will in the world he had no choice but to touch some of the stings, and pain intensified with touch. He knew it because once he had her firmly he said gently, 'I'm sorry, but I'm going to hurry, just bear the pain for a few more minutes,' and then he began to carry her up over the rocks and across the beach.

Jessica did not know how long it took them to reach the hotel room, perhaps only ten minutes, but to her it could have been ten hours. When at last he entered the building and was led through the hall and to a quiet, cream and gold room, she was exhausted from subduing her cries of pain and when at last he stood her down she could only lean against him, praying for the pain to ease.

As it ebbed, he sat her gently down on the bed.

'Good girl.' The words were commonplace enough but coming from Perrello, Jessica judged them to be high praise. 'Can I have the cream in the blue and white tube, please, John? You've used it, of course—how do you feel now?'

'It's marvellous stuff,' John said, sounding surprised. 'Within five minutes of spreading it over my legs the pain eased. Look, shall I . . .'

'No.' The solitary negative was said with a sort of controlled tightness which surprised Jessica into trying to open her eyes, so she saw the look that accompanied the word. It was a look of fury and some other emotion, but since it was directed at

John's back, it did no harm. 'Go and ask the staff for some ice, would you? And a couple of clean towels.'

'Wouldn't it be better if I rang down, got someone to come up? I mean . . . what'll the staff think . . . they don't even know Jessica's a nurse!'

Even in her pain Jessica had to stifle a gurgle of amusement at the obvious trend of John's thoughts. Shut up in a bedroom with a girl in a bikini and nothing else—except a million jellyfish stings—the staff of the hotel would obviously think the worst. If they knew the girl in the bikini was a nurse, however . . . !

'I do not think, John, that the staff will be at all interested in Miss French's occupation. Hurry, please.'

Jessica was quite surprised and rather chagrined at the speed with which John followed the surgeon's instructions and left the room. It would have been a good deal more chivalrous, she felt, had he remained to see that she was at least properly chaperoned, for since his words she had felt, not embarrassed but rather silly, in a bedroom in a bikini with a man, surgeon or no.

However, Perrello obviously felt no such inhibitions. He turned towards her and took her hands, smiling reassuringly as he pulled.

'Up with you. Let's take a look at the damage.'

She stood up, turning as he propelled her round, and could almost feel his gaze raking her blotched and burning body. What a sight she must look—not that it mattered. The pain was still there, from time to time cramping her muscles in spasms.

'They really did a job of work on you, Jessica. I'll start with your legs so hold still.'

'I can do them,' Jessica said feebly, and got a scornful look and a curl of the lip for her pains. He was right, of course, she could not have spread the stuff as quickly and lightly as he and as John had said, as the cream covered the stings the heat and pain began to leave her skin for the first time since the attack.

'Better? Lie on your front then and I'll do your back.'

'On the bed?'

'That's right. Ah, of course, the cream on your legs.' He reached past her and stripped the coverlet, the blankets and the top sheet off the bed. 'There we are; easier to launder than the coverlet. On you get.'

Jessica was in agony; blushing made the stings hurt worse than ever but she felt such a fool! She climbed onto the bed, however, and lay down on her tummy, her head on the pillow and turned sideways, so that she could watch the door. When Perrello's ministrations had reached halfway along her back with the cream spreading its exquisite relief, the door opened and John, laden with towels and a basin of ice, came in. He raised his eyebrows at the sight of Jessica prone on the bed, then grinned.

'Better, honey? Where shall I put all this ice, Diaz?'

'On the dressing table, if you please, and then go and fetch your car and your clothing.'

'Right.' John left, closing the door softly behind him. Perrello finished off her back and shoulders, lifted her long, wet mass of hair to check, presumably, that no stings had penetrated its thickness, then spoke.

'Turn over, please.'

Jessica turned, but sat up at the same time. She said, her voice a little higher than usual: 'I'll do my front.'

'I'd rather finish the job, Jessica. Lie down again, please.'

'No, really, I feel . . .'

'If you share John's first feeling that the sight of you lying on a bed is liable to turn me into a sex attacker, then just take a look at yourself. Red and white stripes, my dear child, do *not* become you. Now let me finish.'

Jessica lay down on the bed again, knowing that facially, at least, red was predominating over white. She waited until the smoothing motion of the cream easing her skin had ceased and then sat up again, only to be again pushed back.

'No, no, *no*! That cream is soothing, but not a cure. For that we'll need the ice-packs and a strong antihistamine tablet every three hours. I'll make ice-packs with the ice and the towels and you can lie face down for a couple of hours, until everything has had a chance to work, then I'll take you home and you can spend the night keeping the ice-packs renewed and making sure you take the tablets. And another time, take advice, don't just ignore it.'

'You said jellyfish were about but we didn't really see them . . . at least, I saw one and we swam round it and probably straight into the others. What were you doing down there, anyway? And in swimming shorts? Oh, that reminds me . . . we weren't on the nudist beach you know, we didn't even know it was there until we swam round the coast to reach the main beach.'

'Turn over now, please.'

Jessica heaved a sigh but rolled onto her stomach and felt the ice-packs cold against her flesh. Looking up and sideways, she saw that he was indeed in swimming shorts and that a pair of binoculars, which had obviously hung round his neck, stood on the floor beside the bed.

'Well? What were you doing at Fontells? And why the binoculars?'

'Here. First tablet.' He supported a glass of water up to her mouth and watched her swallow the small white pill before he attempted to answer. 'Why was I at Fontells? Why not? As for the binoculars, I was birdwatching; it's a hobby of mine.' He walked over to the door and opened it. 'Rest, now. I'll come back in an hour or so.' He closed the door softly behind him.

Jessica lay on the bed, wondering. Birdwatching? Feathered or unfeathered ones? But why should a man who was always being treated to a view of naked bodies on his operating table suddenly take to looking at them through binoculars? Anyway, she was tired, too tired to worry about what Perrello had been doing down at the beach. As she grew drowsier she reflected that whatever his reasons she was very glad he had been there. Poor John, stung himself, could never have coped so magnificently with her pain and confusion.

She might have gone on to analyse her feelings over Perrello's sudden appearance, but it occurred to her that she was feeling even more tired than circumstances warranted. And just why would Dr Perrello have antihistamine tablets in his bag? Far more likely that they were sleeping pills . . . heavens, had she been doped? She struggled up on her elbow and looked wildly round the room, not knowing what she feared but just knowing that she did not want to be drugged to sleep.

But she had had a frightening experience and after all she

was safe here; Perrello might be all sorts of things, but he would not let harm come to her. Reassured and calmed by the mere fact of the surgeon's presence, Jessica lay down again, settled her head more comfortably on the pillow, and decided to foil him by remaining awake.

She foiled him for a further three minutes. Then stings, sunshine, swimming and the little white tablet triumphed. Jessica slept.

'Morning, Staff. Where were you yesterday? My, you don't look your usual cheerful self, not by a long chalk you don't.'

Jessica, bustling on to the ward, pulled a face at Mrs Pontin; it was pretty plain that the whole hospital knew about her escapade with the jellyfish and the dire consequences. She had woken from a long, drugged sleep to find the stings hurting again, the ice long melted, and Dr Perrello sitting on the side of her bed, a syringe poised.

'Don't you dare!' she had yelped, struggling to sit up. 'I won't be put to sleep . . . I'm all right, I feel fine . . . I'm well, I'm . . .'

'Don't treat me to hysterics, Nurse French, it's merely the antihistamine I promised you,' he said coolly. He took her arm and, when she tried to snatch it away, lay the syringe down and took hold of her, firmly, by the shoulders. 'For hysteria, one slaps faces and throws cold water,' he reminded her, and despite herself Jessica stopped struggling and laughed, feebly it is true, but with genuine amusement.

'I'm sorry, but I woke to find you poised over me with that great hypodermic . . . visions of the white slave trade flashed through my mind. It's all right, I'll avert my eyes whilst you torture me yet again.'

'Good girl.' Jessica tried to ignore the virtuous glow which spread all over her at these words. 'As soon as you've had the shot we'll get you off home.'

He had been as good as his word but it had not, unfortunately, been the end of the episode. The following morning Jessica had woken stiff, aching, sore and still dopy and slow. Pat had insisted on calling their GP and he had insisted, in his turn, that she take a day off work.

Now, however, back on the ward, she bustled over to Mrs Pontin's bed.

'You know very well where I was yesterday, Mrs P, but I'll tell you for nothing that I'm a lot better and the stings have completely disappeared. And what's more, I shan't go swimming in the open sea for a long time!'

'Pat said there were notices on the beach. Why didn't you read them, you silly girl?'

'I know, I had a long lecture on the way home in the doctor's car,' Jessica said, pausing by the bed. 'The trouble was, Dr Mariano and I were further up the coast in a little cove and we swam round to the main beach and straight into the shoals of jellyfish that the notices were warning people about. I think you'd better get up now, Mrs Pontin, and sit in your chair for a bit. Here, let me help you.'

Presently, she got Mrs Pontin out and into her chair and began to make her bed. She was still a bit stiff and it was not entirely true that the stings no longer hurt but at least they did not burn and her muscles no longer spasmed.

'They stung your poor cheek, didn't they, Staff?' Mrs Pontin said, as Jessica moved over to the opposite side of the bed. 'Horrid things! You could have been killed.'

'Yes, the doctor mentioned that as well,' Jessica said guardedly. The terrible, biting lecture which had been meted out during the drive back to her flat would certainly not be easily forgotten. She only hoped that John Mariano had suffered likewise, but she had not yet seen him to ask. 'I was very silly, Mrs P, and now I'm sorry. There, your bed's finished.'

'Can I get back into it?' Mrs Pontin asked hopefully, wriggling. 'This chair doesn't fit me.'

'Does the bag get in the way, or the tubing?' Jessica asked, rather concerned. 'I could move a bigger chair through from the day-room, I expect.'

'It isn't the bag or the tubing, it's me,' Mrs Pontin explained. 'I go through the sides; it's the same in the day-room.'

'I see.' Jessica kept a straight face with some difficulty, for Mrs Pontin did bulge over the chair in certain places. 'Well, I'll find you a chair without arms, that will help. Has your drain been checked today?'

'Yes, dear. Nurse Thompson did it earlier. I thought it might come out soon though; several ladies who've had surgery said their drains come out on the fourth day.'

'Well, yours is a bit more complicated,' Jessica explained. She finished Mrs Pontin's bed and moved on to the next one. 'We'll have to have a picture of what's going on inside your wound before we can take the drain away, so you'll go down to X-Ray next Thursday and if everything's going according to plan, the drain will come out a couple of days later.'

'I see. Well, if I can't go back to bed I think I'll trundle down to the day-room. Could you pass me my knitting, Staff? I'd get it myself, only it's the far side of the bed.'

'You really should move around more,' Jessica said, getting the required knitting nevertheless. 'Dr Perrello's got a ward round this morning, he'll want to know how mobile you are and he won't be pleased if you aren't doing things for yourself.'

'Oh, Staff, but I am!' Mrs Pontin's round blue eyes widened into an expression of hurt innocence. 'I'm for ever trotting up and down the ward and going through to the day-room, really I am!'

'I'm glad to hear it.' Jessica watched Mrs Pontin waddle very slowly up the ward and through the swing doors and then returned to her work. When she had got Mrs Webb a bedpan, adjusted the angle of her injured leg, refilled her water jug and admired her latest Get Well card, Jessica went over to Mrs De Sousa, still patiently waiting for her baby to put in an appearance.

Mrs De Sousa put down her copy of *Vogue*, and smiled hopefully up at the other girl.

'Hello, Staff, glad you're back. Them jellyfish! Not that Carl would let me swim in the open sea, not with us having the pool an' all. Still, I reckon you've learned your lesson.'

'That's true. Not only the pain taught me I'd been foolish, but being hauled over the coals by Dr Perrello. I dare say someone told you that he was there, and treated me?'

'Yes, of course. Common knowledge,' Mrs De Sousa said. 'Well, Staff, what do you expect? Fontells is a local beach, not one holidaymakers use much. Except for the nudist bit of course, and that's all English and Danes and Germans. Not there, were you?'

'Scarcely!' Jessica lifted Mrs De Sousa's chart off the end of the bed and studied it. 'Can you tell me, though, as a matter of interest, whether Dr Perrello is keen on birdwatching?'

'Birdwatching? Dr Perrello? Not that I've heard. Why?'

'Oh, no real reason. I thought someone said he did. How do you feel today, Mrs De Sousa?'

'Lousy, thanks. Still, mustn't grumble. At least junior . . .' she patted the mound of her stomach through the sheet, '. . . is still where he should be. It's better if I go full-term they say.'

Jessica agreed with her, warned her not to surprise them all by giving birth on the ward, and continued with her duties. It took her longer than usual to get through all the standard daily tasks but halfway through the morning she noticed the time and decided to award herself a coffee break. She went to the kitchen, made two cups of coffee and carried them towards the private room. She was fond of Mrs Chase and was sure she could now distinguish the friendly and amusing person who was, for the moment, hidden by the symptoms of her disease. In the private room moreover, with the drugs giving the relief she so badly needed, Mrs Chase had blossomed and was now quite popular with the other patients, who sought her out for a quiet chat or a corner where the television did not reign supreme.

Jessica wondered, as she made her way up the corridor, how she would feel when Mrs Chase went under the knife. It was one thing to watch an operation on a stranger, a little harder to see a difficult but rather lovable patient like Mrs Pontin being cut, but someone she felt protective towards and knew well would be, she imagined, more difficult again. It had crossed her mind that Perrello might make a point of operating on Mrs Chase when Sister Cruz was present rather than herself, but it was now an open secret that Isabel Cruz was leaving as soon as she could and on Perrello's regular operating days, when he had a long list, it was always Jessica who stood ready at his elbow.

She knew, moreover, that if Perrello did ask her whether she wanted to assist during the thyroidectomy she would say that she did. The thought of someone else assisting was anathema to her. After all, she knew Perrello's methods, likes and dislikes, better than most, she told herself defensively, and because she was fond of Mrs Chase, who better to be at the surgeon's side to see that all went well?

'Good morning, Mrs Chase,' she said cheerfully, pushing open the door with her hip and entering back first so that the tray and the coffees were safe. 'I've come to share your coffee break, so make the most . . .' she stopped short. The room was empty.

It was thoroughly bad luck that at the moment when Jessica made the heart-stopping discovery that Mrs Chase was not only missing from her room but from the ward as well, Dr Perrello should have decided to start his ward round. So when she burst into the office with a cry of, 'Sister, Mrs Chase has disappeared!' it was not just Sister's round blue eyes which turned a look of startled enquiry upon her. John Mariano, Dr Perrello and Dr Gambas all looked equally surprised.

'Oh, I'm sorry, I didn't . . .' Jessica began, but was interrupted.

'Disappeared, Staff?' It was Perrello looking smug. 'Well, of course, you might have expected that. You put a highly nervous patient in a room all by herself and then she works herself up into a state and before you know it, she's run off. Particularly upon hearing that the operation is now scheduled for tomorrow. I believe I did mention it to you, Sister?'

'You did, Dr Perrello.' Sister's voice was frosty in the extreme. 'I take it that you're criticising me, to one of my staff, when you remind me so sharply that it was I who decided Mrs Chase should go in the private room when it came vacant. May I remind . . .'

'Sister, nothing was further from my thoughts! We agreed, if you remember, that your decision was the right one. But the nursing staff were told that Mrs Chase must be given a good deal of attention . . .'

It was Sister's turn, now, to interrupt.

'Certainly, Dr Perrello. Now shall we hear what Nurse French has to say, instead of laying blame?'

Jessica noticed, out of the corner of her eye, that Dr Perrello's harsh features were darkened by what looked suspiciously like a blush. She also noticed that Mariano and Gambas were suppressing grins. But oddly enough, this did not please her as much as it should have; instead, she found herself wanting to take some of the blame, just to show them. She turned and faced Perrello, looking up into his dark, still rather accusing eyes.

'I didn't know the operation was scheduled for tomorrow, sir, so I am at fault, as you said. Usually I go in to her room three or four times in the course of a morning but this morning I was slow, and Nurse Parkinson had to take a patient down for a barium meal and X-rays so I was behind with my work. I'm afraid I didn't go in to Mrs Chase, as I most definitely should have done, and I'm afraid I didn't come in to Sister's office either, to check the list for tomorrow. But if she's run away it won't be the private room that's to blame, having a quiet place of her own has done her nearly as much good as the medication, I believe.'

'Hm. Well, I'm glad you can admit to a fault, Staff, but I think you'd better start phoning round, to see if you can locate her. She may be home by now, or with a friend. At best she may still be agreeable to returning because once the effects of the proponalol begin to wear off she may become very unstable.'

'I'll phone,' Sister said calmly, taking the receiver off its hook. She started to dial, then put the instrument down again. 'Staff, I've just had a thought. Since the operation is scheduled for tomorrow, might it not be worth checking up at the military hospital? The X-ray department, for instance, might know where she is.'

Dr Perrello looked sceptical, but John Mariano was grinning. He raised a brow at Jessica, then spoke.

'I believe there was talk of Dr Fagandini examining the patient's vocal cords. With her highly charged nervous state, though, I believe he said he'd use an anaesthetic spray, so he may well have taken her over to the small theatre for the purpose.'

'I think not,' Dr Perrello said, 'after all, though Dr

Fagandini would administer the anaesthetic and would want to assist, it is I who . . .'

He was interrupted by the telephone bell ringing shrilly. Sister picked up the receiver and spoke in her usual brisk tones.

'Agamemnon; Sister speaking. Yes, he's here. Certainly.' She handed the instrument across the desk to Perrello saying placidly as she did so, 'It's for you, sir. Dr Fagandini.'

Dr Perrello took the receiver so quickly that it looked perilously like snatching. This time, Jessica too was guilty of suppressing a smile. Surgeons are always right. Except sometimes, it seemed.

'Yes? Yes. Very well, I'll come right away.'

He cracked the receiver back on its rest, turned as if to leave the room, then obviously thought better of it and paused for a moment.

'Mrs Chase is in the small theatre, having just had a local anaesthetic. A misunderstanding, as you thought, Sister. I shan't keep her long, but you'll have to make a fresh cup of coffee, Staff.'

He hurried out of the room with the two younger men following and Jessica, behind them, felt her hand caught in Mariano's warm clasp. He pulled her into the doorway of the dressings-room. He was laughing soundlessly, his eyes sparkling.

'My dear girl, what a storm in a teacup! It doesn't do to put a surgeon in the wrong even temporarily, but I'm sure Perrello will forgive you just this . . .'

'Mariano!' John jumped as Perrello suddenly loomed up before them.

'Sorry, sir, I was just explaining to Staff how . . .'

'Explaining? It should have been clear to you, *hombre*, that I don't approve of my team carrying on their affairs during working hours. Come with me right now.'

John pulled a face but turned and followed the surgeon along the corridor but once Dr Perrello's whitecoated back was towards him once more he turned and blew a kiss to Jessica, mouthing what looked like, 'See you later', at her.

Jessica smiled at him, then turned and went back to Sister's office. Sister was just putting down the telephone.

'Well, Staff, we had a few sticky moments there,' she said cheerfully. 'By the way, Mrs Chase is first on the list tomorrow, which is good of Perrello. After all, we can only request special treatment for difficult cases, we can't demand it. He would have been within his rights to deal with his military cases first and that, of course, would have given Mrs Chase hours of anxiety. At least he's a big enough person to save her that.'

'I'm sorry I rushed in here in a panic, though,' Jessica said, examining the list. 'I hope he doesn't push her further down as a result of this morning, but I remembered everything I'd read about thyroid patients and leapt to conclusions.'

'Never mind, all's well that ends well, not that it's ended yet, but you know what I mean. Keep an eye on Mrs Chase for the rest of the day though, Staff, and make sure the night staff do the same,' Sister advised. She perched her glasses on her nose and pulled a pile of papers towards her. 'To think I once longed for the responsible post of Sister! As for Perrello putting her further down the list, I'm sure he wouldn't. He'd have to face you if he did—you're in theatre tomorrow, of course.'

'I don't think Dr Perrello's afraid of my reactions; quite the opposite,' Jessica said. 'Do you think he'd move her down the list if I was up here instead?'

'Not really. It did just cross my mind that Perrello seems to enjoy putting you in your place on the ward, so I supposed that he was trying to wean you away from us and over to full-time theatre work. He's a strange, rather bitter man, I don't think he ever got over the defection of his first wife, so I always treat his feelings carefully.'

'Meaning I don't? He doesn't like me, you must have noticed this morning that he was hell-bent on getting me into serious trouble, so you see I have to fight back rather hard and can't always take his feelings into account.'

'I certainly don't think he dislikes you, yet in some way I do think he feels threatened by you. Now run along, Staff, or I'll never get these forms filled in.'

Jessica obediently went about her business, but she could not help wondering just exactly what Sister had meant when she said that Perrello felt threatened by herself, a mere staff nurse. It seemed an odd choice of phrase for a surgeon whose self-esteem, one suspected, would render him impervious to threats from a nobody like Jessica French.

However, while dressing wounds, taking blood pressures and checking the pulses of her various patients, she soon forgot conjecture and by the time her lunch-break arrived had hardly thought of Perrello more than a dozen times. It must be a record, she thought ruefully, very much aware of how large the surgeon usually loomed in her mind.

CHAPTER ELEVEN

JESSICA walked into theatre and saw Mrs Chase lying on the table in the classic position, with a support beneath her shoulders so that her head hung down, chin pointing at the ceiling. She was already anaesthetised and looked pale and rather dreadful.

Jessica turned to her trolley, forcing herself to check the instruments whilst the rest of them began their various tasks. Retractors, an aneurysm needle, haemostats, a thyroid enucleator, drainage tubing, Michel's clips, forceps . . . she saw a tracheostomy tube had been included, then Perrello came over and checked that the patient's throat was clear and that Jessica was about to clean the site. As she swabbed, he wandered round to Dr Fagandini's machine and bent over it. Jessica, who had been reading up on thyroidectomy, guessed that he was checking the heart-rate, which would have to be steady before he began.

He returned, as casually, to her side, wandered off and selected a scalpel handle, fitted a blade, changed it for another, then returned to her side once more. Over the top of his mask, his eyes met hers.

'All right, Staff? Not nervous?'

'I'm all right,' Jessica assured him.

'Forget it's Mrs Chase; this is just a patient and one, moreover, who we're going to cure. Now, let's start.'

They never worked in silence, but for once Jessica took little or no part in the lighthearted banter or the more serious remarks which were passed across the table as the operation proceeded steadily. Her whole mind was concentrated on Dr Perrello's hands, his needs and the careful brilliance of what he was doing. She could not have said how long the operation took, though at one stage anxiety was caused by the patient's pulse rate, which began to increase. There was a murmured discussion between the doctors as to how they should proceed, but Dr Perrello and Dr Fagandini finally agreed that since the operation was more than half completed, they should press on with all speed and hope that the pulse would steady of its own accord.

At last, however, Dr Perrello had the tube in to his satisfaction, and began to close the wound with Michel's clips.

'Leaves almost no scar,' he remarked to Jessica, taking them from her. 'Soon be done, now. Let's hope there are no complications . . . not that there should be; straightforward enough.'

'Good. I'll go up and see her in my lunch-hour, if I may.'

'I don't usually approve, you work quite hard enough here as it is, but in fact I shan't need you after lunch; John will operate and Gambas will assist, I'll just keep an eye on them. So consider yourself free from the moment we break for our meal.'

'Thank you,' Jessica said, keeping her voice low. 'Will they give her morphine as soon as she gets back on the ward?'

'I'm sure you can leave that in Sister's capable hands, Jessica.' But at the sight of Jessica's eyelashes drooping onto flushing cheeks he relented, even going so far as to chuckle. 'It's all right, I've prescribed morphine of course. Don't worry, we have your patient's welfare in hand.'

'I know you do, really,' Jessica said. She turned to Ana. 'Let's have a swab count, Nurse.'

'Hello, Staff . . . how are things? I've popped in to cheer up a couple of your patients, I hope that's all right.'

Jessica smiled at Mrs Robyns, now resplendent in a pearl-grey cotton dress with a wide gathered skirt and comfortable low-heeled white sandals. She had a flat wickerwork basket on her arm and it was full of bits and pieces—some silks, some wool, a couple of books, a folder full of snapshots.

'We're delighted to see you back, and looking so well, too,' she assured the older woman. 'What ever do you have in your basket? It looks fascinating.'

'Oh, just bits and pieces that people said they'd like, and the photos of my very own grandson all the way from England.' Mrs Robyns leaned conspiratorially close. They were in the corridor leading down to the wards; plainly she wanted some information before actually entering Room 1. 'How are they, Staff? Mrs Pontin and Mrs Chase, I mean. Oh, and dear little Mrs De Sousa.'

'We had a hair-raising time with Mrs Chase, directly after her operation,' Jessica admitted. 'She was really very ill. We had to send for Dr Perrello, because despite all our care, Mrs Chase haemorrhaged, and then when that was all cleared up and she seemed to be doing nicely the wound started swelling. I was worried, her temperature went up and up . . . and then Dr Perrello came to see her and said serum was collecting and aspirated it. She hasn't looked back since then. As for Mrs Pontin, we're taking out the T-tube presently so it will be curtains round her bed for half an hour or so, I'm afraid. Unless you'd like to pop in and visit her first?'

'Yes, that would suit me very well. And Mrs De Sousa? Is she still waiting?'

'Well, yes and no. She could have gone home, but she got excited, and Doctor decided it was best to keep her in right up to the birth. Then she'll be moved across to the military hospital, of course, where they've proper midwifery facilities. But until then she's better here, with people who speak her language.'

'I'm sure you're right. And where were you off to, Staff, when I stopped you?'

'I was going along to see Mrs Chase. Shall I tell her you're here or do you want to surprise her?'

'Better tell her I'm here, I think. Is she . . . well, how does she look?'

'Fine. The drainage tube in her wound came out after forty-eight hours, so all she's got right now is a light dressing. Tell Mrs Pontin Nurse Hoby and I will be along in ten minutes or so, would you?'

'I'll do that. Thank you, Staff.'

Mrs Robyns disappeared through the swing doors and, muted by them, Jessica heard the welcoming greetings and Mrs Robyn's own brisk, no-nonsense voice answering them. Smiling to herself, Jessica continued on her way to the private room. She had been right in diagnosing Mrs Robyns as a committee person; already she felt she should take care of all the patients on her old ward and do bits and bobs of shopping for them. That basket had been bulging, and not just with a novel snatched off a shelf or a pound or so of grapes. It had contained things which would mean a lot to the recipient and which had undoubtedly caused the giver a good deal of trouble in the finding.

'Good morning, Mrs Chase!'

'Oh, good morning, Staff. I've only just noticed, but hasn't my voice lost a good deal of its hoarseness?'

'It certainly has—you're back to your normal tones, in fact. Well, I told you it wouldn't stay a masculine croak for ever—what was it Dr Perrello said when you asked him about it?'

Mrs Chase, sitting in her easy chair by the open window, coloured and smiled coyly.

'It's unrepeatable to most, Staff . . . as if I'd suspect him of doing a sex-change operation by mistake, indeed! He's been awfully kind, though. He came and talked to me for over an hour yesterday afternoon, not about my condition or anything like that, just about sailing and swimming and how I'm going to go back to England for a few months later in the year to visit my relatives, and Martin's. He told me that he wouldn't be at all surprised if I married again, not at all, because a woman who has spent most of her life happy in her marriage isn't as nervous of repeating the experience as one who's known misery. That's so *true*, yet I'd never have thought of it for myself.'

'He can be very good,' Jessica said cautiously. She wondered what had got into the taciturn surgeon for him to voluntarily visit a patient. But then Sister had said that she thought Perrello was gradually getting easier with people, with nurses and patients alike. Was this a sign that he was getting over his wife's desertion? If so, then perhaps he would start treating Jessica herself like a woman, instead of simply as a colleague.

'You like him, don't you, Staff? He's got quite a way with him when he puts himself out.'

'Who, Dr Perrello?' Jessica smiled at this ingenuous description. 'Perhaps he's never put himself out for me, but I wouldn't say he had a way with him. As for liking him, one doesn't like or dislike senior surgeons, one admires their skill and thinks of them with respect.'

Mrs Chase gave a genuine little trill of amusement.

'Staff, how can you say such a thing! If that was true, no senior surgeon would ever get married!'

'They don't marry nurses, they marry society ladies,' Jessica said, laughing as well. 'No, you're right, I do like Dr Perrello, though I'm darned if I know why. He's quite frequently absolutely horrible to me, and even when he's being businesslike, he's very brisk and cold.'

'Ah well, we don't fall in love because a man is polite to us, necessarily,' Mrs Chase remarked, picking up a lace tablecloth which she was covering with embroidery. 'Women love a man for numerous reasons, and none of them . . .'

'Hey, not so fast!' Jessica laughed. 'I never said . . . well, you never said . . . anything about love! I like Dr Perrello, but . . .'

'Liking often turns to love.' Mrs Chase picked up her cloth and shook it out, then dug her needle decisively into the linen. 'When you got stung by all those jellyfish it was he who pulled you out of the water, wasn't it? Why do you suppose he was there, when you needed him?'

Jessica flirted wistfully with the idea of replying *because he was watching naked women on the nudist beach*, but knew that she was probably being unkind and untruthful. Instead, she said easily, 'Honestly, Mrs Chase, you do leap to conclusions! He was probably just passing by.'

'Oh? And he recognised you out to sea as you were and came down close to the shore in case you were stung by jellyfish? That sounds far less likely than my explanation, to me.'

'And what is your explanation, may I ask?'

'He'd warned you about the jellyfish, Staff, you told me so yourself. He knew you were going to that particular part of the coast and he couldn't bear the thought of you getting yourself into trouble. So he went along to keep an eye on you and was able to help when you needed help.'

'That sounds really nice and I wish it were true, but I'm pretty sure he was there on some legitimate business.'

Mrs Chase smiled but did not answer directly and presently

the talk turned to other subjects and after a bit Jessica got up, collected an empty coffee cup and took it back to the kitchen. There could be no doubt about it, Mrs Chase was improving rapidly and would soon be quite capable of going back to her own home and picking up her life afresh.

Coming out of the kitchen, Pat hailed her from up the corridor.

'Jessica, did you know Mrs Pontin's X-Rays are through, and the cholangiogram shows a free flow of bile into the duodenum, so the radiologist has given us the go-ahead to remove the tube if there's no build-up of bile.'

'Good,' Jessica said. 'Sister said I was to get you to take the clamp off whilst I watched. Do you have time now?'

'I do. Haven't you used artery forceps? It's easy enough but Sister's right, you watch this time and do it yourself next. I keep forgetting there are ward procedures which you theatre nurses never get a chance to use.'

Together, they approached Mrs Pontin's bed. Mrs Robyns, sitting beside it, got up.

'You'll be wanting me to go along to Mrs Chase whilst you see to my old friend here,' she said cheerfully. 'See you in a day or so, Irene.'

Mrs Robyns set off down the ward and Jessica turned to her patient.

'Everything seems fine, Mrs Pontin, so Nurse Hoby's going to clamp off your drain for you, whilst I watch.' She swished the curtains closed round the bed. 'It will be done several times, so the nurse is just going to show me how to use the artery forceps.'

'Oh? Aren't you going to take the drain right away, then?'

'No, not immediately, we have to make sure there'll be no further leakage.'

Jessica stood watching as Pat took the artery forceps and clamped off the T-tube, chatting to Mrs Pontin as she did so. Then, for Jessica's benefit, she removed the clamp and then put it back again.

'If you're in any discomfort call Staff and she'll come running,' Pat said presently, tidying the dressings trolley and brushing her hands together. 'We'll take a look in six hours or so and if you're still all right we'll remove the clamp and see if there's a bile-spurt. We'll leave it off for an hour, then put it back for another six, and if after a couple of days of that there's no pile-up of bile then we'll know we can take the drain right out.'

'I see. Two more days, then. How do you get the tube out? It's stitched in quite firmly, if I catch my nightie on it, it hurts.'

'It won't hurt you at all,' Pat assured her. 'The tube comes away very easily in fact, once the stitches are snipped. But you'll be given a pain-killing injection first, just in case.'

'So long as you're sure.' Mrs Pontin, who had been leaning rather anxiously forward, relaxed onto her pillows with a sigh. 'And then I dare say I'll go home shall I, Nurse?'

'I don't see why not.' Pat swished back the curtains, smiled at Mrs Pontin, and then the two nurses made their way back up the ward, Jessica pushing the trolley. 'You'll manage that next time, I'm sure, but if you need help, give me a call.'

'I'll do that, thank you, Staff.'

Jessica made sure that her work kept her within calling distance of Mrs Pontin and warned the rest of the staff that the T-tube had been clamped, but the six hours passed without incident, Mrs Pontin pottering placidly about the ward and from day-room to toilet block and back just as usual. When the time came to release the clamp Jessica watched anxiously, but there was no spurt of bile to indicate a blockage.

'You're doing very nicely, all things considered,' Jessica told her patient as she clamped the tube once more.'As you say, it won't be long before you get rid of the drain and once that happens, there's nothing to stop you going home, if you feel fit enough.'

'I shall, I'm sure. And having a proper bath will be nice, too,' Mrs Pontin said. 'I wonder if I'll be out before the Fair goes? I do enjoy a Fair.'

'What Fair?' Jessica was pushing her trolley along the next bed, but Mrs Pontin's raised voiced was clear.

'There's a big Fair coming, didn't you know, Staff? It comes every year from the mainland and though it's good fun, you get rowdyism and all sorts. The Casualty department has a hot time of it, I believe.'

'I can imagine. Well, perhaps I'll go and take a look this evening, if I'm able. Tomorrow though, we've a big list in theatre, so I don't want to get too tired.'

From her bed further down the ward, Mrs De Sousa added to Mrs Pontin's explanation.

'It isn't just a Fair, Staff, it's a fiesta. Lots and lots of people, a display of dancing, marvellous costumes . . . all sorts. I've been hoping Junior . . .' she patted her stomach, '. . . would put in an appearance before it begun so I could go. But perhaps I shall anyway.'

'Oh? Is the birth near, do you think?'

Mrs De Sousa winked.

'I didn't say that, But I suppose I could hurry things along, couldn't I? It's so boring here in bed all day, and I'm sure, if I jumped up and down a bit, I could start him off.'

'Goodness, Mrs De Sousa what a thing to say! Jump up and down, indeed!' Mrs Pontin's amused voice followed Jessica as she made her way out of the ward. 'Don't you go having that baby when I'm on the ward, I'm no midwife!'

Nor am I, Jessica thought to herself, as she pushed her trolley into the dressings-room. Everyone does a bit of gynae and midwifery, of course, but she had preferred theatre nursing right from the start. She found ward-work rewarding, but for the first time she realised that, if she had to choose to do one or the other for the rest of her life, she would choose theatre.

Later in the day, walking down with Pat to fetch some sterile packs which were unaccountably missing, she voiced this thought aloud.

'Not that it matters whilst I'm at the Nelson,' she added, 'because obviously I shan't be here for ever. But it has made me see that when I leave, I'd be happier applying for a theatre post rather than remaining on the wards.'

'Are you thinking of leaving? What about the permanent job in theatre over at the military hospital? Wouldn't that be rather nice?'

Pat was gazing at her curiously, but Jessica was concentrating on her reply.

'When Sister Cruz goes, you mean? I'm still not sure.'

'But if you like theatre work best, why don't you jump at it?'

Jessica stared down at her bare toes poking out of the fronts of her white sandals. She could scarcely tell Pat the truth—that she was more than half in love with a man who did not like women very much, and who would simply despise her if he ever discovered her feelings.

'It's not that simple, not here. But later on, at another hospital, I'll go back to theatre.'

'It's because you don't get on with Perrello,' Pat said suddenly. 'And because you *do* get on with Mariano! Ana said the other day that Perrello didn't approve of you and John—is he jealous, do you think?'

'I wish he was!' the words were out before Jessica could stop them. She stared at Pat, appalled. How could she have given the game away so totally? But Pat was nodding wisely.

'He's a fascinating man, don't think you're the only one to have fallen for that machismo, but you've obviously got sufficient sense to realise that you won't get anywhere with someone so embittered. Still, is it so bad that you couldn't work with him full-time?'

Jessica nodded; she could not say it aloud.

'Hmm. And *are* you serious about John? That's what the rumours say over at the big hospital, apparently.'

This time, Jessica was shocked into speech.

'Serious? John and I? No, of course not, we simply enjoy each other's company. Who on earth said it was anything but that?'

'It's theatre gossip, apparently. Don't worry about it, it's probably because you and he talk English together in the rest-room after an op. You know what small things lead to, on a hospital grapevine.'

'Yes, I do. Well, take it from me, Pat, I'm a career girl just at present, not interested in forming permanent relationships.' Jessica pushed the door open and smiled at Zola, behind the long counter. 'We're half a dozen sterile packs missing from our order,' she began cheerfully.

'That's the last, then.' Jessica stripped off her gloves and threw them down, smiling up at John, who had come out of theatre and into scrub up with her. 'It's been a good day though, hasn't it? Dr Perrello finished all the big ones in record time this morning, and now you've got through the rest quickly as well. My goodness, fancy finishing a list with time to spare.'

The pair of them headed for the sinks; Perrello and Gambas were already there, laving their hands and arms. As they turned away she and John slipped into their places and John said casually, 'How about coming out with me this evening, Jess? The first night of the Fair heralds the fiesta and a good time is had by all. What do you say? We could have a meal and then a wander.'

Jessica hesitated. Perrello was standing near and from him there emanated such tension, such stillness, that she knew very well he was waiting for her reply. She knew, too, that he wanted her to refuse—but why should she? He had not asked her himself, she was sure he had no intention of asking her out, so why should she not go with John and have as good a time as was possible?

Yet she found that to say she would go, and feel the annoyance and disappointment which would emanate from the surgeon was more than she was prepared to do. Stupidly, she heard her voice saying that it was a lovely idea, but that she was too tired for an outing tonight. And she saw Perrello relax, saw the tension drain away . . . saw him turn back to Gambas and start to talk about something else.

It brought her to her senses. Rage flowered. She rubbed her hands and arms dry so briskly that they tingled. Why should he let his disapproval be felt, so that she had turned down John's invitation, and then simply walk away, exuding satisfaction because she was not, now, going out with anyone? Any decent man would have turned round and asked her out himself! The fact that, had he done so, she would have been honour bound to refuse, having just refused John, simply did not occur to her, she was far too angry for that. She walked over to where John was standing, joking with one of the nurses.

'John . . . look, we're early, so I'll go home and have a bath and get changed, and then I'll wander down to the square. Perhaps we could meet up down there, if you're going? I won't say I'll definitely be there, because I may really be too tired, but if I'm feeling in the mood for a fiesta, I'll be there. Oh, and we'll have a meal, but we'll go somewhere like Antonio's bar, where we can just have a snack if we're not terribly hungry.'

'That would suit me; but no way will I meet you in the square, during fiesta,' John said firmly. 'I'll pick you up at the flat at eight.'

And because she could see Perrello was listening and because she still felt sore at his obvious disapproval of her friendship with John, she said that if he was coming up to the flats he might as well mount the stairs and share her meal, and he said that would be fun, and she could see the lines deepening round Perrello's mouth and the cold, hurt look in his eyes, and she told herself she was glad, and it served him right, and she left the theatre suite, at last, with her hand in the crook of John's arm and her mind and heart untouched by the laughter which bubbled on her lips.

'I don't know why you asked him back for a meal, but you did, and I respect your right to do so, and I'm going out,' Pat said firmly, standing in the kitchen doorway in her low-cut, flame-coloured chiffon dance dress, with a matching scarf tied round her hair. 'Did you really think I'd stay here to play gooseberry to you and John Mariano?'

'I thought you'd be here; you wouldn't play gooseberry,' Jessica said crossly. 'Oh, Pat, now you'll make it look much worse than it is.'

'Rubbish, no one will know. And anyway, you invited him. Look, you aren't really scared he'll come the big lover or something, are you? I don't think he's the type.'

'Of course I'm not. Oh, go off then, and have a good time. Don't wake me when you stagger indoors in the early hours.'

'Ha! The boot will probably be on the other foot. Have a good time yourself, and give John my regards.'

It proved an enjoyable meal after all, though. Jessica cheated a bit by doing an extremely simple main course—steak and salad—and then dazzling John with a much more elaborate pudding. She flambéed apple pancakes in brandy and then spread strawberry icecream over the top which effectively cooled the dish down and made John's evening, or so he said. They finished the meal with coffee and cream floaters and then some mint chocolate wafers, and even Jessica was beginning to relax by the time they cleared the table. John wanted to help her wash up, but Jessica was firm. That would be done next morning, before breakfast; right now, she wanted to see this fiesta that she had been told about.

Villa Castello was *en fête* all right. By the time they left the flat it was dark and the square was crowded with people. Men on horseback, elaborately costumed, moved to and fro, children ran and screamed and begged their parents for money for the Fair, women wore their best and strolled languidly along, many with flowers tucked behind an ear or in a waistband.

'We'll go on the Fair, first,' John said in her ear, for the din was terrific. 'Then we'll come back here in time for the horses.'

'Fine. What do the horses do?'

'Goodness, woman, don't you know? They're wonderful, trained in the Spanish school, like the Lipzaner stallions, but all on the island and all ridden, reared and bred by local men. They don't do much this evening, it's just a parade more or less, but tomorrow they'll give all sorts of displays and so on, for charity and for the fiesta . . . the saint in question, whose Saint's Day we are celebrating, must have been fond of horses, for they're the main attraction.'

'I see. Well, I love horses, so that should be fun, but I also love Fairs.'

The Fair was a large one. Hand in hand, so as not to get accidentally parted, John and Jessica wandered along the lines of stalls. They had a go on the bumper cars, shrieked and slid down the tower chute, whirled on the merry-go-rounds and ate various concoctions, including a cold Spanish omelette which proved far more delicious than it looked. Then they made their way to the children's theatre, which was being held in a courtyard which led off the main square. John managed to find them a couple of seats and he bought two glasses of shandy, a bag of popcorn, and they waited for the performance to start.

It was spoilt, slightly, by the fact that the play was an ancient one which called for the children to wear huge papier-mâché heads representing the main characters and this muffled their childish tones, so that the words were difficult to follow. However, John knew the story and told her what was happening and she managed to enjoy the brilliant colours of the costumes, the spirited caperings of the little actors and the singing, which, since it was done by children merely clad in peasant costume, was not spoilt by the artificial heads.

When the performance was at an end the children, obviously at a pre-arranged signal, produced fireworks from somewhere and began to let them off. Rockets soared, Catherine-wheels whirled, jumping-Jacks jumped and leapt, and Jessica was just remarking to John that this could be pretty dangerous, when the accident occurred.

There were several theories, afterwards, as to what had caused it, but at the time all that Jessica saw was the child wearing the Negro head with tight grey curls all over it, screaming as his mask became full of smoke and flames licked and sizzled in the wig.

Jessica jerked at John's arm and pointed; the two of them began to fight their way through the crowd, many of whom were still unaware that anything unusual was happening. The two of them reached the child just as his mother did; she shrieked, grabbing the little boy, screaming that someone must help, her son was being burned alive and before either John or Jessica could stop her she had picked him up and was staggering with him across the crowded courtyard, plainly with no other thought than to get him to water . . . but the fountains had been turned off whilst the play was acted out, and in any event, the child's clothing was beginning to smoulder where fragments of his headpiece had fallen off. There was no time to lose.

'Grab his body,' John snapped to Jessica. 'I'll heave on the mask. If we can get it off . . .'

Jessica snatched the child out of his mother's limpet-like grasp and tried to invert him so that the head would be easier to remove, but the mother was clearly hysterical and seemed to be doing her best to get in the way. What was more, the wig and the artificial head were blazing and incredibly hot. John could not get a purchase on the material for long enough to give a sustained tug and the child, from struggling and screaming, had gone ominously quiet.

'Here!' John let go of the mask and stripped off his shirt. He wrapped his hands in its folds whilst the mother continued to shriek and to try to take the child from Jessica, then he grabbed the mask. A cloud of smoke, a smell of burning nylon, a long heave from John whilst Jessica clung grimly, and then the artificial head was off and the little boy's face popped into the air, his cheeks scarlet and wet with sweat, his hair plastered to his head. His neck was badly burned and the sides of his face were blackened, but by some miracle his hair had not caught and Jessica thought, thankfully, that he should live to tell his frightening story to his own children.

'You're a grand girl!' John took the child from her just as another firework exploded within a foot of them. 'My God . . . get them to clear the kids out of the way, can you? Jessica, we'd better get the lad out to the square—there's a good chance of getting an ambulance out there, in fact there's usually one waiting nearby—drunks, you know.'

Together, they fought their way across the crowded courtyard. Around them the good-natured people surged and called out, touching the child, reassuring the mother that all would be well. A good few were drunk, Jessica realised, but even so they made way for the small group.

And then another firework was set off and this time it went fizzing along the ground. A woman screamed, a man swore, and a shower of embers, falling from a more successful rocket, set alight another of the grotesque wigs.

From that moment it was pandemonium. Jessica clung grimly to the back of John's jacket and together they fought their way through the panic stricken people and out into the main square. As they left the courtyard all around them people were screaming to each other to help a child, or to get a woman to the ambulance.

But there, in the square, beneath the palm trees, was an ambulance. John made for it and arrived first but close to their heels came others. Men, whitefaced, carried children whose clothing and wigs still smouldered, women limped along, their singed skirts held away from their legs. Clearly, things had got very out of hand. John climbed into the ambulance with his burden, laid the child on the bunk and then came over and spoke to Jessica.

'I'll go with the ambulance, Jess—will you come with me? My bleeper's gone off, I imagine this isn't the first ambulance to set off for the hospital by any means.'

'Yes, I'll come . . .' Jessica was beginning, when she was interrupted, kindly but firmly, by the ambulance man.

'No. Sorry, señorita, but it won't be possible. There are too many people needing treatment. Sorry.'

'She's a nurse . . .' John began, but Jessica took the point.

'It's all right, John, they'll have plenty of nurses at the hospital but they'll need all the doctors they can get. I'll hang on here for a bit and then make my way home. See you in the morning.'

He nodded ruefully, taking her point.

'All right, love. Take care, now. Isn't that your flatmate over there in the orange dress? You could join her. Don't forget, when a Spanish *hombre* gets a drink or two inside him he can get very amorous! See you in the morning.'

Jessica waited until the ambulance had driven away and then looked round for Pat. She thought she saw a glimpse of the orange dress on the far side of the square and was about to make her way across there when the first of the horses minced into the central space and she forgot everything in admiration both for the horse, the rider, and those who followed him.

The horses themselves were spectacular. All jet-black stallions, at the very least sixteen hands high, their coats polished to gleaming ebony. Caparisoned in scarlet and gold, they came across the square with the dancing steps of great power leashed, and Jessica gasped at the perfection of their strong, muscled bodies.

The riders, too, deserved a second and then possibly a third glance. They were dressed in skin-tight white riding breeches and long black boots, in white, ruffled shirts and tight black coats, whilst each man had a red rose in his buttonhole and a low-crowned, wide-brimmed black hat on his head.

But before she had fully taken in the pageantry of colour before her, the horses began their display. They formed into twos and each beast moved with his partner, leaping into the air at a word of command, rearing up on their hind legs like heraldic beasts and holding the pose for moments on end, taking great leaps from that position, and then dropping onto the ground again, to take off in a perfect half-pass to cross the square corner-wise and start again on the smooth and classical poses.

The rider who had entered the square first was obviously in charge, his horse reared the most proudly, jumped the highest, but Jessica did not realise she knew him until his mount, jerking his head with dismay when a child darted right underneath him, stayed still for a second and then moved sideways unexpectedly, putting his partner out of step. The rider was taken by surprise and the black hat tilted a little and the dark face, the harshly held mouth, the narrowing eyes as he fought to bring his mount back into line with its partner, proved to belong to Diaz Perrello. He looked magnificent, totally in control, and the stallion was grand, a strong and muscular creature which looked a perfect match for the man astride his back. As man and horse cavorted across the square again Jessica caught Perrello's eye; he gave her his slight, sardonic smile and then they were off again, heading for the other side of the square.

Jessica turned to her neighbour, a fat little woman she had never seen in her life before, and addressed her without a thought. What on earth was Perrello doing up on that horse?

'Excuse me, señora, but the man at the head of the troupe . . . did my eyes deceive me, or . . .'

'It was Dr Perrello, from the military hospital,' the woman said, and gestured to the retreating horses. 'The priest was his partner. You will know them all, señorita, but they are difficult to recognise in costume—all so tall, so dark, so handsome!' She sighed with pride, glad to be able to talk. 'My son was the last rider, he's just leaving the square now. He is the youngest riding this year, so I am very proud.'

'So you should be, señora. And do the men own their own horses? Are they all men from Villa Castello?'

'Mostly they are from Castello, but there are some who now live in Malon or even further afield. Yes, they own their own horses; when a stallion is put to a mare there is great interest in the foal, for if it is a true black then it will go to someone who will ride in the fiesta. The horses are the best. None are cut, all are stallions still.'

'And where will they go now? Home? Or do they go on somewhere else, to take part in some other display somewhere else?'

'They'll go home now, but tomorrow they will give displays all over the town. Tomorrow night, if you come down to the square, you will have to be very careful, very discreet. The men get drunk and a woman alone would perhaps be accosted. Tonight it is family fun, but tomorrow night it is wild, dangerous even. The younger men ride their horses into the houses and out onto the balconies . . . the horses are trained, but even so people can get hurt.'

'People got hurt tonight,' Jessica said soberly. 'A little boy was quite badly burnt, in the courtyard where the play was held.'

'So? Yes, such a thing often occurs. But tomorrow night, señorita, come out with your *hombre* or not at all. Take my word.'

'I will.' Jessica looked around her and spied the orange dress moving away from the square. 'Oh, excuse me, señora, I see my friend is leaving. She'll walk home with me if I go now.'

Despite the lateness of the hour and the fact that the display was over people still lingered in the square and surrounding streets. Jessica managed to miss Pat yet again and knew she ought to be heading for home, but she, too, wanted to stay. Vendors were selling hot doughnuts which smelled delicious, a shop had a window open and chips were being handed out wrapped in newspaper, reminding Jessica sharply of Manchester on a Saturday night. Someone shook a bottle of beer and then opened it; foam spurted high into the air and soaked several passersby. Everyone laughed and shook their fists and the would-be beer drinker gazed with maudlin sadness at his now half-empty bottle.

Jessica was biting into the delicious softness of her first doughnut when she saw quite clearly, across the square, her erstwhile patient, Diane De Sousa. She started to smile and wave when it suddenly occurred to her that Mrs De Sousa had been tucked up in her hospital bed that very afternoon, grumbling that she might miss the fiesta . . . no, saying that she would find a way to get to the fiesta! Another quick look, and Jessica realised that Mrs De Sousa had recognised her and was sliding through the crowd as quickly as she could.

The little monkey, Jessica thought wrathfully, she's slipped out of the ward and now she's going to slip back in, having had her fun. And what if something awful happens to her, hurrying the mile and a half back to the hospital in her condition? Suppose she starts to give birth in the taxi? Suppose she can't get a taxi? There must be several thousand people from Puerto Malon here tonight, and since the last bus must have gone hours and hours ago, most of them will be catching taxis presently.

Walking as fast as she could, she pushed her way through the crowd and followed Mrs De Sousa, who was well ahead. Jessica kept her eyes fixed on the blue and white stripes of what she now recognised as Mrs De Sousa's best nightie, and hurried along. When her patient left the crowded square behind and made for the dark and narrow sidestreets she did not hesitate, but plunged down the first one after her. The girl must be mad, coming out in a nightie in her condition, but mad or not, Jessica was determined to catch up with her and see her safely back to her bed. Recriminations might well follow—but not until she saw Mrs De Sousa safely back where she belonged, with trained staff at hand for any emergency which might arise.

CHAPTER TWELVE

It was dark in the alley, but for the first time that evening Jessica realised that the moon was shining, for now that she was away from the lights of the main square and its surroundings, it was only the moonlight which lit her path.

She thought for a moment that she had missed Mrs De Sousa, then she saw a tell-tale flicker of movement ahead. Her patient's nightie, drained of colour by the moonlight, was showing as zebra-like black and white stripes but it was clearly the same garment. Jessica followed determinedly, skirting an entrance into a narrow, cobbled court and making for the slightly larger lane which led out from it.

She realised after two or three minutes that she was lost, but did not worry unduly; the town was small, the alleys and streets, though both narrow and winding, nearly always ended up in the main square. She would find and capture the erring Mrs De Sousa and together they would find their way back to the main square. By then it was even possible that one of the ambulances would have returned, or they could always ring up for an ambulance car, or of course, in the Spanish manner, they could simply commandeer a car to take them to the hospital by waving one down with a white hanky.

Mrs De Sousa led her quite a chase, but in the end she caught up with her simply because her patient took a turning which led only into one of the enclosed, silent courtyards which were dotted all over the town. She had slipped in easily enough through the gateway, open, no doubt, because all the inhabitants were still revelling in the square, and had hidden behind an ancient water butt, but Jessica has seen a tell-tale whisk of striped material as she rounded the corner and had relentlessly pursued her.

Now, having seen from Mrs De Sousa's crouching shadow where she was hiding, she approached the water-butt, rather cross and more than a little breathless.

'Mrs De Sousa,' she began, trying to sound reasonable yet firm, 'you really are . . .' she stopped. Mrs De Sousa was still crouched in the shadow, but it was not the crouch of someone hiding from a friend, it was clear that the girl was in some discomfort. She raised her face to Jessica's and her eyes were dark with fear, her skin sweat-streaked.

'Oh, it's you, Nurse. I've got . . . I've got an awful pain.'

'Good lord, Mrs De Sousa, what do you expect, running like that in your condition?' Jessica said, with a briskness she was far from feeling. She cast a hunted look round her and realised, with a sinking heart, that this was no ordinary courtyard. It was surrounded, not by houses and friendly blocks of tattered flats, but by warehousing and commercial premises. There was no hope of help from the residents, then!

'I didn't want you to know I was out,' Mrs De Sousa muttered. She took a deep, steadying breath, started to try to stand, then sank down again with a moan. 'Oh dear, what have I done? I've got an awful pain!'

'Sit back then, whilst I go and fetch help,' Jessica said. 'I shan't be long, probably I'll find someone in the next street . . . just stay there.'

'No, no! Don't leave me, Staff . . . please, if you leave me I'll die of fright and how would you find me again? Please stay, I'll be all right, give me a minute and then the pain will go, I'm sure it's only because I ran so hard, and then we can go back to the square together.'

'We-ell . . .' Jessica was beginning, when Mrs De Sousa suddenly gave a sharp exclamation, stretched out her legs, and began to pant.

'Nurse, it's started!' she said. She didn't sound nearly so frightened now, but far more matter of fact. 'Well, what a place! Now I know just what to do, so don't you worry. Only don't you dare leave me.'

She seized hold of the hem of Jessica's dress and Jessica, reassured by her sudden calmness, knelt at her side.

'I won't leave if you don't want me to, but do remember, Mrs De Sousa, that I've never delivered a baby in my life. Couldn't I just . . .'

'Call me Diane,' the patient recommended. 'Can you time the contractions? They seem awful close to me, considering the pains only started twenty minutes ago.'

Jessica shot out her wrist and the two of them peered, in the moonlight, at the small face of her watch. It showed ten minutes to midnight.

'Right. Now if the relaxation classes and books are right, and I'm still in the first stage, I shouldn't get another for . . . oh . . . oh! Hold on, Nurse.'

There was a short pause, during which Jessica felt she could almost share the contraction which was tightening its grip on her patient. It lasted, by her watch, for a whole minute, before Mrs De Sousa—Diane—began to relax.

'Sorry, the books *are* wrong. I reckon that was no more than five minutes from the last, possibly less. Nurse, you may never have delivered a baby before, but if you ask me you're going to do it quite soon!'

Jessica smoothed the damp blonde curls off the younger girl's brow and smiled as reassuringly as possible.

'Well, they say taxi drivers, stokers and airline stewards deliver babies, so I suppose I'm as capable as the next man! I feel I ought to be boiling water and finding sharp scissors to cut the cord with, but . . .'

A hand, falling on her shoulder, nearly made her die on the spot, but Mrs De Sousa, looking up and past her, gave a wide welcoming smile.

'Hello, Dr Perrello, fancy meeting you here like this!'

Jessica's heart did a leap of sheer delight before she told herself, firmly, that it was simply relief, and waited for the surgeon to tell Mrs De Sousa what he thought of her. But she wronged him. He crouched down beside her, and for a moment his hand gripped her arm comfortingly, then he addressed the younger woman as though this was the most natural place to meet in the world.

'Decided to surprise us all, Mrs De Sousa, and give birth to that baby on fiesta night? Well, I don't think much of your surroundings, but otherwise it seems a fine idea. How far along are the contractions, do you know? I can get back to the square in five minutes and drive my car down here, but I wouldn't want to leave Staff if the birth is imminent. I'm no gynaecologist, but I've delivered babies before now.'

'They're about four . . . no, three minutes apart,' Mrs De Sousa said as soon as she could speak. 'Oh, and I do believe it's getting lower . . . the pains are changing . . . I do think something's going to happen quite soon.'

'Then in view of the poor visibility I think I'll hurry back for my car. At least then you can recline on the back seat and we'll have some light.'

Jessica wanted desperately to object, to say that she would go, but it would have been stupid and pointless. She had no idea where his car was parked and she remembered the crowds in the square and the sheer impossibility of getting through the people fast. Dr Perrello, she was sure, would find a way and anyway, he could drive and she could not.

He stood up, then did a surprising thing. He pulled her to her feet and stood for a moment looking down at her, his hands resting lightly on her hips. He was very serious, yet she could sense that he was amused by the whole episode.

'Will you be all right, Jessica? I'll be as quick as I can. If the child does get itself born before I get back don't panic, don't try to cut the cord, just sit yourself down and hold the baby, having first dangled it by the feet and smacked it for the first cry. I'll send someone to keep you company if I find anyone who isn't drunk.'

'I'll be fine.' Jessica was as full of panic as the night was full of moonlight, but she had no intention of showing it. Dr Perrello trusted her, and she would not let him down. After all, she had little enough to do; she must simply stay with the patient and hope that the child would put off being born until someone else arrived.

He patted her shoulder, smiled, waved to Mrs De Sousa and turned on his heel. Once he was out of the courtyard, Jessica knelt beside her patient once again, trying to look cheerful, competent and optimistic all at once. He would not be long, she was sure of it!

Diaz Perrello left the courtyard, walking with long, determined strides. Knowing something of Mrs De Sousa's medical history, he meant to do his best to get her back to the hospital before the child was born—certainly she must be at least in the ambulance and not on a filthy cobbled floor, alone but for a girl whose experience of midwifery was limited, to say the least.

It was lucky, he told himself severely, that he had happened to see Nurse French in the crowd. What had made him put Satan, his most valued stallion, into the hands of the rider next to him, what had made him hurry back to the square when he should have been grooming his horse and getting out of his riding gear, was more than he was prepared to conjecture. So far as he was concerned it was good fortune which had led him back to the square in time to see Nurse French disappearing into one of the dark and winding alleys which led to the poorer part of the town.

It was equally fortunate that he had decided to follow her. After all, she was a foreigner, without parental support. She needed someone to look after her and she worked for him—worked well, what was more—so what more natural than that he should take what care of her he could? He did not want her to be hit over the head and raped in a dark alley if he could prevent it. The thought, indeed, made him go cold all over.

By now people were beginning to drift away from the square and those that were left were the young and heedless. He stared hard at faces as he pushed his way to where his car was parked, but there was no one he trusted to help Jessica. The girls were too young and foolish, the men, all of a sudden, seemed far too swaggeringly self-confident. He spotted a medical student, changed course to go towards him, changed course again, heading for the car once more. No! He would go back to her himself, no one else was to be trusted with something so precious.

He was in the car and revving the engine to clear the crowd out of his path, a white handkerchief in his hand to indicate that he was on medical business, when he realised that he had no idea exactly where the little courtyard was situated. He shoved the car into gear with wet palms and began to inch towards the alleyway he had emerged from. How many times had he turned right and how many left? He had been led by the light and the noise of the crowd after he left Jessica, and of course following her he had been intent on keeping her in sight, he had not given a thought to the direction in which they were heading. He wound down a window and seized the arm of a passing youth.

'Hey, *hombre*, I want to find a courtyard . . . cobbled, surrounded by tall buildings . . . there's a water butt on the left-hand side of it, the gates weren't closed.'

The youth laughed.

'Such a description fits almost every courtyard in Villa Castello, *amigo*! Did you notice anything else? The number on a door? A flowering shrub in a pot? Anything like that?'

'No, I was in a hurry.' He made a decision. 'Jump in, will you, I'm a doctor, a patient needs my help urgently, she's having a baby. Can you drive?'

'Sure.' The youth laughed again and Perrello realised that he was by no means sober. 'I've even got a licence!'

'Right. Then will you drive this car, slow and steady, up and down the alleys, whilst I get out and take a look in each courtyard? It'll be quicker.'

Had the youth not been drunk he might well have asked how a doctor came to be searching for a patient whose address he did not know, but as it was he simply climbed into the car, revved the engine, fiddled with the gearstick, and then drove down the alley Perrello indicated.

'I won't take you to the east,' he remarked as they entered the tunnel of blackness between the high old buildings, 'because there are no houses or flats that side, it's all warehousing and commercial premises. We'll turn right here.'

They turned right. The big car crept on into the dark.

'It's all right, Diane, someone will come quite soon now,' Jessica said, but she might as well have saved her breath; Mrs De Sousa was not in the least concerned with anything right at this moment other than what was happening to her. She had struggled into a sitting position, with Jessica's help, and was leaning half on the water butt and half against the wall, and was beginning to push the baby out. Apart from mopping her brow, holding her hands when she held them out, and praying, there was little that Jessica could actually do. She could not stop gazing hopefully at the entrance to the courtyard whenever her attention was not fixed on the mother-to-be, but apart from that she could only kneel right where she was, on the rough cobbles, and do her best to comfort her patient in between contractions.

'It isn't a bit like they told us in relaxation classes,' Mrs De Sousa said breathlessly at one point. 'How I wish it was lighter! I think it would be easier if we had a light.'

But no light save for that of the moon was forthcoming, so she and Jessica worked on, together, to get her baby born.

'That's the last one, Doctor,' the young man said presently, when Diaz Perrello returned to the car after what seemed like his umpteenth fruitless search round a dark little courtyard. 'Tell you what, why don't we drive back to the hospital, see if she's got herself an ambulance car by now? Someone will have found her, that's what it is. They'll have taken her in to the flat or the house or whatever to have her baby in comfort. I shouldn't worry.'

'No. I've a better idea. I'll play it by ear.'

Dr Perrello got out of the car, leaving his driver open-mouthed, and set off. At first he simply wandered up one street and round a corner, down an alleyway and up another, but suddenly his slow walk became purposeful. The car was left behind as he strode, for now he was following an instinct older and more reliable than mere memory. He was searching for someone who meant a lot to him, concentrating not on finding a particular courtyard but on a particular person.

He left the residential district behind very quickly and went forward confidently, into the commercial property. His mentor, following, exhorted him not to waste his time but Perrello felt all the quiet satisfaction of one who is now on the right track.

Presently, his heart beating hard, his hands and forehand clammy with sweat, he rounded a corner and headed straight for the entrance in the high brick wall. He was right, he knew it!

* * *

'One more push, my love, and you'll have a dear little baby,' Jessica told her patient. 'Come on, I'll hold both your hands and we'll both work hard . . .'

Mrs De Sousa grinned, her teeth flashing in the moonlight. She began to push, pulling on Jessica's arms until the older girl wondered if they would leave their sockets, and then, as the contraction eased, Mrs De Sousa gave a tiny crow of triumph.

Jessica had risen half to her feet as she tugged, but now she dropped quickly to her knees again. Just in time to deliver Mrs De Sousa's pink, wet, startled-looking son.

Diaz Perrello ran across the courtyard; he had not run like it for years. Jessica knelt on the cobbles. She was holding a baby up by its feet and even as he reached her she smacked it lightly on its small, curved buttocks. A whimpering squall, rising slowly to a shout, emerged from the tiny figure and Jessica cradled it in her arms.

She was not aware that she had company until Dr Perrello's arms went round her. He gave her a hard squeeze, baby and all, and plonked a quick, warm kiss on the side of her face.

'Well done!' he said, and his voice sounded young, eager, without reservation, Jessica thought wonderingly. 'Oh, Jessica, well done!'

'What about me?' Mrs De Sousa enquired, sounding rather injured. 'I gave birth to him, all Nurse French did was to stand by!'

'Yes . . . sorry. I got carried away.' Perrello had, Jessica realised, fallen on his knees too in order to hug her. She could only stare up at him as he got to his feet and went over to the big car which was now just nosing into the courtyard. He opened the door and got a bag out of the boot, then he said something to the driver and immediately the headlamps came on, full beam, lighting the scene as if for a theatrical performance.

'Here we are, then. We'll just clean things up a bit and then I'll get my young friend there to drive us all to the hospital. And you, Mrs De Sousa, can explain to me and to the staff just what you were doing in town, in your nightdress, giving birth to a fine baby boy, when you should have been tucked up in bed on the ward.'

'I don't mind if they're all cross, not now,' Mrs De Sousa said contentedly. Jessica had handed her the baby, small, bare, damp but drying now in the warm night, and she could do little other than smile down at the small face so near her own. 'Will he be all right with nothing on?'

'He'll be fine, it's a warm night. Cuddle him up, that's right, and we'll lift you into the car. You'll be back in bed before you know it.' Perrello's voice had not changed, Jessica noticed; it was still more relaxed, warmer, than his voice had ever sounded before. He finished what he was doing and turned to her. 'Jessica, give me a hand with our patient, I dare say she'd rather hold on to her little son.'

Together, the doctor and nurse carried the woman over to the car and laid her gently on the back seat. But she struggled to a sitting position, leaning forward and thanking the driver for his trouble.

'It's a pleasure, señora, and I wish you and the baby well,' the young man said politely. 'Have you finished with me now, Doctor? If so, I'll get off home; it's not far from here.'

'I'll give you a lift,' Perrello offered, but the other shook his head.

'No, thanks all the same. It's quicker to walk. Good night, señora, señorita . . . Good night, *ninõ*.'

He left them and Perrello tidied his instruments into his bag and then opened the passenger door, ushering Jessica inside.

'We'll get straight to the hospital, and then I'll take you back to your flat,' he said authoritatively. 'Come along, no time to waste.' He lowered his voice. 'I'm sure Baby De Sousa is fine, but I'd like to make certain.'

'Well, Jessica? What a night, eh?'

Perrello took her arm as they left the hospital building and turned her towards the car-park. Dawn was greying the sky in the east and they were both very tired, Jessica stumbled as she walked but his hand was on her elbow, guiding her, and as they reached his car he slid it round her waist for a moment.

'Tired? Never mind, we'll neither of us ever do a better job than the one we've just completed. A fine boy! I am happy for her, and for her man.'

'You keep saying he's a fine boy because she's calling him Diaz, after you,' Jessica said, smiling as she climbed into the passenger seat. 'I still think she could have called him after me—Jesse James was a fellow, after all—but she said I'd be in his names somewhere, so I suppose she'll call him José or something, as a second name. It would be close enough.'

'Marriage is a fine institution,' Perrello said dreamily, as he drove through the still dark streets. 'If one is fortunate enough to find the right woman, there can be no happier state. Mr De Sousa is a lucky man.'

'I'm sure you're right and it's very nice to be married, for some,' Jessica said repressively. 'But others, like myself—and you, Dr Perrello—are probably best off single. I enjoy my career.'

He slowed the car and turned to look at her. His eyes rested on her almost tenderly, she thought, confused. What a wonderful thing was birth, if it could make Diaz Perrello regard marriage as a fine institution and herself with equanimity!

'Jessica, you're being foolish. Why don't you admit that you'd like to be married? To the right man, of course.'

Jessica's heart began to thump. She looked at him, opened her mouth to reply, hesitated, then spoke.

'To the right man, yes. But I've not met him yet.'

'Haven't you?' The car had stopped. He had drawn it close to the kerb and now they just sat there whilst the engine idled and looked at one another.

'N-no.'

'Jessica . . .'

One moment they were sitting in their respective seats looking across at each other and the next, Jessica thought wonderingly, they were in each other's arms. All the feelings she had been repressing for weeks and weeks simply rose up and boiled over and Jessica clung, kissed and fluttered against his chest just like a silly, lovesick teenager.

Presently, he put her away from him. He was smiling that slight smile which scarcely seemed to touch his lips but which warmed his eyes and changed his whole expression, charging it with lightness.

'You are a career girl, eh? You think you are best off single?'

'Dr Perrello, kissing doesn't mean . . .'

'Jessica, I came to my senses after weeks and weeks of struggle last night. I'd been telling myself that I could manage without women—any women—and that I was happier by myself than I'd ever been even when Amanda and I had been first married. And then along came this skinny know-all of an English nurse . . .' he paused to give her an enigmatic smile and to catch at her upraised hand. '. . . Hear me out, Jessica. Then along came this heartbreakingly pretty English nurse . . . why aren't you trying to hit me now?'

'I never stop people from speaking the truth,' Jessica said demurely. 'Go on . . . then along came this pretty, intelligent English nurse . . . ?'

'Yes. And for the first time for years, I found myself caring about a woman. Oh, at first I don't deny that I cared only to take you down a peg or two, but even that, my darling, was because you had dared to come into my quiet bachelor existence and make me see that there were more important things in life than self-sufficiency. And I found myself wanting you more and more, not just in the physical sense but in all sorts of ways. Why did you think I turned up so opportunely at Fortells beach that afternoon?'

'I thought you were watching the naked ladies on the nudist beach,' Jessica said frankly. 'Weren't you?'

'No, I was not. I was down there on the off-chance that you might need me. I thought John might . . . oh, I don't know. I only know that I wanted to be with you, yet I despised myself for what I thought of as a weakness. And then I found I was visiting the ward more often in the hope of seeing you, hanging round the nurses' flats to watch you go in and out, even sailing always on the Villa Castello side of the water to catch the odd glimpse. And when I saw you tonight, alone in that huge crowd . . . when I knew how rowdy the men can get, how they will treat a girl who is not of Villa Castello . . .' he stopped speaking, and Jessica heard him grind his teeth. 'I thought, this is my girl, and it's about time I told her how I feel, and I came looking for you. And when I found you, that second time, with the child in your arms . . .' He sighed, running his hand down her back and making goosepimples appear all over her arms. 'Ah, then I knew that it was you I wanted. Will you marry me, Jessica?'

'It's all so sudden,' Jessica complained, safe in his arms. 'You've never even been particularly nice to me. In fact, there were times when I thought you hated me.'

'No! But I wanted to hate you, because you disturbed me and upset all my nice, bland ideas.' He let her go though, and leaned forward to start the car's engine. 'Oh well, I dare say I deserve to suffer a little longer. If you can't make up your mind I've only got myself to blame. I'll just have to . . .'

'Yes.'

Perrello promptly cut the engine.

'Yes? Yes you'll marry me?'

'Trying to be humble doesn't suit you,' Jessica said in an exasperated tone. 'It's perfectly clear that you think you're a marvellous catch for a mere nurse, and . . .'

He swept her up in his arms again, kissing every bit of her face he could reach, down her neck and across her collarbones. When at last he stopped they were both breathless.

'Well? Do you still think I believe myself to be doing you a favour?'

'No,' Jessica said in a small voice. 'Only you didn't say . . .'

'What? What was it I did not say?'

Jessica put her arms very tightly round him and said loudly, 'Diaz Perrello, I love you very much.'

He laughed, but she could hear the little tremor in that laugh.

'I *see*! Jessica French, my darling Jessica, dearest Nurse French, I love you much, much more!'

NOW ON VIDEO

Harlequin Romance movie™
Silhouette
CLOUD WALTZER
CIC VIDEO

Harlequin Romance movie™
Silhouette
LOVE WITH A PERFECT STRANGER
CIC VIDEO

Two great Romances available on video . . .*

from leading video retailers for just £9·99 R.R.P.

The love you find in Dreams.

*from Autumn 1987